PUCK'S PROERTY

A BAD BOY BIKER ROMANCE

STEAMY BIKER ROMANCE SERIES

MONIQUE MOREAU

Cover Design by Cover Couture
www.bookcovercouture.com

Photo (c) Lindee Robinson Photography

MEET MONIQUE!

Join Monique's Newsletter (and receive goodies and release information): https://bit.ly/SteamyReadNewsletter

Follow her on TikTok @moniquemoreauthor

Like her Facebook Page: https://bit.ly/MoniqueMoreaufb

Follow her on Instagram: https://bit.ly/MoniqueMoreauIG

Follow her on Book Bub: http://bit.ly/MoniqueBookBub

Learn all about Monique's books: MoniqueMoreau.com

1

———

PUCK

Puck threw down a card on the chipped tabletop.

Glancing up at the icicles hanging down from the barred windows of Duchess County Jail, he swore under his breath.

Fuck, what a way to start the new year.

He shifted on the hard bench, bolted to the dusty cement floor. His eyes crawled down the peeling paint of the cinder block wall and skated over the heads of the inmates in the housing unit. He had to get the hell out of here. And fast.

He'd almost blown a fucking gasket after seeing Sammi in court, at his arraignment earlier that morning. She generally disobeyed him, driving him insane with her antics, but that straight-up pissed him off.

He'd thrown Sage, his lawyer, a mean look before losing his shit and getting carted away by the guards. Hadn't he explicitly told her to keep Sammi out of the courtroom? He didn't want his *baby* sister seeing him in cuffs. But she was tenacious and stubborn as fuck, so he shouldn't have been surprised that she flouted a direct order.

The thought of his little sister brought his gut roiling to a high boil. At the age of twenty-one, the girl had never been left alone a day in her life. Having raised her since she was thirteen, nothing could stop him from protecting his kid sister. *Nothing until now, that is.* Being behind bars limited a man's options.

After his outburst, he was bundled into a van, musty with stale body odor, and thrown back in gen pop, the recent term he'd learned for the general population of inmates. Smacking another card down on the ugly-ass table the color of puke, Puck lifted his head when he heard the unit door clang open. Who the fuck should waltz in like the asshole he was but Whistle, his Squad brother.

Shooting him a wide grin, Whistle shifted the thin plastic sleeping pad over his shoulder and followed the correctional officer's finger toward a cell. He adjusted the bundle of bedding in his arm and ducked past the steel-plate door of the enclosure.

The brother got his ass thrown in jail to keep him company. Christ. The boy followed him like a goddamn puppy, giving Puck the added burden of watching out for him. If anyone had impulse-control issues, hell, that would be Whistle. Besides...his pretty-boy looks would get under some fucker's skin up in this joint. That face was a brawl waiting to happen.

Five minutes later, Whistle crossed the expanse of the housing unit and took a seat beside Puck, a shit-eating grin on his face.

Concentration shattered for good, Puck threw down a random card with a grunt. "What in the fuck are you doing here?" he asked testily.

Whistle's face fell so fast it was almost funny. Almost. Shrugging sheepishly, he bowed his head and mumbled, "Got arrested. Fightin'."

Angling his head, Puck side-eyed him. "Again?"

Whistle gave an embarrassed shrug. Shaking his head, Puck let out a sigh. The same age as Sammi, Whistle was a hot mess of a brother. Patched in by the skin of his teeth. Loyal as a bulldog, he liked to act dumb as fuck. At his age, Puck was bustin' his ass. Prospecting, working a shit job, and keeping a sharp eye on Sammi. He'd barely slept for two years. His gaze swept over Whistle critically. He seriously doubted the boy would survive in the world alone. Puppy-dog or not, though, now that he'd patched in, he was as good as blood.

Crumbling his cards in his fist, he slammed them down on the metal table with a loud smack and declared, "I'm out." The men he played with gave him chin lifts of recognition as he got up from the table with a tilt his head, a silent command for Whistle to follow.

Walking to a deserted corner of the large space where men milled around, played cards, and basically wasted their time away, he propped his shoulder against a wall and asked, "What the fuck happened?"

"Had to keep you company," Whistle admitted serenely.

Puck gritted his teeth. "Christ, Whistle, I'm a grown-ass man. I don't need a keeper in here, watching my back. There aren't any brothers from other clubs and everyone else is scared enough not to fuck with me."

"It's your first rodeo in this place, but I've been here seven times. I know how it works and who's who. I can help. Everyone needs someone at their back. Even you. I'll be out soon, but I can be an extra pair of eyes for the next couple weeks. Told Sage why I did what I did. She was mad as hell, but she promised to take things slow on her end."

"Motherfucker, are you insane? It'll be my job to watch out for *you*. You're making my life harder here."

"Nah, I'm good in jail. I know how to play the system."

Cocking an eyebrow, Puck looked at him dubiously. Whistle nodded in response. "It's the truth. I know the COs, the correctional officers. They haven't changed much since the last time I was in here."

Scrubbing the bristles on his jaw, Puck cursed softly. "Christ, you're a pain in my ass."

❋❋❋

WHISTLE WAS UP AHEAD of Puck, with his tray of food in the chow hall. The beige-colored cinder block walls, fake-wood Formica tabletops, and green-painted doors were what passed as decoration in this cesspit. Puck grabbed a still-wet flexible tray from a stack, a spork from the wire basket for utensils, and took the plate of slop handed to him by an inmate dishing out food from a huge tray of steaming chili. Moving down the line, he scooped up a small bowl of what might or might not be mashed potatoes.

His eyes flicked up, passing over several men in front of him, and zeroed in on Whistle. The kid was talking to a monstrosity of a man. Shaved head. Big and powerful, the guy flexed his shoulders as he said something to Whistle. The kid tensed and growled back. He spoke too low for Puck to hear, but he'd seen enough in this cage to know a "heart check" when he saw one. It was an established inmate's way of testing a newbie.

Without hesitating, Puck clenched the spork in his fist, flew past the men in front of him, and landed a fist in the monster's chest. The spork crushed against his pecs, but no matter. Shaking off the splintered plastic, Puck balled his fist and slammed a left hook against the fucker's cheek. The familiar sound of crushed bone sounded in the now-silent chow hall, followed by a howl.

Pain radiated up Puck's arm, vibrating like a tuning fork. A crescendo of sounds exploded as trays and plates clattered to the cement floor and inmates flocked to the fight, surrounding Puck and the monster in a tight circle.

A chant began.

Cu-jo. Cu-jo. Cu-jo.

Great, just his luck. The bastard was named after a rabid dog.

Shouts from the COs rang off the high ceilings.

Back teeth grinding, Puck didn't have much time before the COs would swoop in to break them up. From his side, he saw Whistle busy fighting another man. At least that man was about his size. Whistle let out a whoop. The idiot was fucking enjoying himself.

Adrenaline pumped in Puck's bloodstream as the monster he was struggling with grabbed him by the throat and slammed him down on the cement floor. *Oomph!* Pain crashed against his skull and down his spine. Ten fingers tightened around his throat. *Fshh.* He gasped for air through the crushing of his windpipe. Twisting and writhing on the floor, Puck tore at the fingers around his throat, but to no avail. His eyes burned like a motherfucker, his face flushed, and his chest was about to explode. Black crowded the edges of his vision.

Giving up on the fingers, he jammed his thumbs into the inmate's eye sockets. The cocksucker expelled a tortured *gahhh* and pulled back, giving Puck the chance to wedge his forearm against the guy's throat. With enough leverage, Puck loosened the hold on his own throat. With wheezes and snorts, they were locked in a battle for survival. Puck jabbed his elbow in the bastard's face. With a grunt, he slid off one of Puck's legs, freeing it. Instantly taking advantage, Puck kneed the motherfucker in the nuts. A yelp of pain screeched in his ear.

Before he could do more, the fingers wrapped around his windpipe were pried off. An instant later, the asshole's weight was off him. Blinking up, Puck massaged his neck muscles as he heaved in a deep breath and swallowed around the burn of his throat.

COs had their hands all over him, hauling him to his feet. His swaying body was yanked around, and manacles were clicked around his wrists.

"Motherfucker! You're a dead man," the big guy yelled from over the shoulders of the COs circled around him as they shoved him toward the exit.

Taking in gulps of air, Puck's gaze found Whistle, who was being taken away as well. Twisting his head over his shoulder, Whistle mouthed *thanks, brother*. Puck gave him a chin lift and a wink. Blood dripped from Whistle's nose and the side of his face. He shook his head and laughed before he got shoved hard in the back by a female CO's baton.

"Not even two fucking days and already in a fight? You a troublemaker, boy," the CO barked as he tightened the cuffs on him. The circulation to his wrists was cut off, but, hey, at least he could breathe again.

2

AVE

Ava parked her bright orange compact Nissan near the front entrance of her father's Harley Davidson dealership for her weekly outing with Kat.

Having been born in the bosom of the Renegades MC, her little sister derided her Nissan as "the Clementine." She was here to see said bratty sister for their long-standing Saturday afternoon date. Since Kat spent as much time at the dealership as she did at home, it was a natural meeting point.

Stepping into the shop, Ava inhaled and then released a simple, quiet breath. The one downside of meeting Kat here was the risk of bumping into her father. Seventeen years after he'd dumped her and her mom to go off with a biker chick, a needle pricked her heart whenever she saw him. She loved him. Of course she did...but his serial cheating had changed the course of her life at the ripe old age of twelve. Although she'd made the best of it—like her relationship with Kat—she couldn't let go of how he'd ruined her childhood with his betrayal.

Stomping the residual dust of snow off her sturdy leather boots, Ava took in the place. She may be ambivalent about her father, but she loved the shop. The dealership was literally as large as a church. The vaulted ceiling was made of cherry-wood, and broad windows graced the four walls, blazing with bright sunlight. It was as ostentatious as a cathedral, only with Harley Davidson posters and emblems adorning the walls in the place of saints. A hundred bikes in perfect rows, like pews, displayed the popular Softail, the Sportster, the Touring, and the Street lines.

Strolling past the bikes to her left, her hand caressed the handlebars. Riding was the one aspect of bikers that she had no reservations about. Once upon a time, when her life had been free, she'd ridden a Sportster 883 Super-Low. She'd owned a refurbished one that her father had gotten her, one of the few gifts she'd accepted from him. It felt like a lifetime ago.

"So, when are you going to buy one?" a feminine voice came from behind. Ava whirled around and smirked at her sister, who had her arms folded across her budding chest and her hip cocked out to one side. *Sassy.* Ava always took a moment to herself to enjoy the bikes when stepping into the shop, and her sister almost always stomped on her little moment of peace.

"When you turn eighteen and can ride along with me."

Re-crossing her arms, the girl tapped her toes and hmphed. "This isn't about me. You should get one for yourself." Oh, but she was getting a tad too big for her panties, this one.

"You get a few piercings and you think you're a badass. How many are there, hmmm?" Ava counted off as she flicked gently at the teenager's eyebrow, nose, and lip. "Only three, but you're already rude as can be."

Face bright and open, the girl flung a wave of blue hair over her shoulder and gave Ava a fake punch. Grabbing her fist, Ava scooped her up and swung her around in her arms.

"Ava!" she shrieked. "Put me down before I scratch your eyes out. I'm too big for this!"

Ava dropped her to her feet, arched an eyebrow, and swatted away the teenager's pointed, manicured nails.

"What your father lets you get away with," she said with a soft shake of her head.

Kat's lips pursed up in a little moue. "He's your father, too."

When he became a single dad, Ava had stepped up and they'd essentially co-parented Kat for the past seven years. She sometimes envied her sister's easy camaraderie with their father. Meanwhile, her relationship with him was either distant or strumming with underlying tension, punctuated by rare moments of appreciation. He was the cause of some of the worst times of her life, but he'd also showed up to take care of her bills for rehab and college. Expenses her single mom could've never swung on her own the way he did. And he'd done it without recrimination or complaint. She begrudgingly respected him for that.

Breaking through her thoughts, Kat announced, "Hey, I wanna show you the new ones that came in."

"What's the rule when I come through the door, Kat?"

Her bottom lip jutted out in a disgruntled pout. "I leave you alone."

Ava might be torn about her father and keep the brothers of his club at a distance, but bikes? No need to cut off her nose to spite her face.

"You make me sound like a monster. Girl, I'm going to take a little time for myself and meet up with you at the counter."

"I want to go with you," her sister whined. Ava reached out and stroked back a rogue wave of electric-blue hair. Her dad may indulge her, but it didn't make up for her lack of a mom.

"I need a breather, sweetie. Give me a little bit of time—"

"Kat!" a baritone voice rang from out of an office behind the counter.

The girl's chin dropped to her chest, and she groaned. "Fantastic. He's found me."

Ava rolled her lips inward and stifled a chuckle. "Go on. I'll catch up with you in a bit."

Escaping, she zigzagged through aisles until she reached the secluded back and ended up near the 48s. She caressed a line of them. The big, fat front tire, the gleaming chrome, the Harley logo branded on the tank. She slipped onto one in a natural riding position. Closing her eyes, she was on a country road, her thighs vibrating from the motor, butt soaking up the bumps. The shocks on this model were nonexistent, but no matter. She liked a rougher ride, the way the engine opened up with a loud rumbling that reverberated through her core.

The only time she let herself go, the only time she felt free, was when she rode. Although she rarely had the time nowadays, riding was freedom from worries, emotions...everything. Bowing her head, she strained against the shoulders of her jacket. *Remember, freedom and lack of rules haven't been your friends.*

Hopping off, Ava paced away from the bikes and toward the front, where Kat waited impatiently. Chatting and joking with Kat, Ava gathered up her belongings and was halfway to the door when a massive hand wrapped around her upper arm. "Ava."

She stilled and blinked down at the four-inch-wide fingers banded over her skin. She sucked in her stomach. *Dad.* He rarely made an appearance on the floor.

"Get back here soon, y'hear?"

His hand quickly slipped away, but her gaze remained on where his fingers had been. He was rarely demonstrative. It simply wasn't their way.

Peering up at him with a frown, she mumbled, "Yeah, okay."

She'd come for a dose of solace, but there was always a tightrope of tension between them. Circling an arm around Kat's shoulder, she inhaled the sweet scent of bubblegum lip gloss. It settled her frazzled nerves.

Outside, in the crisp winter air, she released the girl's body and clicked her fob to open the car doors. "Come on, let's get some bubble tea."

3

PUCK

CO pulled Puck out of the hole, snapped cuffs on him, and walked him over to see the social worker, where he was supposed to "talk" about the fight.

For fuck's sake, he didn't know what was worse: being locked up or being forced to talk to a shrink.

Sure, he was glad to be out of solitary. He'd been dealing with heart palpitations, lying on the plastic-covered cot that crackled every time he moved when the lock to his cell disengaged. He swiped a few beads of perspiration along his hairline with the thumbs of his shackled hands as the CO knocked on the closed door. A muffled voice instructed them to come in. The officer pushed the door open for him, and he sauntered in, ready to get this bullshit over with, when his feet froze in their place.

His breath caught in his throat.

Ava.

Mother*fucker*.

Sitting behind the desk, one hand primly laying on top of the other, she raised her gaze to his. Her hazel eyes went round, mouth parting slightly. Dark mahogany hair cascaded down the sides of her face, much longer than when he'd last seen her.

Eight long years ago.

She wore a brown plaid suit jacket that engulfed her slim form, but she had the same build. Who could forget a tall, lithe body like hers? Or her high, round tits topped with delicious berry-tasting nipples?

His head cocked to the side as he observed her carefully. She'd always been the hippest person in a room, but her suit was...drab. Where was the party girl dressed in sexy little dresses, stripping nude any chance she got? Sassy, spirited, crazy. Here, she was dressed in an androgynous suit that didn't flatter of her slim figure, with subtle but definite curves. Her hair was the only sign of her femininity.

A frown creased his forehead. This woman had no laugh lines around her big eyes or her lush, sensual lips. The glint of mischievousness and humor was gone from her large doll-like eyes.

Instead, they stared out at him, serious and grave. It had been a long time, but he wasn't used to this look.

"Ava?" he asked with a rasp, his mouth suddenly dry.

She jerked slightly; calling her name had pulled her out of her own reverie. Instantly, her eyes shuttered, changing the color of her irises and sealing off the windows to her soul.

Officer Dipshit, as Puck had coined him, handed her his file, and said harshly, "You know this inmate? He just got into a fight." Concern laced his tone as he asked, "Want me to stay?"

Puck bristled at him.

"No, I'll be fine, Derick," she mumbled, her eyes fliting away from Puck's. "He's a kid from my old neighborhood."

Derick? His eyes swung to the CO and then back to her. *She's on a first-name basis with this jackass?* Guess it was to be expected since they worked in the same facility. Still, Puck didn't like it.

He didn't like the man or his manner when it came to Ava. Ava was *his*, dammit. He recoiled slightly. No, she hadn't been his for a long time. He'd made sure of that, hadn't he?

Eyes roving over her, the CO asked, "You sure?"

Dipshit was checking her out. *Oh, hell no. Fucking NO.*

She tilted her chin toward Puck's hands in cuffs. "I'll be fine. Would you please uncuff him?"

Dipshit looked at her hesitantly.

"I know Mr. Rossi, Derick," she explained. Why did she have to explain herself? Dipshit didn't want to let this go.

Head down and sifting through the Puck's folder, she continued, "Come back in thirty minutes to take him back to his cell."

Damn, the husky tone of her voice had always turned him on. Apparently, today was no exception.

Dipshit seemed reluctant.

With a little huff, she glared up at him and clarified, "We don't have another social worker available. Until the county allocates enough funds to pay for a second social worker, we don't have a choice. God knows we need one."

Officer Derick Dipshit pressed his hand on Puck's shoulder. His muscles tensed with the urge to resist, but he wasn't going to fuck up his one chance at seeing Ava. Even though he'd recuperated fast, he was still reeling from the shock.

His eyes roamed over the room for other clues about her. What she lacked in personal appearance she more than made up for on her walls. One was plastered with motivational posters in soft pastels, calling for compassion, feelings, and promising confidentiality. There were knickknacks scattered on her desk, on the low bookshelf behind her, and on the institutional filing cabinet against one wall. A large dream catcher hung above her head, facing him. Christ, if only it'd catch the bad dreams that plagued him at night in this hellhole.

Under Ava's watchful gaze, he consciously relaxed his body and allowed himself to be pressed down into the seat facing her.

"Behave yourself," the officer tossed out before leaving and softly shutting the door behind him.

Asshole.

He wasn't a fucking kid, and he sure as hell didn't hurt women.

Once Dipshit was gone, his gaze returned to Ava.

Damn, she was as stunning as ever. There was her long hair, which he knew glittered red in the sunlight, her multicolored eyes, and her lush, plump lips. He knew what it felt like to have those lips pressed against his. Or wrapped around his dick.

Fuck, he was getting hard, thinking about it. Sex with Ava had been spiritual, and it wasn't because they'd been high half the time. It was phenomenal no matter what they'd drank, smoked, or snorted. Hell, stone-cold sober and fucking her brought him to the highest of heights. Their bond just was, like the sun rising at dawn or setting at dusk. Like the turn of the seasons. Their lovemaking had been a phenomenon, like the Northern Lights. That's what fucking Ava was like. Spectacular. One of a kind.

It's the reason he didn't have an old lady, a baby mama, or even a steady fuck. After he broke up with her, he'd kept tabs on her for years. Many a time, he'd been tempted to show up on her doorstep after he got his head on straight. But in the end, he'd decided it was best to let sleeping dogs lie. Did he regret it? Fuck yeah, he did.

Now—all bets were off. Ava was back in his life, and like

catching sight of a deer in the crosshairs of his hunting rifle, she was his.

Sweeping her soft, burnished chestnut hair over her shoulder, she inspected him with guarded eyes, shooting him a *fuck you* look. Hell, she was so off-limits, she might as well have been wrapped in yellow police tape with "caution" stamped in block letters.

Behind it, he caught another emotion. One he'd seen only a handful of times. One she kept carefully under wraps. Swirling in the yellow, copper, and green shards of her irises was sorrow. That sentiment was emphasized in the corners of her mouth, which drooped slightly, and then reinforced in her soulful eyes.

Breaking the silence that had descended between them, she politely inquired, "Damien, how are you?"

"I go by Puck," he replied. A notch formed between her perfectly arched brows as she shifted in her seat. "I patched into the Demon Squad MC seven years back, and my road name is Puck. That's the only name I answer to."

"Puck."

His name rolled softly off her tongue, and swear to God, it was like listening to a fuckin' angel calling his name. He wanted to hear her say it again. Better yet, he wanted to hear her scream it out loud while creaming on his cock.

Glancing down, she opened his file and read the details of his arrest. "Alright then, why don't you tell me what happened in the cafeteria?"

"I'm not gonna tell you about beating a man's ass in the fucking cafeteria, Ava. How have you been? How's your mom? Your sister?"

Her body stiffened, starting with the word *mom*. Her fingers curled around the file. The crunch of the heavy paper stock was loud in the small office. He chased a flurry of emotions across her face, and none of them were good.

She took in a slow breath through her nostrils and firmly stated, "We're not here to catch up on the past. You're Puck now, not Damien. I'm Ms. Evans, not Ava. After so many years, we're basically strangers to each other, so let's keep it that way, shall we?"

He deserved that slap on the wrist, but it didn't stop a red haze from blanketing his vision for a moment. They'd *never* be strangers. A deep well of experience existed between them, and nothing would sweep it away.

"Bullshit. You'll always be Ava to me." He leaned back in his seat, the top of the metal chair digging into his back. "Don't care how many years have passed." His eyes raked over her. "You look good. More than good. You look fucking beautiful. I know you stopped using long ago. Went back to school. Became a shrink."

"Not a shrink. I'm a social worker with a master's degree in Criminal Justice."

"Yeah?" A corner of his lips tipped up. "There you go. I knew you'd pull yourself together and do good. I'm fucking proud of you, Ava. You always had a smart head on your shoulders."

"Then, why'd you—" She cut herself off with a slashing motion of her hand. "Anyway..."

"Though," he continued, undaunted, "can't say I like what you're wearing. You're fucking gorgeous."

He paused, his eyes gliding over her once again. "Gor-ge-ous." He enunciated the syllables.

Angling his head, he changed his mind. "Nah, come to think of it, I'm glad you're all covered up, working around these fuckin' assholes. I didn't like the way Officer *Derick Dipshit* looked at you."

His eyes sharpened. "You're not dating that fucker, are you?"

Her mouth parted. "Are you kidding me? You haven't seen me in eight years. *Eight. Years.*"

Through gritted teeth, she ground out, "And you have the audacity to comment on the way I dress or how a colleague speaks to me? Are you out of your mind?"

A smile broke on his face. "There's the Ava I know."

"Shut up, Damien. I mean Puck. Just shut your mouth before you say something unforgivable. Do you know what I'm doing with Derick?"

His jaw tightened. Damn, how could he forget her attitude, or that smart mouth of hers, when she got heated?

She tapped her chin with her index finger, her eyes burning into his. "Hmm, let me think."

Her eyes flared wide. Her mouth popped open in an expression of surprise. "Oh, wait, it's none of your business."

She leaned forward and spoke slowly, enunciating every word as if speaking to a child. "Because you aren't part of my life and haven't been for *eight* years."

"Watch your tone of voice," he snapped.

"Don't say something stupid, and I won't have to watch my tone, *Puck*." She spat out his name like it was a curse. "Unfortunately, I'm the only social worker at Duchess County Jail, but if I weren't, I'd transfer you in a heartbeat."

His lips flatlined. It was more than a slap on the wrist, but she was right. He'd forfeited any rights he once had. Tell that to his fuckin' heart with her sitting not three feet away from him. Usually, he was laid back when it came to chicks, but Ava was different. Always had been, since the moment he laid eyes on her a lifetime ago.

Picking up a ballpoint pen, she scribbled something into his file. "I'm ordering you to attend an anger-management class. You always were a hothead. Clearly, nothing's changed. I'm certain you lost your temper when you pistol-whipped that poor innocent man. Bad enough that got you in here, but then you go ahead and get into a fight the day of your arrival? That's a shot on your record. Since your drug test came back clean, I can safely assume you were neither drunk nor high. So, temper it is."

He snorted. "That poor innocent man was a fucking wife beater, and I wasn't pissed off when I beat him up. Did that shit to teach him never to hurt a woman." Ava's head shot up. "As for the fight, I was protecting a brother. He's a kid and a pretty boy. Had to back him up."

"Are you trying to tell me you *used* to have a temper, but now you're in control?"

"No, but that doesn't mean I don't have a handle on it."

Ava massaged her creased brows.

He leaned forward. "You okay?"

"Fine, fine" she muttered with a wave of her hand. It was an obvious lie. She pressed her forefinger and thumb hard into the middle of her forehead and her temple.

"Migraine," he asserted knowingly, leaning back into his chair and crossing his arms over his chest. She'd struggled when they knew each other. One of the many reasons that put her on the path of using the way she did.

"Seeing you can bring one on," she snapped.

He gritted his teeth at her saltiness. *Calm down.* The decision to terminate their relationship had been unilateral, and as painful as it'd been for him, it had been far worse for her. It come as a shock to her. They'd been madly in love and she'd been adrift, with no goals or aspirations besides the next hit or the next party.

He'd had his work, the club, and Sammi to throw himself into. Two years had passed before he came up for air, and by then, the pain had subsided. Fuck, he was witnessing only a fraction of the pain he'd caused her. He'd been young, stupid, and grieving when he'd broken things off between the two of them, but breaking her heart was his biggest regret.

"Fuck, babe. I wish I could help you."

"Don't *babe* me," she snapped. Releasing her head with a frustrated sigh, she dropped back in the chair. Again, emotions warred on her face. Finally, she sighed and asked hesitantly, "H-how old is Sammi now? Twenty-one?"

"Oh, it's alright for you to ask me questions?" he grumbled.

She narrowed her eyes. "I'm asking because at her age, she probably still lives with you. If that's the case, then you'd be worried about leaving her alone. Which means you'll want to get out as soon as possible. I'm trying to be helpful, for her sake if not yours. What's your bail situation?"

"Bail denied by fucking Judge Korman."

"Ahh...Korman. Yeah, you're not getting bail." Flicking her pen against the desktop, she raised her eyes above his head, lips pursed. He couldn't help staring at those lips. Her gaze returned to him. "I think you should consider attending the anger-management class. It'll be a good look for you, considering the shot on your record for the fight."

He lets out a sigh. "You're right, I'm worried about Sammi. That's my greatest problem right now. If it gets me outta here, then I'm down."

She gave him the first small but real smile. "I know how important she is to you. Okay, so I'll put you down for the class. Make sure you don't get into another fight or accrue another infraction."

"Yeah, okay."

Ava bent her head as she scribbled into his file. A rebellious wave of mahogany slipped off her shoulder and swept over half her face. She tucked the errant lock behind her earringless ear with her finger. Her unvarnished fingernails were neatly clipped and filed into half-moons. Another change. She used to wear loads of jewelry and paint her nails crazy colors.

It was like she'd leached all the color and beauty out of her life.

A pull tugged at him from the center of his chest. He followed the sensation and leaned forward until he was mere inches away from her. Her scent drifted toward him, knocking him sideways. Tahitian vanilla mingled with coconut and mango. It was the same balmy, tropical scent that always got his cock to stand at attention. Thank fuck his oversized jumpsuit hid his growing erection.

He growled low in his chest. He'd taste her again, he swore. He didn't know how or when, but it was happening. *They* were happening.

Seemed only fair to warn her of what her future entailed. "Ava," he called.

She lifted her face toward him, her eyes flaring slightly in acknowledgment of his proximity.

"I promise I'll have you again. In my life. In my bed. This time, you're not going anywhere," he vowed to her.

Sparks flew from her eyes. "Oh, yeah?" She leaned forward until her sweet breath fanned over his face and said in a throaty tone, "Well, let me set you straight right now. That's *never* going to happen. Maybe you don't remember how it went down between us, but I certainly do. You were the one who broke up with me. Go to hell, Puck."

"There were reasons for that—"

Pulling away, she cut in, "I agree, and that's why I never ran after you or tried changing your mind. After your mother's death, you did what you felt was necessary for both you and Sammi. You were shocked by her death and having full custody of Sammi. I understood it then, and I understand it now. While I may respect your decision, it doesn't change the fact that you threw away what we had. You threw *me* away, Puck."

The stark pain bleeding from her almost brought him to his knees. He'd readily slam them down on the scuffed floor and crawl to her on his hands and knees. Swear to her he'd never do it again. He knew about her dad. How he'd cheated on her mom and then ran out on them, leaving them to fend for themselves. "It was hard as hell. I get that, babe."

Her palm went up, front and center in his face, shutting him down. "Don't *babe* me. Don't call me by anything other than my name. The only relationship between us is a professional one."

She paused for emphasis. "Social worker and inmate."

Her walls clanked down between them, like the jailhouse door that shut his ass in this shithole.

She wanted to play it this way. Alright, he'd allow it. For now.

"I'm not going to argue with you," he announced. *I've done my duty and put you on alert. You're a grown-ass woman. Just be ready*, he silently declared.

"Good, because you don't have a leg to stand on," she replied pertly. Checking the clock above the doorway, she stood up.

As if on cue, there was a knock on the door.

Fucking Officer Derick Dipshit was back.

"Good luck, Puck."

"Oh, babe, I don't need luck," he drawled.

She didn't have the opportunity to respond with the door opening, but she made sure to shoot him a deep scowl.

Puck took in his competition as Officer Dipshit stepped inside, unimpressed by his thinning hair or slight paunch.

Unfortunately, a man's physical attributes didn't mean a whole lot to Ava. She wasn't superficial; character and connection were far more meaningful to her.

Giving the other man a slow once-over, he couldn't imagine she had any kind of connection with this idiot. Of course, she may have lowered her standards. Enough things had changed about her.

One way or another, he'd find his way back into her office. This was providence, and he wasn't about to fuck up again. Derick Dipshit be damned.

4

AVA

The instant the door closed behind the men, Ava slumped back in her chair.

She expelled a pent-up breath and dropped her head back against her chair. Thankfully, once Puck was out of her presence, the pulsing pain in her temples began to recede. The audacity of that bastard.

He'd always had a cocky swagger about him, even as a teenager. Ava could hardly believe the nonsense that spewed out of his mouth. Seriously, the man was delusional if he thought he had a chance of getting back with her.

She glanced down at her dowdy pantsuit. Good God, why would he even want to? She looked like shit. Professional yes, but otherwise, she looked horrible. Of course, she purposely dressed badly. She wasn't looking to get hit on by an inmate, a CO or any other employee.

Time in the hole must have twisted his mind if he was entertaining the idea of being with her again. She hadn't measured up the first time around, and the pain of that knowledge reared its ugly head yet again.

Despite his absurd declarations, seeing Puck left her

rattled. Even now, her heartbeat was going fast. She'd managed to maintain a cool demeanor while in his presence, but her hands still trembled slightly. Puck was always so impulsive. Clearly, some things never changed.

Her lips twisted in a wry smile. Funny, she'd seamlessly transitioned into using his new name. It fit him. Mischievous. Mercurial. Clever, oh-so clever. And, she reminded herself sternly, never to be underestimated.

While it was crucial that he not be taken lightly, it was a waste of time to dwell on or overanalyze their conversation. First of all, she'd probably never see him again. She worked mostly with inmates who struggled with substance-abuse issues, and his drug test had come back squeaky clean. She wasn't teaching the anger-management class, so if he stayed out of trouble, he wouldn't be back. And Puck wasn't risking another fight to sabotage his chances of getting back to Sammi.

Secondly, he was unpredictable. One moment, he supposedly wanted her. The next, who the hell knew. He'd flip-flopped before. No reason to imagine he wouldn't do it again. Barely any time in her presence, and he was already pronouncing that he'd have her in his bed again. She rolled her eyes. *Puh-leeze, what a flake.*

The only one he was steadfast with was Sammi. Ava had always admired the way he took care of his little sister. Seeing what Puck had done when his mother died had inspired Ava. She'd made a conscious decision to separate the resentment she felt toward her father from Kat and had cultivated an independent relationship with her. It began even before Kat's mother took off, leaving her father and Ava to finish raising her. And it'd paid off. She had a loving relationship with someone she adored.

Just because Puck was loyal and dedicated to his sister

didn't mean he was capable of that kind of consistency with a partner.

But seeing him *had* been a shock. Eight years on and the man had filled out from the nineteen-year-old boy she'd known. Filled. Out. Even wearing an orange jumpsuit a size too large, she'd noted the outline of his hard chest, tufts of chest hair peeking out from the V of his opened collar. Or his strong forearms, the cords of sleek muscles bulging as he'd laid his arms on her desk earlier.

And his face. Jesus, he was handsome, in that rugged way of his. It could wreck a woman's resolve. *Any woman besides me, that is.* She'd experienced the lack of devotion that lay beneath that gorgeous olive skin of his. The image of him hovering so close to her, shimmered in her mind's eye. His jet-black curls bouncing slightly as he moved his head. His deep chocolate-malt eyes staring at her, ringed by long black lashes. Hair and eyelashes like his were wasted on a man. Then there were his high cheekbones and that strong nose above a generous mouth. She knew exactly how those lips felt, pressed against her own, sliding down her throat or over the slope of her breast. Or even lower...

She sucked in a breath. *Don't go there. It's the lack of sex that's affecting you this way.* She'd left the past behind after Sasha's death. The drugs, the partying, and most definitely, the man. Losing her best friend so soon after their breakup had been a doozie.

There was a soft knock on her door. A knock she recognized.

"Come in," she called out.

Derick popped his head in. "Busy?"

"Not at the moment. Come on in," she invited him in with a wave of her hand.

Derick had showed interest in her, which she found

surprising, considering how badly she dressed the three days a week she worked at the jail. Being the only social worker with a degree in Criminal Justice at the Agency, she'd been a shoe-in for the position. At five foot nine, she was tall for a woman, so she always appreciated height in a man, and Derick definitely had that. He was neither as fit nor drop-dead gorgeous like Puck, but she wasn't looking for a random hookup. Not that she overthought her mild flirtation with Derick. It was simply nice to chat, lightly tease, and joke with a guy. That was it.

"On my fifteen-minute break," he said, holding up the Styrofoam cup of coffee. He placed another one on her desk. "Here's one for you. Cream and sugar, how you like it."

He'd done that before, and she appreciated the gallantry of his gesture. Taking a sip, she smiled at him before placing the cup down. "I always feel the need for an extra coffee on Mondays. Thanks."

Sitting down across from her, he crossed an ankle over his knee. Steadying the cup on his knee, he asked, "How's the day going so far? No one giving you trouble, are they?"

Derick always started his conversations this way. Making sure no one was bothering her. "All good. A day like any other."

"So...you knew the last guy?" he inquired in a careful tone.

"Yep," she replied succinctly. No way was she going into her past with Puck. It had been bad enough seeing him. Seeing the way his eyes had lingered on her. It risked going to her head, rummaging inside, and rearranging it ways she could not permit. Could she even do her job correctly with him? Her chances were about as good as a roll of the dice. Hopefully, her professionalism wouldn't be tested again.

At one time, she'd fallen hard for him. It had been deep and wild. Wild like the breaking waves, crashing against sharp, rugged cliffs. That's where she'd end up if she wasn't careful. Crushed against a jagged rock, left to bleed to death. Like before.

After a small lull, Derick asked, "First time you see someone you know?"

"Yeah," she replied. "Has it happened to you?"

"On occasion. Had my elementary school teacher in here once on a drunk-and-disorderly conduct charge. Explained a helluva lot about fifth grade."

Ava let out a peal of laughter. "I bet it did. It's a little shocking to see someone you know, but we're working in the county jail, so it's to be expected, I suppose. People from all walks of life pass through here."

Derick brought his coffee cup to his lips and swallowed.

Another lull. Racking her brain to move on to a different subject, she asked, "Anything special go on out there today?"

Derick shifted his foot on the linoleum floor. "Nah, it's quiet. Winter's slower. Less arrests makes for less inmates. Less inmates makes for less work," he replied in a singsong.

"True," she replied, nodding. Derick may fall on the boring side of the spectrum, but he'd always been kind and respectful toward her. That was worthy of her esteem. Better than falling in love with a hot, charismatic mischief-maker who broke one's heart.

Jiggling his foot a little, he pressed his lips together and then pushed them out in a silly raspberry sound. "Here goes nothing," he mumbled. Taking in a deep inhalation, he lifted churning eyes to her and said, "Maybe you wanna go out and have dinner sometime?"

Ava blinked rapidly several times. They'd been taking breaks together for a couple of months, and he'd never gone further. Frankly, she'd given up on him, wondering if she'd misread his cues. What bad timing. If he'd only asked the day before... Sheesh, if he'd asked an hour before, she would've jumped at the opportunity. *Damn Puck.* His reappearance had pulled her up short. "Uhm..." she trailed off. *What do I say? What do I do? Gah!*

Jumping to his feet, he blurted out, "I sprung this on you. I get that. Shouldn't have done that."

"No, it's not that, Derick. I just...it's just..." Dammit, she was stammering. The memory of Puck was too hot and new, like a match thrown on a powder keg of lust that'd been sitting in a corner, undisturbed for so long that she'd forgotten it existed. The bastard had fallen back into her life, completely unwelcome, and stirred up a hornet's nest of emotions.

"Well, thanks for the chat. Nice break on the days you come here. I love my fellow officers, but sometimes we know too many details about one another. If I had to listen to one more story about Brian's mother's digestive problems, I'd have to use my gun on myself."

Awkward. Ava chuckled self-consciously. Unsure how to respond, she followed his lead and pretended he hadn't asked her out. "No worries. My door's always open. If you're going back on the clock, can you bring over the other guys who got into the fight with Mr. Rossi?"

"Sure thing," he said. Lifting his coffee cup in a goodbye salute, he stepped out into the hallway. Just before closing the door, he cautioned, "Never a good thing to get sappy about someone we see in here. We gotta remember. They're here for a reason," and softly shut it behind him.

Smacking her hand on her forehead, she groaned loudly. She had to get her head on straight quick because she'd let a perfect opportunity pass her by. Hopefully, he wouldn't avoid her, because next time he stopped by, she intended to ask him out.

5

PUCK

Puck was back in his regular cell, *thank fuck.*

After almost five days with only his mind and a Bible in a six-by-eight-foot solitary cell, he was about to lose his damn mind. Baring his gritted teeth, he shuddered at the memory of the walls closing in on him. Nah, he was pretty sure he *had* lost his damn mind.

Kingdom, his president, and Sage kept a careful eye on him. Or as much as was possible from the outside. They were most likely the reason he was already back in with gen pop. Pregnant or not, Sage worked relentlessly for him and Whistle.

It'd been hell, but it wasn't like he'd had much of a choice. For a new inmate like him, a fight was inevitable. The only question was *when* it was going to go down.

Puck had spent most of the mind-numbing hours focused on Ava, daydreaming about her and...plotting. Hey, it was better than going insane, worrying about how Sammi was holding up, or how he was going to get out of this fuckhole.

Lying on the top bunk, over the threadbare piece of cloth

the county passed off as a blanket, Puck hung one ankle over the other and went over his plan. There was no doubt in his mind that this was more than a coincidence. They'd lived in the same small city in New York for eight years and never crossed paths. And their paths could've crossed because her father was in the Renegades MC. Although not a real club like the Squad, there weren't that many bikers in this city. They tended to overlap.

But it happened after enough time had passed and they'd both matured. Their stars were finally aligned, and Puck was determined to have her again. Tomorrow, he had an appointment with Sage before his preliminary hearing with Judge Korman. Dumbass that he was, he'd opened his big mouth and answered the arresting officer's questions in the cop car. His confession was due to the adrenaline rush from taking down Kerri's abusive ex. His misstep had cost him big because it supplied Korman with enough evidence to go ahead with a grand jury.

Puck shut his eyes. Since he was likely stuck in jail for a good amount of time, he'd convince Sage to get him seen by the social worker. Lucky for him there was only one, and her name was Ava. Once he was alone with her behind closed doors, he'd set his plan into motion.

There was a scuffing of shoes by his door. Eyes snapping open, Puck rolled onto his side. Whistle poked his head in.

"Hey, brother," he called out to the youngster. "They let you out, too?"

Whistle stepped inside the small space, circled around the open toilet, and jumped up on his bunk bed. Puck moved his long legs, clasped Whistle's hand and gave him a gruff hug.

"Whattup? You go crazy in there after a few days, or what?" asked Whistle with a chuckle.

"Mad-dog crazy. Fuck, the echoes alone can drive a man insane."

"Yeah," Whistle replied. "Good to see you back, brah. I've got my preliminary hearing later today. Sage thinks I'll get bail this time around."

"Good, I can't have you around me. You're too fuckin' tempting for the motherfuckers up in here."

Whistle's gave him a lopsided grin. "You're jealous, is all."

"Yeah, that's it," he scoffed and smacked him lightly on the side of his head. Whistle had started hanging out at the club at the age of seventeen, although Prez, the president of the Squad at the time, decreed he couldn't prospect until he was legal. Along with Prez, Puck had adopted Whistle.

"Appreciate what you did for me, getting your ass thrown in here to check up on me. Don't do it again, though. I need you on the outside. The Box is the hottest spot for MMA fighters, and Loki's being run ragged, especially with Abby pregnant." He scratched the growing scruff of his chin. "Cutter was splitting his time between the Squad Bar and the Box, but he was put full-time on the Box. That leaves me alone with the bar, and I was charged with figuring out how to make the place pull in a profit. You need to move in there because some underhanded shit is goin' on. Live and breathe that fucking place. I need you to do the dreaded liquor inventory. How much stock we have at the beginning of inventory, how much stock we have at the end, and how much stock we receive in between. Not sure if someone's stealing or giving out product for free, but I kid you fucking not, we ran out of Hennessey."

"Someone's stealin'," said Whistle with a sage nod of his head.

"Can't jump to any conclusions when we don't have an inventory usage report, can we? It's the most popular alcohol we serve. I want your eyes open and everywhere, Whistle. The

Squad can't afford to carry a whale like that for long. Babies are poppin' out of two old ladies within the year. That makes their men nervous. They want to know they can provide for their families. We gotta hustle and make money."

"Sure thing, boss man."

"And you need to settle down," Puck continued, firming up his tone.

Eyes wide, Whistle pulled back. "Whaaaat?"

"You heard me. You're too fuckin' wild. How old are you now?"

"Twenty-one, goin' on twenty-two."

Puck grimaced. "Yeah, too fuckin' old to be pulling this shit anymore. At twenty-one years old, I was saving for a down payment on a house. Going to fuckin' parent-teacher conferences for Sammi. I kid you not, motherfucker. You buy yourself a sleeping bag or borrow Loki's roll-up bed since he doesn't use it anymore, and camp out at the bar. Ask Loki how to do inventory, take a class online, I don't care fuck-all what you gotta do. Do it and figure out why we're bleeding cash like a gutted heifer."

"Fucking hell, Puck."

"Don't curse at me. I'm the one stuck in here, twiddling my fucking thumbs while the world is going about its business. I'm charging you with a job. You find out something, you come here and tell me. Unless it's an emergency. Then, you hit up Kingdom. Hear me?"

"Yeah," Whistle grumbled.

"You've been living the high life. Crashing at the club is fine, fucking bitches is normal, but you've got to do something with yourself, yo. You won't be so quick to get your ass back in here if you have goals. I've fucked around like you, but I always had my eyes on a prize."

"Count Time," was bellowed out into the common area

outside their cells. Whistle slipped off the top bunk and landed on his feet. He stepped aside for Puck to join him on the floor, and they walked out of his cell. Each took a side of the entrance, backs to the wall, as the CO strolled down past the cells with clipboard in hand.

6

AVA

Ava's door was usually open unless she was in a meeting, in a session, or she had to concentrate on paperwork.

She was typing away on her keyboard, updating case reports, when there was a light knock. Glancing up, her fingers lost control when her eyes landed on Puck. *What the hell is he doing here?*

Officer Bryant prodded Puck inside. "Hey, Ava. How ya doing? Here's your two o'clock."

"Uhm...I don't recall having an individual with Mr. R-rossi this afternoon." she stumbled a bit over his last name. She pressed her lips together and clenched her fingers into fists.

"I just put them where they tell me," he said with a shrug.

"My lawyer didn't contact you?" Puck asked.

"I don't think so, but I've been swamped since I got in today, so I haven't checked my voicemail messages yet," she replied, waving her hand over the piles of case files and other paperwork. "Or done more than glanced at my emails."

Puck dropped into the chair facing her. "I can explain."

Ava's eyes narrowed slightly. She glanced up at Bryant's

bored face and back at Puck's composed, determined expression. Taking in a deep breath, she asked Bryant to take off his handcuffs. He did so, gave her a nod, and shut the door behind him.

Ava saved her work and logged out of her computer to give herself a chance to process Puck's presence. Jeez, his size alone was unnerving. He was so much bigger now. Her eyes flicked over the top of her computer screen and then quickly skittered away. Not only was he bulkier, with huge biceps that flexed as he crossed his arms over his broad chest, but he oozed power. The kind that could wriggle through any chink in her armor.

From the first moment she set eyes on him years ago, their attraction had been explosive. Their sex life as well. As much as she hated to admit it, she hadn't had an orgasm with a man since Puck. She could make herself climax, and she could certainly enjoy herself with men, she'd just never had the two occur simultaneously since him. Another annoyance on her long list of grievances.

Ava squirmed in her seat. The heaviness of his stare acted like a balmy, humid breeze over her heated skin. Or like the caress of a calloused hand. She felt it move from the crown of her head, down the length of her hair to her breasts and then swoop back up to her face. Taking a deep breath, she came face to face with his handsomely rugged face and soulful eyes.

This was the one who'd broken her heart. Left her and never made an attempt to reach out. True, at the time, she wasn't an ideal partner, but he hadn't given her a chance to change, to redeem herself, or be there for him when his mother died. Staring into the warm depths of those dark eyes of his, her heart melted, and she was finding it hard to maintain her irritation.

He started, as if taken by surprise, and the mood was broken.

Gripping her hands tightly on her lap, she inquired, "What can I do for you, Puck?"

"Ava," he rasped out.

The longing in his tone took her aback. She plucked at her heavy wool sweater. Licked her lips. Swallowed hard around the lump in her throat.

"W-what did you want to discuss with me?"

"Fuck, babe, you don't know what it does to me to look at you. You look like a fuckin' angel. So soft and pretty. I've been in the hole for days. Just got released into general population yesterday."

She inhaled harshly. "You were in the SHU that long?"

"Yeah, but it doesn't matter." He shook his head. "Seeing you makes the hell go away."

"I'm sorry you had to go through that. I'm so sorry, Puck," she heaved out, reaching over her desk and grabbing his hand. A wave of electricity pulsed through her fingers and up her arm. Shit, she shouldn't have done that. Quickly, she released it and clasped her hands together. Biting hard on the inside of her cheek, she slowed down her breathing. *Focus. Be professional. Focus, dammit.*

"I'm glad seeing me makes you feel better, but I don't want you to think that we could...you know...be together. I understand it's hard to be here, but you'll get out and reunite with Sammi and your club. You'll go back to living your regular life, and everything will return to normal. Most importantly, you'll feel normal again."

His right eye twitched almost imperceptibly. As a social worker, she'd learned to read micro facial expressions, but even more than that, she knew him.

"You think I'm saying this because I'm stuck in here? That I'm desperate, and that's why I want you?"

"Well, it's to be expected. You're a red-blooded male, and

we know how active you are." *What in God's name are you saying? Shut up and stop babbling.* She cleared her throat. "This is a crazy situation, and on top of that, you were in solitary. The stress of being in isolation could lead anyone to start thinking things they usually wouldn't...think...of..." She trailed off. *Oh, just shut up.* Years ago, she would've grabbed at any chance to be back with him. *Anything.* That was before she'd built up a resentment the size of the Grand Canyon. The point was that he was basically a trapped animal.

Abruptly, Puck leaned over and was in her face, his fingers pinching her chin. "Listen, Ava, and listen real fucking good. I want you because you were the love of my fucking life. I don't have an old lady. Never had a long-term girlfriend. Why? Because no one could hold a candle to you. Hell, just the way we fucked was off the charts. Sure, I wasn't going to approach you again after the fucked-up move I made years ago. But fate, destiny, whatever you wanna call it, brought us together. So that's what we'll be. Together. I don't give a fuck that I'm an inmate. I don't give a fuck whether we're in here or out there." He jabbed his finger toward the door. "We *will* be together."

Her jaw clenched tighter and tighter as he spoke. By the time he ended, she was scraping her back molars together like the wheels of a grinder. She wrenched her chin out of his hold and seethed, "What in the hell are you going on about? You haven't seen me in eight years. Simply because, by *sheer* chance, we happen to see each other again, you've taken this to mean we're meant to be together? That's plain crazy! My life won't be dictated by a random event, and I'm certainly not going to have you make a decision on my behalf. I left those impulsive, crazy days behind me when Sasha overdosed. I'm not going back to living like that."

"I'm sorry about what happened to Sasha."

She swallowed down the rush of emotions that came up

whenever she thought of her best friend and roommate. The trinity of remorse, sadness, and hopelessness crashed into her. Ava cursed herself for the umpteenth time for not having read the signs that her drug use had gotten out of control. The irony of all ironies was that Sasha's drug dealer, a man by the name of Kingpin, was currently serving time at Duchess County Jail. Puck was housed in the same jail as Sasha's true killer. Ava had made it her personal mission to follow his trail into criminality and testified against him during his parole hearings on more than one occasion.

Puck continued, "I wanted to go to you. I was at the funeral, y'know."

Her eyebrows popped up and grazed the edge of her hairline. "I didn't see you."

"I made sure you didn't. You were wrapped up in your grief, and I took cover in the woods on the edge of the cemetery. You weren't exactly expecting me."

He'd come that close to her and still stayed away? *What the fuck?* "Why didn't you show yourself?"

"The day wasn't about me; it was about Sasha, and I didn't want to add to your pain. As much as I wanted to wrap my arms around you and hug you tight, I'd lost that right, and I wasn't about to make your life any harder than it already was. I stayed till the last car left. Afterward, I visited her myself and told her my goodbyes. Had a bucket full of apologies to hand out to her."

She imagined him at Sasha's grave, praying out his sorries. They'd been good buddies, the two of them. Ava's gaze dropped, and suddenly there were tears. Dammit, she didn't do tears anymore. Regardless, they were there, salty and running down into her mouth. She wiped them away roughly with the back of her hands, but her vision remained blurry. She was furious for breaking and prayed he didn't reach for her. She wouldn't have the strength to push him away.

Thankfully, he didn't. A bunch of tissues were thrust under her nose, and she attacked them with desperation. Grabbed them and buried her face in them. She swerved around in her chair, giving him her profile. After sobbing quietly for a few minutes, she pressed her fingertips into her eye sockets. Her shoulders shuddered as she struggled to regain control.

"I'm so sorry, baby girl. I'm sorry I wasn't there to hold you. I'm sorry it happened. She was a funny, sweet girl. A good girl. Like you."

She sniffled. "I haven't spoken about her in a long time. None of my friends knew her. I broke off with that crowd after she ODed. Went back home to my mom with my tail between my legs. Even took money from my father to go to rehab and get clean. You can imagine how much pride I had to swallow to do that."

Unexpectedly, he came behind her desk and dropped to his haunches. Facing her, he caressed her hair soothingly. "And you did good. You did real good. You fought those demons and made something out of yourself. I knew how good you could be, and you went beyond my hopes and dreams for you, girl. I regret how things ended between us. I was in a fucked-up state of mind after my mother died in that car crash. Out of my mind in grief. I reacted on impulse, and by the time I looked back and realized my mistake, it was too late. The damage had been done."

His hand felt so good, gently smoothing down her hair. He wrapped his hand around the nape of her neck, pulled her into his chest, and kissed the top of her head. She leaned into the hard warmth of his chest, the spicy male scent of him enveloping her. Like patchouli and cedar ground together with a mortar and pestle. Her eyelids grew heavy. She let them fall and breathed in his masculine fragrance deeply, letting it soothe her.

A low growl rumbled in his chest, shuddering through her core. Suddenly, he was back on his feet, stepping back to take the seat across from her. Her eyes fluttered open. What had she just done, leaning into him? God, how could she forget how dangerous he was to her? Like a hypnotist, he held the power to lure her in and sweep away her inhibitions. He was as dangerously addictive as drugs, and she'd do well to remember how drugs ended Sasha's life.

Wiping her nose with the Kleenex, she threw it in the wastepaper basket beside her desk. Her eyes rose to his and held on. Crisply, she said, "What do you really want from me, Puck?"

"I told you what I want. My decision isn't based on the fact that I'm stuck in this hellhole. It's not desperation, or whatever other wack-ass reason you're coming up with. That's not how I roll. I want us to be together again."

Her hands trembled, and she crammed them beneath her thighs to stop from shaking. Casting her head down, she said, "I think solitary confinement has gotten to your head. You're used to club women. Look at me," she plucked at the hem of her oversized turtleneck sweater.

"You're hot as ever—"

Her head snapped up. "I'm not fishing for compliments."

"Didn't say you were. Just telling it like it is." He tilted his head to the side, looking at her as if he could see beneath the layers of bulky clothing. "I know exactly what you look like, and I can't wait to lick every fucking inch of you. You've matured, and I already know you'll taste better than before. Better than I remember. Better than I imagined while I was in the hole. And, woman, let me tell you, I have a damn good imagination."

"You can't know that," she muttered, even though his honeyed words rolled over her, melting her against her will.

Rolling her eyes up to the ceiling, she said, "Puck—"

Suddenly, a thought popped into her head. Once there, it rapidly morphed into a germ of an idea. Her gaze snapped to his. "Speaking of Sasha, have you seen Kingpin out there?"

Sasha's former dealer.

Puck's jaw clenched hard, muscle pulsing against his jawline. "Yeah, it's like a reunion from hell up in here."

She inhaled deeply and then blurted out, "He's the one who gave Sasha her last screwball. There's no way to prove it, but I think he cut it with fentanyl. Can you imagine what adding fentanyl to heroin and meth does? It kills, that's what it does. It killed her, but nothing could be traced back to him. He's been arrested on a charge of possession with intent to sell more often than I can count. I've even testified against him at his recent parole hearing because I'm positive he's still using."

"You work with him?"

"Yes. Can you imagine?"

"Isn't that a conflict of interest?"

Ava pursed her lips in frustration. "Why, yes, Puck, how very observant of you. Although it doesn't seem to concern you when it comes to the two of us. I've grown up in this town. I'm bound to meet people I know, but I'm also the only social worker on the payroll. How I feel about him doesn't impact my ability to help him get clean, if that's something he wants to do. It was years ago when he last saw me, and I never bought from him. Although I may have partied hard, I wasn't that far gone. Not the way Sasha was toward the end. He hasn't said or done anything that suggests he recognizes me."

She clenched her hands into fists and shook them. "He

comes in and out, in and out of here like it's no skin off his back. They always catch him on something, but never anything that will put him away for good, like...oh...say manslaughter. He gave Sasha her last hit, so he's directly responsible for her death. Soon, I'm certain he'll be free again, peddling drugs to teenagers and doing God only knows what. It's frustrating as hell."

Puck's eyes sharpened. Leaning back, he eyed her carefully as he asked, "How badly do you want to get him?"

"Bad," she breathed out. "So bad, Puck. You can't imagine."

"What are you willing to do for it?"

Her head jerked back. Eyes narrowed, she asked suspiciously, "What are you suggesting?"

His gaze locked on her. The intent she saw there sent a shiver down her spine.

"I can find out more. For you." He paused for a beat. "For a price."

She stabbed her forefinger at him. "I knew it. You want to use me, but I don't have the power to get you out of here."

"Christ, woman, the price is *access* to you. To touching you. Kissing you." The pitch of his voice dropped. "Licking you."

Her blood slowed to the speed of molten lava then sped up as if she'd taken a hit of meth. "What?" She clenched the sides of her head. This guy was going to drive her crazy. He was stubborn to the point of madness.

"Ava, listen to me. We're both here. Sure, I could wait till I'm out to pursue you, but I don't want to wait. I want you to take me on as a client and have individual meetings with me. While I'm with you, I'll be free to do what I want to do to you."

"What in the—"

"*Annnd*," he talked over her, "in exchange, I'll get close to Kingpin and find out what I can about his activities, in and out of jail."

"H-have you lost your mind?" she sputtered out. "I don't know what you want from me, but you can't possibly think I'd fall for you again. Not now. Not ever. Not you." Her voice trembled slightly as she hissed out, "I fell for you once, and it *crushed* me. What kind of fool do you think I am that I'd ever open myself up to you again?"

She let out a sigh of exasperation and staring him in the eye, declared, "You're a flake, Puck."

7

PUCK

"*A flake?*" Puck reared back at the insult.

"I've never been a flake in my life. I stepped up and took care of Sammi. I'm a loyal member to my club. Hell, I just came out of the hole for weighing in on a fight to protect a brother."

What in the ever-loving fuck was she talking about? He was one of the most stable men he knew. From a young age, too.

"Yeah, but you flaked out on *me*," she shot back in a bitter tone. Her hands grasped the edge of her desk like she was holding herself back from lunging over the desk and throttling him. "How do you explain that? Was it that you weren't in love with me?"

"You know that's not true."

"I know nothing of the kind. If you loved me and you're not a flake, then how do you explain what you did to me? To us?"

Christ, what a mess. He wouldn't have broken up with her so abruptly had he been able to read the future and find himself in the shithole he was squatting in now. At nineteen, he'd had much less finesse. Okay, maybe finesse wasn't the right word to describe him on a good day, even now. He came in more like a wrecking ball, that much was true. Fuck his life, but the past was the past. No use in wishing it were any different.

One thing he'd learned is to fight for what he wanted. If he backed down any time a barrier was thrown in his path, he'd never have risen to become sergeant at arms of the Demon Squad MC. Being sergeant at arms was no walk in the park; his club wasn't for pussies.

"I wasn't a flake," he replied patiently. "I was young, confused, and trying my best to deal with a difficult situation."

Ava rubbed the center of her forehead. "Fine, you're right. Whatever. It's in the past. I don't even know why I brought it up. Let's get to the more relevant topic. Kingpin." She lifted her eyes to his and pinned him in place. "What do you know? There's always rumors flying around in this place. That's part of life when you have five hundred men behind bars. What have you heard?"

This was a quick change in subject. In the wrong direction. She seemed to dismiss his side of their little bargain, but he'd play it her way. For now. After all, he was confident in the array of ways and means he had at his disposal.

Inhaling slowly to calm his temper, he took his time replying. "Haven't heard anything. Haven't been around long enough 'cause I got into that fight the day after I arrived, but now that I'm back, I'll mix with the others. I've already proven myself, and I'm a biker. That means something in a place like this," he concluded with a shrug.

He noticed her fingers had loosened their grip on the desk, and she was nodding encouragingly. Her eyes left his face, flittered around the room, and then returned. She swallowed. "This could be dangerous."

He smirked. "You worried about me, all of a sudden?"

Flames ignited in her eyes. "Yes, I'm worried, you asshole. I'd be worried for anyone. It's not personal."

Oh, yeah? He'd make sure it got personal real soon. "Babe." He leaned forward, and her lips pursed together in disapproval. His gaze wandered over her face, dropped to those lips pressed in a thin line, then farther down to her tits. He couldn't see much, but his memory filled in the blanks. His eyes slowly dragged back up to meet hers.

Taking her chin, he tipped it up and asked, "Did you conveniently forget what I said about helping you out? You think I'd do this for free? Fuck, no."

She pulled her chin away and mocked, "Oh, I heard. I chose to ignore it because your proposal's ridiculous. You can't be serious."

"Dead. Fucking. Serious." He dropped his voice, low and stern.

She raised her hands in supplication. "Puck, come on. Really? You can't want me. You broke up with me. There's no point in resurrecting the past."

"We're not resurrecting shit. I'm looking toward the future, and that future includes you. I've always wanted you, Ava. That's never changed. You might have gotten away from me if we hadn't crossed paths, but we did, and that changed every-thing. This is how it's gonna be." He reached over and took her chin again. Any excuse to touch her, he'd take. "Believe it. This is happening. *We* are happening."

Her jaw dropped open a little, and he felt her warm, moist breath whisk over his fingers. Her lips were wet and kissable. The tip of her tongue peeked out of the corner of her mouth, and he bit back a moan.

She shook her head and then pulled away. Again. That shit had to stop, but he couldn't deny enjoying the thrill of the chase. He hadn't chased anyone before, not even her. They'd fallen into bed together the first night they met.

"I don't think so," she replied, a stubborn tilt to her chin. A challenge. God, that got his blood stirring, and his cock.

"C'mere," he crooked his finger at her.

"What? No!" she protested.

"Come on. It won't be so bad. You'll see. Maybe you can pretend to forget what it was like between the two of us, but I haven't forgotten a damn thing. Let me remind you. Might change your mind."

Ava squeezed her eyes shut and gritted out between clenched teeth, "I don't want my mind changed."

"Ava," He growled low. It was the tone he used on Sammi when she was being a pain in his ass. Never seemed to work on her, but Ava was a different creature altogether. She wanted him. It was obvious in the racing pulse at the base on her slim throat. The way her tongue had played peekaboo when he held her chin. The way her body tilted toward him ever so slightly as he spoke her name.

Then, she pushed away and folded her arms over her chest.

"*Avaaa*," he repeated, putting more warning into it. Her head whipped to the side in rebellion. "You gonna be naughty? Do you remember what happens to naughty girls?"

She inhaled sharply and froze. Oh, yeah, she remembered alright. Turned out her memory was as good as his. Hell, he still jerked off on occasion to the punishments he used to give her. Mounting her from behind as he grabbed a bright pink ass cheek. Her tight pussy shuddering around his cock as the flat of his hand rained down on her buttock.

"The longer you make me wait, the longer I'm gonna make you wait," he taunted. "If you want me to find out about King-pin, you're gonna have to work with me here."

She shoved her chair back with a screech and stood up. Shoulders squared, chin held high. "Fine, but you won't make me come. I'm not going to have an orgasm with you. Do. Your. Worst. This is about Sasha's killer for me. Not a thing more."

Go ahead and tell yourself that, baby girl.

He patted his lap. "Here."

She stomped over to him, her eyes flicking over to the door. He leaned over and jiggled the little lock on the door-knob of her office door. Couldn't keep anyone out for real, but it would give them time to separate, should anyone try the door. Either way, Puck was keeping an ear out for anything that happened in the hallway. Turning in his chair, he stretched out his legs for her to come and stand between them. She practically vibrated with a mixture of emotions. Her eyes flashed, but he knew this woman inside out. It wasn't simply anger and frustration swimming in her eyes. Unless one counted sexual frustration.

She wore a pair of slacks under the bulky wool sweater that engulfed her. Tapping his lap for her to sit, he waited as she shifted from foot to foot. Huffing out a curse, she plopped down on his hard thigh and almost bounced off. He grabbed her by the waist and settled her on his thigh. He was fit—of that there was no doubt. In solitary, he did so many crunches and sit-ups, he'd stopped counting after a thousand.

Even though she sat primly on the edge of his thigh, he felt the spread of her warm, plump backside. Taking a deep inhale, he breathed in the light fragrance of her herbal shampoo mingling with her unique vanilla-and-mango scent, and fucking *salivated.* Christ, he could fucking soak in that scent. It drowned out the odor of urine and unwashed bodies that had taken over his sense of smell since being in the hole.

The florescent lighting from the ceiling lamp was strong enough to bring out the auburn highlights of her long hair.

His large hand raked through her tresses, and she gave a slight shudder. *That's it, baby. Let go.* How many times had he picked up a woman with hair almost like hers, fucking them from behind while calling out her name? Yeah, he'd never forgotten her. She was tall, but being six foot three himself, and bulked up like he was, he dwarfed her slim frame.

His other hand landed on her thigh, which flexed underneath his hold. She'd always been an athletic little thing. Running marathons, stuff like that. He leaned in until his nose was in her throat and scented her like a damn dog. Tugging her turtleneck down, he nuzzled into the side of her neck, and his lips glided softly down the slim column of her throat.

His tongue flicked out for a quick taste. *Fuuuck!* She not only smelled like vanilla, but she damn-well tasted like it. Ironic, since she didn't like to fuck vanilla. The contradiction only made her more enticing. This woman had been complex at twenty-one. He couldn't begin to imagine the many layers to her now. He *did* know one thing, though: he'd be taking his time peeling them back, one by one. Revel in everything he did with her.

Ava's body was motionless, but he felt the humming under his touch like a swarm of buzzing locusts on a hot midsummer's night. He could almost hear her blood sing. Heat rose to the surface of her skin, flushing hot under his ministrations.

"Damn, baby, you taste so fucking sweet. I bet that lickable pussy is as tasty as ever. You slick for me yet?"

She didn't answer. He bit down on the juncture where her throat met her shoulder, and she yelped. "Answer me," he warned with a growl.

She shook her head, her bottom lip pulled inward and bitten by the top row of her teeth.

"Do I need to check myself?" he asked in a husky rasp. She didn't answer. "Guess that's a yes."

Her legs were pressed tightly together, but his fingers caressed the seam of her thighs. "Open up for me, angel." She tossed her head. His tone hardened in just the way she needed it. "Open up, or the deal is off."

After a long moment, she relaxed her muscles. He grunted out his approval, not a moment's regret for blackmailing her. Not when all the signs of her body were chanting *yes, yes, yes.* He was giving her incentive for what she wanted anyway. It was her heart she feared for. And he got that. She had every right to be fearful, and he knew that heart of hers was hidden away, regardless of how her body responded to him. Didn't mean he was gonna stand down, though.

He knew this girl. She had a stubborn streak when she put her mind to something. Not everyone came out of rehab and ended up with a master's degree. It happened, but not *that* often. If she didn't want at least part of what he was offering— okay, *demanding*—she wouldn't be spreading her thighs a tiny bit wider.

He couldn't wait to taste that sweet pussy. Wasn't gonna happen now, but fuck, did he want her bad. Releasing the top button of her brown slacks, his fingers caught the tab and pulled the zipper down. They slipped inside and underneath the elastic band of her panties and hit the warmest, wettest little slit he'd ever had the privilege of touching. Burying his face into the crook of her neck, he groaned out, "Fuck, fuck, *fuck.*"

His index finger swiped at her entrance, and she squirmed, opening her thighs wider and pushing her tight cunt toward his finger. Damn, must have been a long while since she was last fucked right. The thought more than pleased him. Her hips began to move, and sweet little moans slipped out. Dropping her head back on his shoulder, she lifted her hips off his thigh and moved faster. Soon, her hot body writhed in the air, and her even hotter pussy ground against the heel of his palm as he inserted another finger, and then another.

Ring, ring, ring.

Ava's head snapped up. She grabbed his hand and yanked it out of her pants. Staggering forward, she grabbed the receiver of her desk phone. "H-hello?" she stammered in a rush. Puck grinned at her shortness of breath.

Shoving at him with her other hand, she stumbled to her feet. Her eyes flew to her open zipper and then up to the wet fingers he sucked into his mouth. Her eyes bulged when he moaned out his appreciation for her taste. Yep, she tasted even better. He gave her a shrug. He wasn't letting a drop of her go to waste. And fuck him because it turned out that her fragrance was stronger and muskier in his mouth. Damn. His tongue could live in her pussy for breakfast, lunch, and dinner. He might try that once he was out of this place and had her spread out in front of him like a feast, on a proper bed.

Frowning, she quickly moved to her side of her desk and answered, "Yes, this is she. Oh, yes, Ms. Cameron. I actually have Puck with me in my office at this very moment." Her expression was pinched. Lips flattened; her eyes narrowed in on him. Was that jealousy? He almost burst out laughing. Sage was the president's old lady. And pregnant, to boot. Even if none of that were true, Ava had nothing to worry about. He was quite enjoying her little fit. Proved she felt something for him, despite her serious misgivings.

"Yes, why don't I have him returned to his unit, and I'll give you a call back." She grabbed a sticky pad and pen. "What's the best number to reach you?" She scribbled down Sage's number and responded to whatever Sage was saying with an "Mm-hmm. Very good. Speak to you soon."

Ava hung up the phone, sagged into her chair, and scowled up at him. "She's very concerned about you."

"She's my president's old lady. Ava, it was never an issue of other women."

Chewing her inner cheek, Ava drummed her fingers on the surface of her desk.

He lifted his chin and said, "Make sure you're decent."

Her eyes dropped to her crotch. Giving him a look that would maim a weaker man, she lifted her sweater and righted her slacks. "She can't know about us. Or about Kingpin."

"'Course not. I'm not a snitch."

"Very honorable of you," she snipped. "Too bad you had to go ruin it with a touch of blackmail."

"Hey, it's nothing more than a little incentive to push things along since I'm trapped in here." He pointed to the door. "If I was free, I'd pursue you the normal way, but I'm an inmate in this fucking place. I have no rights. No power. I'll damn well use whatever leverage I have to get what I want. Am I proud of it? Not particularly. But I'll be damned if I'm gonna stay helpless in this shithole," his features hardened, and he stared her down to make sure she understood that he wasn't playing around, "or let you slip away. Twenty-four hours a day, I'm treated like a damn dog. Being inside this office with you is the only time I feel like a fucking human. A fucking man. Sue me if I want a taste of that honey of yours. It's the closest thing to heaven in this place and I'm not giving it up. No way. No how."

"God, Puck," she breathed out, a stricken look on her face, but her cheeks flushed a nice pink. Yeah, he wasn't in a pretty place in his life. He was wearing a prison-issued bright orange jumpsuit with the word INMATE stamped on his back, but he took comfort in his ability to arouse her. That was a good sign, at least.

Throwing up her arms, she huffed out, "Okay, fine. You win. Two sessions a week; that's the most I can do. Don't get greedy and ask for more. I'm jeopardizing my professionalism as it is, so don't push your luck."

His heated, hungry gaze skated down her shitty outfit, knowing exactly how good her supple flesh felt under his fingers. His fingers curled into fists. How good she tasted on his tongue. "I'm a greedy fucker when it comes to you, but it'll do."

"Since I work in addiction, I'll tell them I think you're using. Shouldn't come as a surprise since 65 percent of inmates meet the medical criteria for having a substance-use disorder of one kind or another. You'll have to attend your choice of either Alcoholic Anonymous or Narcotics Anonymous meetings to legitimize my theory. Satisfied?"

"Good enough," he agreed.

Lifting the receiver of the phone to her ear, she requested a CO to come pick him up. After hanging up, she said, "Make sure you stay out of trouble. Do I need to see your friend as well? The one you got into a fight for"

"No," he barked out then pulled back and inhaled smoothly. He wasn't letting that pretty-lookin' kid around his woman. Brother or not, Whistle's eyes alone could charm the panties off almost any woman, and he hadn't locked her down just yet. "He's getting out soon, anyway. Which is for the best. He's a brother, but he's also a distraction." *Like you, but you're the kind of distraction I want.* "Then I can focus my energy on finding out more about Kingpin." *And focus on you.*

There was brief knock, and the door opened to a CO. Officer Dipshit, again. Fuck, the man was constantly around Ava. Another bolt of jealousy speared through Puck. Here he had to blackmail his way back into Ava's presence when this fucker could mosey into her office any damn time he wanted.

Standing up, he nodded once to Ava and held out his wrists for the cuffs. He focused on lifting his feet, one after the other, away from her. His muscles screamed in protest, but he had no choice. But, if he bided his time, he'd be pounding into her, bent over the desk, with her heart securely wrapped around his little finger. Hopefully, that CO didn't get to her first.

8

AVA

Ava massaged her forehead. What the hell had she agreed to?

Did it matter as long as she got Kingpin's poison off the street corners and out of schools? Seven years later, she still missed her closest childhood friend. Ava had Kat, but she'd been so busy raising her little sister, going to school, and helping her mother that she hadn't the time or energy to build another tight friendship like that.

Another part of her was also scared. What if she did, and that person disappeared like Sasha and Puck had. There was no doubt she was a little lonely. Although she'd never regretted walking away from the old crowd, she missed their easy camaraderie.

Sinking back in her chair, she tapped on her keyboard to open up her computer screen as fantasies of getting Kingpin danced in her head. After three long years of following his trips in and out of jail, she was a step closer to getting him locked away for a substantial amount of time.

Through the open door of her office, the speaker crackled

and announced the jail library was closing in fifteen minutes. If she was lucky, he'd be off the streets forever. Her journey began during an internship when she was finishing up her graduate degree. She was shadowing a social worker at the Green Haven Correctional Facility, a maximum-security prison half an hour away. It was the closest Kingpin had come to serving real time for one of his many crimes.

Her thoughts drifted toward Puck and his touch. A hot shudder coursed through her traitorous body. Not only had she found herself in the arms of a man for the first time in two years, but it wasn't just any man.

It was Damien. *Puck.*

His scent alone brought back memories of them lying on her mattress on the floor of the apartment she'd shared with Sasha. Pillows had lain, cast off on the floor like sun-bleached debris on a vacant beach. The hot summer breeze came in through her bedroom windows. The apartment was down the street from a fire station, and the sound of ambulances and fire trucks blared through the night. Their sweat-lined bodies intertwined together as they fucked for hours through the sweltering heat of the August nights.

At nineteen years old, he was already a stallion, and he hadn't even been that experienced. She'd taught him how to go down on a woman. The way he'd spoken about licking her pussy advertised he had his fair share of women since then. Talking dirty was new. Before, it had been all moans and grunts between them, neither of them experienced enough to consider talk at all, much less explicit talk. Clearly, that had changed in the past eight years.

He may have aroused her, but she couldn't afford to catch feelings for him. Never that. She huffed out a laugh at his indignation when she'd called him a flake. Undoubtedly, he was solid with the people he'd committed himself to. Once upon a time, she'd been one of those people and remembered well what it was like to be cosseted by a man like him. Protected. Coveted. He was an expert at making a woman feel wanted and desired. It was one of the things that had made it such cold, miserable hell when he turned her away.

Her mind meandered back to the day he'd ended their relationship. Her belly had dropped when he gave her the double-whammy that his mother was dead and that he was breaking up with her. She knew their relationship was a cause of stress between him and his mom. Till then, he'd never told her how bad it had gotten. Admittedly, she hadn't been a great influence, but if he'd told her, she might've changed. She wouldn't have called him out to so many parties at her apartment or the record shop where she'd worked.

If given half a chance, she would've done things differently because she was head over heels in love with him. His mother had died in a car accident right after arguing with Puck. He'd made his decision, halfway out of his mind with grief and guilt. Damn him. Thinking about it brought back the harsh agony of that day. Briefly, it'd been overshadowed by Sasha's death. Then, they'd merged together into one ball of grief and lived as a consistent ache in her heart for years afterward.

That one decision was the flakiness she saw in him. She'd given in to his demand today but there wasn't much coercion. Who was she kidding? She wanted him to touch her. But in no way did that mean she'd allow him to pry open her heart. Hard pass on that one.

✳✳✳

SATURDAY, Ava picked up Kat from the dealership for their regular bubble-tea date. Her father was on the floor *again*, so she was forced to endure a strained chat with him. He even suggested she stop by during the week to have dinner with him and Kat. Was he having a midlife crisis or something? Recently, he seemed to be trying to breach the divide between them. Almost as if he were remorseful. *Yup, definitely a midlife crisis*, she mused as she nudged Kat out of the dealership door toward her little orange Nissan Versa.

"Is the Clementine still here?" Kat cracked like she did every single time Ava picked her up. As if making fun of her car for being little and orange was going to somehow push her to buy a bike for Kat to ride on. Yeah, not happening.

"Hardy-har-har," Ava replied as she clicked her car open. "I'd like to see your first car. Oh wait, your father spoils you like the brat you are, so he'll buy you a fantastic car, and I won't be able to tease you about it. Oops, my bad."

"He'd buy you a fantastic car if you'd only let him. You know he likes to show his love by buying stuff, but you rarely let him spoil you. Whatever. Even if I end up buying my own car, I can guarantee you what it won't be. It won't be *orange*."

"It was on sale," she defended as she slid into the front seat and quickly turned on the heat.

"You wonder why? They couldn't afford to offload these cars at full price. They had no choice but to put them on sale. Otherwise, they'd be stuck with that trash inventory, like, for-ev-er."

Ava tightened her grip on the steering wheel. She loved her little sister, but teenagers could try the patience of a saint, and she was no saint. She counted to the number ten and then repeated *patience, patience, patience* to herself.

"So how was your week?" asked Kat.

"Good," Ava squeaked out, a frown tunneling between her brows. How could the thought of Puck not pop into her head at that question?

"Why do you look like that? Ohmigod, is something wrong with Rita?" Kat called Ava's mom by her first name.

Ava gave her sister a quizzical sidelong look. "No, what would make you say that?"

"You had a weird look on your face, and only one thing would get your face screwed up like that. Me or your mom. I'm fine, so it's got to have something to do with her. Did she get any news from the doctor?"

Ava pulled to a full stop at a stop sign and put on her left-turn signal. *Click-click-click.* "She's fine." Her mother was breast cancer-free over a year now.

"Then, what is it?"

Silence. Bothering her lower lip, she mulled over whether she had the guts to bring up the subject of Puck with her teenaged younger sister as she took a slow turn onto a main road.

"You're starting to worry me. What is it?"

Ugh. Teenage emotion. So dramatic. She should've lied, but now it was too late. Kat was onto her. It was easier to simply come out with the truth. "Damien. I saw Damien. In jail. He goes by Puck now. He's a member of the Demon Squad," she blurted out.

Kat turned large, saucer-wide eyes toward her and punched her lightly in the arm. "Shut. Up."

"I kid you not," Ava confirmed. Kat knew everything there was to know about the clubs in Poughkeepsie and the surrounding area. It was a tight community, even if her father's MC would technically be considered weekend warriors by the likes of the Squad.

"The Demon Squad," Kat said in a hushed, awed tone. "They're a badass club, and those bikers are, like, sizzling hot. Every man I've laid eyes on from that club could be on a Harley calendar. One hot biker for each month. Seriously, it's sick."

"Tell me about it," she muttered to herself.

"What?"

"Nothing," she replied quickly.

"You saw him in Duchess County?"

"Yep," she grumbled. "He's an inmate."

"Did you talk to him? What's he like now? Hot? I was too young to really notice, although I remember he had kind eyes," Kat gushed.

"Yes, I did speak to him briefly. He's...attractive. I-I'm his social worker."

"He's a druggie?"

Ava shot her a warning look. "Kat, what did I tell you about people who are struggling with addiction?"

"Sorry," she mumbled, only slightly chastened, but she rebounded immediately with a, "So is he?" Kat knew about her past. Not the details, but she knew Ava had struggled with drugs, got clean, and dedicated her life to helping others fight the same fight.

"No, he's not. I'm going to have sessions with him for other reasons, related to my job, of course."

Her sister's perceptive eyes coasted over Ava's face. Kat had grown up fast with a deadbeat mom who'd left her. Besides that, the girl was smart as a whip. "How did it feel? Being around him?"

Too good. "Not great," she replied. *Both are true.*

Kat flopped her hands on her lap. "Wow. You haven't seen him since I was what? Eight?"

"Seven."

"Eight years, then. And he's an incarcerated biker. What's he in for?"

"I can't tell you that," she responded patiently.

"Is it bad?" she asked in a hushed tone.

"It isn't a good thing, although there was one redeeming aspect about it. Bottom line is he broke the law and he will most likely do time. He doesn't have a sympathetic judge. On the other hand, he has an incredible attorney. Her firm has a great reputation." Based on Sage's exaggerated concern, Ava bet that Puck had probably banged her. Asshole. Like her father, who at one time had banged anything that wasn't nailed down.

Motioning her hands in a "tell me more" gesture, Kat asked, "Aannd...what was it like...to see him? Did you still feel something for him?" Kat had kissed a boy, or at least that's what she'd divulged to Ava, and she was definitely curious about sex. They'd had the sex talk, the how-to-pleasure-yourself talk, the consent talk, the how-to-be-a-badass-bitch talk, and the sexual-assault talk. Ava had made sure to cover all the bases. She wasn't letting her kid sister walk out into the world of sex without being as informed as possible. Ava also tried to answer Kat's questions as honestly as possible. Of course, she hadn't had sex in a couple of years, so she hadn't had much to answer for in a while.

Ava cleared her throat as she pulled into the café where they always went for their bubble-tea dates. "Well...it was a shock at first. I was attracted to him," she admitted slowly. "Even in his orange jumpsuit. He's definitely grown into a man's body. He was always tall, but he was almost slim back then. Now, he's bigger and wider. Lots of muscles," she swallowed around her suddenly parched throat, "everywhere." She let out a huge gust of breath. There, that was honest.

"Did you touch him?"

"What? No!" Okay, that last question put a screeching halt to honesty. No way was she admitting to touching Puck in a government correctional facility *while on the job.*

"What if he was out? Would you have done something? Do you want to do something?"

"What's with the twenty questions?" Ava griped as she turned off the engine, grabbed her purse, and got out of the Clementine.

Kat followed her out, buttoning her coat and clutching her cell phone to her chest as a cold gust of wind flapped at her coat tails. Shutting the car door, she said over the hood, "They're legitimate questions."

Ava clicked her fob to lock the car doors and waited on the curb for Kat to reach her. As they walked to the café, Kat admitted, "I remember him. He was funny. Used to play with me. Pay attention to me."

Yanking the door to the café open, she gestured for her sister to enter and answered bitterly, "Yeah, but then he broke up with me out of the blue, Kat. Out of the blue. You may have been too young to remember that part." She remembered one time, when she was babysitting Kat at her mother's house. Puck had stopped by, and she came out of the kitchen with snacks to find him down on the floor, helping Kat construct her newest Lego Friends building set.

They got to the counter and ordered their bubble tea. Oreo for Kat, Black Milk Tea for Ava. She paid, and they slid over to the end of the counter to wait for their drinks.

"In a way, you should thank him for dumping you."

Ava gave her an unamused look. "Is that so?"

"Yeah, because it started you on the path you're now on. I know other things happened. Bad things. But you wouldn't be where you are today without them, and the changes began with him dumping you."

"'Dumping,' hmm...nice choice of word there. You're right, but I also don't think you should reward someone for screwing you over."

They grabbed their bubble tea and took seats at a table by the window. After taking a long suck from the wide straw, Kat continued, "I think it's because of dad. You haven't forgiven him, and he's the first one who ever screwed you over. Even if you wanted Puck, you wouldn't open yourself to him, because you haven't gotten over what dad did. Doesn't help that he piled more crap on top of your abandonment issue."

"Look who's so smart, huh? Abandonment issue, she says now. Who's to say he even wants to be with me?"

"Really, Ava? You're a catch, and I'm not saying that because you're my sister. You know I don't roll like that. Besides the fact that you're a great person, you're, like, *hawt*. You have the figure of a model, without being too skinny. You still have boobs, and you have a beautiful face."

"Ha! You clearly don't remember how I dress at work," she scoffed.

"Please, that's bullsh—" She trailed off at Ava's hard glance. Kat's eyes turned soft as she asked, "Don't you want a boyfriend?"

"Of course I do. I just want to make sure it's the right person. I want what I had with Puck. That connection. The intimacy. But with the security of knowing I won't get hurt. That my heart will be safe." For that to happen, it would need to be with anyone *but* Puck. The irony was not lost on her.

"To do that, you have to take a risk."

"Easier said than done." Ava placed her hand over Kat's. Her younger sister looked a lot like her father, with bright intelligent eyes, although she had her mother's heart-shaped face and blond hair. Ava had long stopped resenting her little sister and the fact that her existence was the final nail in the coffin of her parents' marriage. Once she'd turned her back on her misguided anger and embraced the little girl who'd always looked at her with adoration, Ava's heart filled with love for her sister. She'd never told Kat, but taking care of her had helped Ava pull out of a deep depression after Sasha's death. "The beauty about you is that your spirit hasn't been crushed or even dimmed. Not one bit. Even with what happened with your mom, you're still you. A bright, shining light of laughter and sassiness."

"Part of that is your fault," she teased.

"Thanks, sweetie. I try my best." Looking out the window, she confessed, "You know, in my heart of hearts, I believed Puck was my person. That he saw me and would love me forever." She pressed her lips together. "Turns out I was wrong. I've been wrong twice, and I'm not sure I could survive another disappointment. If I go for a guy, it should be someone who's the opposite of Puck. There's a CO at my job who's nice. Someone like him might do. But Puck," she shook her head as she chewed on the tapioca bubbles, "that's a no-go."

Kat took a long sip and chewed thoughtfully. "That's what you need to do. Get out there. At least hook up with someone."

She shoved Kat's shoulder. "Oh, you know a lot about hooking up, do you?"

"I know it's something you do when you want to have sex, and I think sex might help. Break the curse you've been under since Rita got sick."

It's true that after her mom's diagnosis, Ava had dedicated herself to her family and her job, leaving little time for fun and play. "Okay, Ms. Know-it-All, and on that note, this discussion is officially closed. Now, tell me about your week."

Enough about her private life. She loved sharing with Kat, but there was still a difference in maturity between them. Kat needed a mother figure, not a friend. While their relationship might transform over time, Ava was supposed to be there for Kat, not the other way around.

9

PUCK

CO Dipshit was the one to bring him to Ava's office this time.

This CO, above all others, annoyed the hell out of him.

Puck side-eyed him as they walked alongside each other from Puck's housing unit to Ava's office. Perhaps it was because Dipshit was so damn obvious about crushing on his Ava. It pissed him off to no end that he couldn't shove his fist into the fucker's mouth and let him know, in no uncertain terms, whom she belonged to. This woman was his *property*, dammit. A woman he couldn't get out of his head. Seriously, with the monotony and boredom of life behind bars, he was fucking obsessed.

At the same time, he was trying to get close to Kingpin. They were in the same housing unit, but it wasn't as easy as it seemed. The man had protection; he was always surrounded by his minions. Puck didn't know if it was because he was connected to someone with serious clout or if he *was* the clout. Either way, he had to try, for Ava's sake. It was clear as day that she felt responsible for Sasha's death, and if keeping the bastard behind bars made her feel better, then he was all in. Kingpin manned the card tables, where much of the gambling went on in the unit, so that's where Puck found himself most of the day.

As Dipshit knocked on Ava's office door, Puck's heart thumped against his ribs. *Boom-boom, boom-boom, boom-boom.* After waiting so many days to see her, it was nerve-racking as fuck to be seconds away from seeing her. He awkwardly rubbed his clammy palms, stuck in manacles, against the trousers of his jumpsuit.

Dipshit swung the door open to reveal her shutting the drawer of a metal-gray filing cabinet. Was it his imagination, or did she look different? Why, yes, she did. For one, she was wearing a skirt. Even though it fell just above her ankles, it was a vast improvement to the bulky, shape-hiding clothes she'd worn previously. At least he could see her silhouette. His gaze skimmed down her figure. He never would've thought that ankles, covered in black tights no less, would be sexy, but there it was. More proof he was obsessed.

Puck swallowed and licked his parched lips. Damn, but she was fucking gorgeous. Long, thick waves of hair toppled over her shoulders, begging to be wrapped around his fist. Her wide hazel eyes were like two jewels, outlined in dark lashes. Was that lip gloss covering her full lips?

Dipshit did a double take. Puck wasn't the only one who'd noticed a difference. Swear to God, he was going to fuck that man up for the audacity of lusting after his woman.

Nodding toward Puck's handcuffs, she greeted them. "Good afternoon, Derick. Mr. Rossi. Please take his cuffs off for our session."

Derick looked up at her sharply but did as she asked. Rubbing his wrists, Puck took a seat and waited for the asshole to leave.

"You don't have to call ahead. I'll be back in exactly an hour," Dipshit declared. Then he turned to Puck and gave him a hard stare. "Behave yourself."

Puck gave him a *fuck you* stare but provided a simple, tight-lipped, "Yes, sir."

Ava gave Dipshit a smile broad enough to have Puck grinding on his back molars. Hell, if she kept that up, his molars would be pulverized to dust by the time he was released. "We'll be fine. I can handle Damien."

"That's what I'm worried about," Dipshit muttered under his breath. Gripping his knees, Puck kept his eyes cast down. If he looked at the cocksucker, there'd be a smackdown of epic proportions. He waited until the door closed behind him. The instant Dipshit's footfalls receded down the hallway, he let out a hissed curse. "The man's a fucking asshole."

Ava was back in her chair. "He's not so bad."

Puck gave her a look that had her hurrying to add, "At least to me. The system is based on an adversarial model, Puck. Believe me, it's not easy to work here, and there are people who've committed heinous crimes."

"Don't defend him," he ground out.

She raised her hands in surrender. "Okay, okay. I'm not taking sides. I'm quite aware of the failures of the criminal justice system."

He nodded stiffly. Puck wasn't about to waste their precious time arguing, and if he hadn't been suspicious of the man's motives, he might be grateful someone was looking out for her. Fact of the matter was he was straight-up jealous. That man was free to come and go into her office anytime he wanted. He was free to see Ava. Hell, he was just...free, period.

Puck's spine hit the back of his chair. The realization struck him hard that, for the first time, he felt insecure. He was always proactive, decisive, even if the decision was to kick back and do nothing for a bit. He couldn't exactly ask her to strip and lay herself out for him, like he wanted to. He wanted his hands on her like he wanted his next breath, but this wasn't one of his random hookups. Nor was it a date. Not that he dated. But he would've made an exception for Ava.

While it was awkward and artificial, he had to find a way through the morass of the past and the minefield of the present to a safe, neutral place. "How's Kat?"

Ava jolted slightly, an expression of surprise tattooed on her face, but she graciously answered, "She's good. Really good, in fact. Her mother actually left her and my father a few years back, but I stepped in to help raise her. By then, I was clean for a few years and back in college. I scheduled my classes in the mornings and evenings so I could pick her up from the school bus and take care of her in the afternoons. Helped with homework, made her and my father dinner, and then left when he got home from the dealership." Her face broke into a wide smile, full of love, that almost brought him to his knees. If she'd only look at him that way again. "She's fifteen now. A teenager." She rolled her eyes. "She has an opinion on everything."

"Impressive."

Her smile slipped, and he wanted to make a joke, do anything to get that bright, authentic grin back on her face. "Not really. You did much more for Sammi. In a sense, I have you to thank for my relationship with Kat. The way you took care of Sammi was a model for me. You re-arranged your entire life to take care of her. I wasn't required to do nearly half that. How is Sammi, anyway?"

It was Puck's turn to smile broadly. "Great. She's fucking great, although she's stubborn as hell and drives me up the fucking wall. She started her own business as a personal stylist two years back. I was able to front her the start-up money, and she's blowing up. The first year was a little rough, but she has a good eye for the stuff she does. Talented as hell. Sweet and caring. Well, at least to her clients, she is. Me, not so much." He ended with a satisfied chuckle.

"How old is she again?"

"Twenty-one years old. Legal to drink. Can you fucking believe it? There were days when I sat at the kitchen table with a past-due rent notice in my hand, thinking, 'What in the hell am I going to do?'"

Her eyes softened, building an urge in him to yank her into his arms and kiss her silly.

"But you did it."

"I did it. Me and a helluva lot of luck. Going to the Squad saved our asses. Prez took me under his wing like the son he never had. Took good care of us until I got patched in and could get my hustle on. Then it was game fucking on. I stuck my hand in any pot of money there was to make. No lie, it was tough as hell. Took me another year until I was comfortable bringing her around the club. The Squad is like a family. They pitched in to look after her so I could focus on making real money. Bought us a small house so I'd never have to hold an eviction notice in my hand again."

He looked down at his hands. Hands that had done whatever was necessary...for a cut of the profit or for the sake of the brotherhood. Thank fuck, the Squad was out of anything illegal. The money wasn't as great, but after this stint in the slammer, at least he didn't have to factor jail time on behalf of the Squad in his life plan.

"I didn't like how it ended between us," Ava began, "but I understood it. It was a bold move on your part, and that move was an example to me when it was time to make my own bold moves." Ava's serious-yet-melancholic eyes remained steady on his, jabbing his heart with remorse.

"I was a fucking kid, Ava," Puck clarified. "For real, if I'd known I'd be sitting across from a woman as fucking gorgeous as you've become, that I'd have to fight to make her mine again, I would've made different moves. You were spirited then. Tack on the maturity in you now, and there are layers I can only dream about. It fuckin' tears me up that I don't have the privilege to touch you whenever and however I damn want to," he concluded, in a bleak raw tone.

"Who says we would've stayed together? That I would've stopped partying and been there to support you?" she said softly. There was no strength behind her words. She was simply being kind. Polite.

"Bullshit. I underestimated you. Seeing you now, seeing what you've accomplished, and then hearing you talk about Kat, I know I made the mistake of my life. There's no doubt you would've been there for me."

"Yes," she replied bluntly, her eyes stark. "I would have."

There it was. The truth. He wasn't one to shy away from it. He hadn't shied away from it back in the day, when he decided her lifestyle wasn't conducive to his new responsibilities. He wasn't going to shy away from reality now.

"You're right. I was wrong, and I'm man enough to admit it," he stated plainly, hoping against hope it would mean something to her. That it'd suffice.

Ava's eyelids fluttered shut, and she took in a deep breath. "It's not easy talking about these things, but I appreciate your acknowledgment. You *did* underestimate me, and that hurt. You thought I was superficial, that I'd chose my lifestyle over you and Sammi. It cut me deep."

Seeing how much he'd hurt her made him want to crawl out of his skin. He'd do anything for another chance. To redeem himself and his dumbass mistake, because this woman deserved the world on a platter, at the very least she deserved his heart. He'd give her anything she desired. Anything. The fear that she wouldn't give him another chance clawed at his throat like when that inmate had tried to choke him out. Breathing was becoming difficult, and his vision was starting to close in. Focusing on her, he expelled a huge, shuddering breath.

"Never again," he said vehemently, leaning forward and taking her hand. Her eyes snapped open and flared wide at his touch. Although he wouldn't admit it to her, his mother's last words had infiltrated his young, immature mind and twisted it against her. *She's bad for you, Damien. She's bad, and she's going to ruin you with her parties and drugs. You're the man of this house, and she's going to tear this family apart.* His mother had been wrong, but what did his besieged juvenile brain know about right and wrong? They were the last words of his beloved mother before her car was wrecked by a drunk driver. By following her wish, he though he was honoring her memory. Not that he'd share these thoughts with Ava. It'd be cruel. Especially since the decision was his to make and he'd made the wrong one. Hands down. *Wrong.*

Lifting her hand, Puck pressed the tips of her fingers against his lips. "When I woke up from the nightmare two years later, the realization of what I'd done crashed down on me, but it was too late. It would've been an insult to show up at your house, even if it was only to beg you for forgiveness."

She gave a harsh chuckle. "I would've slammed the door on your face and called the cops."

He smiled against her soft fingertips. "There you go. C'mere." He tugged at her fingers and gave her a chin lift.

Ava pulled her hand away and folded her arms over her chest. His heart dropped to his belly.

"I thought we were getting along. There's no need to take things further."

"We are getting along, but we'll get along even better with you on my lap," he growled, gripping the arms of his chair to prevent himself from lunging at her.

Her chin lifted at a haughty angle. "What if I don't want to?"

Glancing at the clock on her wall, he noted he didn't have time to lose. He sure as hell wasn't fucking around. Time to pull out his joker card again.

"We have an agreement, don't we?" he responded with a cocked eyebrow. He watched her expression like a hawk. She compressed her lips together in a flat line and shook her head slightly. "Yeah, this is where our little agreement comes into play."

He heard her foot tapping underneath her desk in an irritated staccato. They glared at each other in a showdown. Finally, she broke, flinging her head to the side. *Bingo.* Huffing, she stood up, flicked her skirt to the side, and rounded the wide desk to him. He spread his legs, but stubborn girl that she was, she halted right outside of the circumference of his knees. Curling his fingers around her hip, he drew her in closer, inch by inch, until he wrapped his arm around her waist and brought her down to his lap. She was so fucking soft. Her sweet breath fluttered against his neck. Her ribs felt delicate under his fingertips. His index finger caressed a minute spot beneath her breast, gently grazing the underside. That little motion eased her stiff posture.

Drawing her even closer, she ended up nestled on his lap, up against his front. He clenched his jaw tight as her bouncy tits pressed against his chest. Fuck him, but he had to force himself to not reach forward and taste her. On her collarbone, her neck, her cheek. Really any part of her that was exposed to his tongue. The enticing scent of tropical vanilla danced around him, enfolding him in a bubble of sweet and sensual wholeness. That, along with the comfort of her supple body up against his, transported him to a Caribbean beach, lying in a hammock in the shade of a tree on.

✳✳✳

OHMIGOD, *ohmigod, ohmigod.* Ava's heartbeat banged out a rapid drumbeat against her rib cage. She was on his lap, pushed up against his hard chest. His arm banded around her in a tight embrace. His finger touched her with a delicacy that made her almost swoon. Ava hadn't been touched in so long. She was a carnal creature at heart, although she'd locked those desires away to deal with the demands of her job, taking care of her mom, and mothering Kat.

She wasn't being touched by any random man, either. This was *Puck,* the only man who'd ever made her feel something. A stream of bittersweet memories rushed her, reminding her of what it was like to be sheltered and cherished by this man. He had an innate ability to make her feel treasured. Memories of the sexathons they'd had flashed through her mind. The first night they met, she'd tumbled into bed with him after one kiss. She'd never found that sexual chemistry with any other man, and the femininity she hadn't bothered with for so long spread its wings like a new fledgling, bracing for flight.

A part of her wanted to let go, but fear kept her tethered to the here and now. Even though he acknowledged that he'd been wrong, she couldn't risk her heart to another one of his arbitrary "decisions." A torrent of vying emotions tumbled through her. The desire to settle into him and enjoy the hardness of his chest strove against the jangling nervous energy of playing with fire. Sensing her inner struggle, he lay a gentle hand on her head and caressed her hair.

"Lean against me," he ordered in a quiet voice. The sounds of a CO and an administrator walking past her door sifted into her office. She froze, biting down on her bottom lip till the steps faded down the corridor. When she freed her bottom lip, it stung from the pressure of her hard bite.

The low, dim light reflecting off the flat gray clouds of the winter afternoon filtered through the metal grid encasing her window. Quiet settled between them as he stroked her. The sensation of his calm yet demanding touch sparked tingles through her. Mixed with his cedar musk, the slow up-and-down rhythm of his chest cavity as he breathed lured her in. Ultimately, she sank into him and laid her cheek against his shoulder.

His other hand landed on her knee, and his fingers brushed small circles before moving up her thigh. Stroking her thigh from end to end with his entire palm, his fingers flexed involuntarily from time to time. A shiver coursed through her each time his hand squeezed. Her eyelashes quivered at the sublime, beatific sensation that overtook her at his ministrations.

He exhaled, feathering the wisps of hair near her forehead and covering her in the sweet scent of his breath. Her nostrils flared. Self-control slipping, Ava tilted her head and reached upward to graze her lips along his jawline. She gave it a small nip.

Abruptly, his mouth crashed down on hers, demanding entrance. She opened in a gasp, and his tongue entered, invading every inch. His fingers raked through her hair, enhancing the sensation of his laving tongue.

She shifted in his lap and butted against his stiffening cock, pressed along her outer thigh and hip. God, it took up space. She'd forgotten exactly how large he was. Hungry, she slid her hand over his lap, knuckles bumping against his abdomen. Her fingers wrapped around the girth of his thick shaft, tugged upward, and smoothed over his crown, round and blunt in her palm. He moaned into her mouth. The vibrations triggered little shocks that shuddered down her limbs, causing her control to slip further. His mouth turned shameless, kissing her deeply, *devouring* her. The claiming strokes of his tongue lit a fire in her.

Pulse throbbing out a harsh, needy rhythm, she lost herself in him. It'd been so long, and his talented tongue wooed her out of any lingering inhibitions. She'd take advantage of this—the intense physical rightness between them—for as long as it lasted. Her tongue danced, parried, and thrust in response to his. Her other hand shimmied up the long length of his torso and grabbed onto the ends of his hair at his nape. Gripping and twisting them, as if to keep her from floating away.

Breaking their kiss, Ava shifted off him and stood up. His hands reached for her, tugging her closer until he realized she was pulling up her stretchy, ribbed skirt high enough to straddle him. Her knees fell out of the gaps between the armrests and the back of his chair. He cupped her neck and delved back in. She palmed the hard planes of his chest as she twined her tongue with his. God, he tasted like ambrosia. Truly the food of the gods because nothing, and she meant *nothing*, tasted as good as he did. He tasted like a beach bonfire on a chilly autumn night, the scents of smoked firewood and sea salt in the air.

Tunneling into her hair, he pulled her away. Breathing raggedly, his smoldering gaze roved over her face. Her eyes, her nose, her mouth, and then back to her eyes.

"Fuck, baby, you're like a wildfire," he said, his voice rough and harsh as if he was as affected as she was. His eyes were wide and dilated. It wasn't like they hadn't kissed before, but maybe, like her, he'd forgotten the punch of a simple kiss. Her heart fluttered like a tipsy butterfly against her rib cage.

His teeth scraped over his bottom lip, and then he captured her mouth again. Threading her fingers in his curls, she brought his head down at the same time as she arched to rub herself against his solid chest. It felt so fucking good, his fingers digging into the flesh of her ass.

Ripping his mouth off hers, they bumped foreheads. He heaved out, "Fuck, lift your skirt for me. I wanna see you."

Shifting back on his lap, she took the hem and slowly dragged it up until her black and deep-purple lace panties were showing. His gaze was riveted on her.

"Holy fuck, you wanna drive me fucking crazy." His gaze lifted and drilled into hers, almost angry. "That's it, right?"

She exhaled a husky giggle. "This is what I wear."

"Since fucking when?"

"Since I became a grown woman with a job and could afford to indulge once in a while," she replied, somewhat tersely.

"Unbutton your top," he commanded in a strangled voice, his chiseled jaw tight and rigid. She knew what he was checking for. She quickly unhooked the buttons of her blouse and exposed the matching black and purple lace demi bra. She wasn't large per se, but her chest was a decent size. He'd certainly never complained before.

"You were made for sin, baby girl, and I'm the worst kind of sinner. I see how a man would kill," he cupped her breast, his gaze riveted on his thumb, swiping back and forth over her peaked nipple, "for a woman."

Her lower muscles clenched with need. She arched into his touch, wanting something rougher, but she knew better than to push him. He'd get there eventually, but he'd hold back if she got feisty. He liked to tease her, test her. Or at least he had in the past.

His other hand dropped between them, his knuckle grazing her mound. She stifled a moan as his knuckles went up and down, up and down. Hooking a finger on the top of her panties, he lifted the band off her abdomen and peeked down. The peek turned into a stare, his eyes darkening from chocolate to a lusty tar-black. She was dripping wet. Smooth, blunt fingertips grazed down her pussy and teased her folds open.

"Oh God, Puck," she breathed out. *Please touch me, please touch me*, she wanted to plead, but she pinched her lips together to prevent her words from escaping. Meanwhile, she suffered under the torture of him playing with her clit or exploring the length of her slit, everything but penetration. He liked to banter with his touch, keep her on the edge of sanity for a while before giving her what she needed.

She peered up at him. His expression caused her to get slicker around his digits. That did the trick because the instant her juices rolled down the length of his fingers, he thrust them upward. Her head rolled back on her shoulders, spine bowed, and breasts jutting out brazenly.

A firm grip, almost angry, caught her jaw. His fingers tilted her face up until her gaze was locked with his, eyes roiling in lust and anger. His hand slid down and wrapped around her throat, holding her head suspended as he thrust ruthlessly into her pussy.

"This cunt. Always so goddamn hot. Is it hot in general, or is it hot for me, Ava? Tell me," he seethed against her lips. Pleasure building, she lifted and thrust down onto his thick fingers. His hand pulsed around her throat, and she swallowed around the pressure. "Answer me, goddammit."

She heard the jealousy in his tone, the need to know that he mattered. She fought his demand by shutting her eyes. No, she wouldn't answer.

"You want to fucking come?" he withdrew his fingers and gave her pussy a slap.

She hissed out low. "What do you think?" Her eyes snapped open and threw him a glare.

He gave a little chortle. "Then, answer."

Fuck the orgasm! She shoved the heels of her hands against his chest. No way was she going to be vulnerable. She struggled to get off him, but there wasn't much she could do when he tightened his grip on her throat. His fingers circled her clit languidly, gently, not at all what she wanted or needed. She bared her clenched teeth at him.

"Tut, tut, not playing very nice. When your man asks you a question, you answer like a good girl. Let's start with some-thing easier, then. With the way your tight pussy is throbbing, I'd say it's been a long time since you last came on a cock. Am I right?"

"Fuck you," she spat out.

Angling his head, he gave her a look of disappointment. "You're not making the right moves for a woman who wants to come," he taunted. His hand left her clit and came around her to grab an ass cheek. "Need a little swat to remind you of who's boss? Or would you rather get *fucked* into submission?"

All of the above?

She growled in response, eliciting another chuckle from him. He wanted to know if he was special? Fuck him, he didn't deserve an answer to that question.

His tone got hard. "Get up," he said as he pushed her off his lap and onto her feet, all the while keeping a hold on her throat. "Lift up your skirt." She struggled against his fingers, but she didn't have much wiggle room. Fisting clumps of her skirt, he rucked it up to her waist.

"Take your panties off," he demanded.

"No," she countered, shaking her head with what wiggle room she had. He crowded her backward until she was flat against the wall. Damn him, the fight in her was quickly morphing into pure, white-hot lust.

His tongue flicked out to the corner of his lips. "So fucking hot when you fight me. You know how that turns me on."

Tucking her skirt around her waist, he let go of her throat long enough to tear her panties off her. *Riiip.* Her mouth dropped open. Hand back around her throat, he brought the ripped panties to his nose and scented them before letting them drop. Cool air whisked over her skin, but her clit throbbed with desperation. She shifted from foot to foot, rubbing her thighs to get some friction going. His wolf-like black eyes were on her the whole time, watching every reaction as she struggled to hide them.

"Take out my cock."

Her gaze bounced around the walls of her office as she licked her parched lips. Good, this she could do. Reaching for the zipper of his jumpsuit, she dragged it down tooth by tooth and reached inside. There was his swift inhale of breath, but other than that, he stayed still. His thick cock felt so silky smooth and hot in her hand. She groaned when her thumb smeared over the pre-come. Oh God, she wanted a taste of that. So. Bad.

"Now," he crooned, his face twisting in unrefined pleasure. "It's time for this hot little pussy to come all over my cock."

"I'll go down on you. I'll suck you off."

"Oh, no, angel. You might've gotten away with swallowing if you hadn't been stubborn, but it's too late for that. You've got a lesson that needs learning, and I don't do things by half measure. I might not be able to smack that ass the way you deserve; nice, hard, and long until you're begging me to stop. Someone walking past your door might hear. So the only option is to take this tight cunt."

He thrust two fingers inside of her, forcing a harsh gasp out of her. "I'm gonna take it over and over again until you recognize who owns you. And you better fucking wait for my permission to come." He angled her head up so she had no choice but to look at him. "Make damn sure you wait, Ava."

Her eyelids fluttered at his command. She loved when he took control and got rough. Holding back until he gave her the go-ahead made her come all that much harder.

Releasing her throat, he yanked her off the wall and bent her over the desk. One firm hand fell on the small of her back and slid down to palm her bare ass. Goose bumps pebbled her blistering, hot skin. Puck stilled for a moment, listening for sounds in the hallway. She cocked her head but heard nothing until...*smack*.

"Fuck," she snarled, pain blooming on her left butt cheek. Might not be as hard as usual, but his hand certainly landed with precision. The searing heat traveled to her core, leaving it pulsating with want.

Three more slaps rained down in rapid succession. She whistled out a deep, dark exhale. It'd been a good spell since she was handled like this, since she heard the distinctive sound of her flesh getting smacked.

"Ripe. As. Fuck. Your ass is as bratty as your mouth. It needs a good session to get it the shade of pink I want, but we can't chance someone overhearing us, can we, my dirty little angel? I'll have to find another way—" A sharp hiss flew over her head as the blunt tip of his cock swiped against her drenched opening.

His hand rested on her nape, holding her down as he gave

a forceful thrust. They moaned in unison. Once he bottomed out, her inner walls spasmed against his length. God, but he felt massive. Bigger than she remembered. The rough glide of his cock as he withdrew and slammed back in felt oh-so good. It was everything she'd been missing with other men. It was like home.

"This how you like it?" he rasped out, a quiver in his rough voice as his stiff cock filled her again. She should be mad at him for taking her like this, but each time she opened her mouth to voice a complaint, the slide of his cock wiped her mind blank. Her mouth strained wide, lip curling at the incredible sensation of his fucking. Saliva dribbled out of her gaping mouth on the folder beneath her cheek.

"Tell me," he demanded. Each thrust shoved the desk forward a bit, rattling the drawers.

"Yes! This is how I like it. You know that, dammit."

Fingers found and tickled her clit, sometimes gently, sometimes not so gently. He gave her clit a flick with his nail. She jerked back against him.

"Nice, I like that," he moaned. She loved the feeling of being crammed chock-full of his thick cock, with his fingers playing her and the occasional slap. There was nothing like it.

He pulled all the way out with a wet sucking noise. "My cock's nice and slicked up with your juices, girlie."

He slammed back in, eliciting a tortured groan. Hovering over the edge of an impending climax, her eyes rolled to the back of her head.

"Don't you dare fucking come," he warned, "or I will keep you on the edge for weeks. Don't test me on this, Ava."

Banging her head lightly against the top of her desk, she gritted her teeth to hold herself back. In a heartbeat, he had her right back to the last time they'd lain together.

"Never had a cunt this hot and sweet. Christ, you were made for me."

She shuddered. His dirty talk was winding her up too fast. She was familiar with his cock and fingers, but the dirty talk was new. New, and provoking. Rearing back against the firm hold on her nape, she arched her back and lifted her hips to meet his brutal pounding. Between her trembling thighs, she clamped down in a futile attempt to prevent his withdrawals. The pressure was more than she could handle, but she clenched her fists and bore down hard, tensing herself not to come. She held on. Held on tight.

"I need—" She broke off with a high-pitched keen that she smothered in the folder as he sped up behind her, battering into her, the wet *slap slap slap* of flesh on flesh invading the small office.

"Come," he intoned gravely, his voice a little thready toward the end. She exploded spectacularly. A full-body spasm powered through her as she flew over the edge and fell down a rabbit hole. Down, down, down she went. For how long, she couldn't say. She lost touch with reality. Everything fell away but the feel of his cock. A SWAT team could've burst in and trained a hundred guns on them, and she wouldn't have heard or seen a thing. Other than the cock taking her from behind. Forcing her submission by orgasm.

Short, brutal jabs became arrhythmic as Puck tensed behind her. Teeth suddenly clutched at the soft flesh of her shoulder. A growl tore from his throat and roared around her flesh as his hot seed jetted inside her.

"Fuck, Christ, are you on the pill?" he rasped out against her ear.

"God, yes." They'd been so consumed that it hadn't occurred to them until now. A tiny ball of want in her chest rebelled, as if saying, *yes, I want his come to mean something.*

She told it to shut the hell up. Clearing her parched throat, cheek glued to the file beneath her cheek, she said, "Don't worry, I won't get pregnant."

Puck didn't reply. No thanks or comment expressing relief. Braced above her on locked arms, he continued with light thrusts for a bit longer. Then, after a deep sigh, he pulled out.

Slumped over the desk, she lay there, breathing heavily. Enjoying the soreness that spelled fulfillment of a woman well used. She heard the teeth of his zipper. Then a hand took her hip, another her shoulder, and he peeled her off the desk. Disorientated, Ava's body was of little use to her. Holding her against him, he grabbed tissues off her desk and wiped her up. He found her panties and tried tucking them in his jumpsuit until he realized he couldn't take them with him. With a dry chuckle, he gave them one last forlorn look, brushed them beneath his nostrils and then leaned over and slipped them inside her top drawer.

Settling heavily on the desk, she rearranged her clothes with shaking hands. What had she given up in fucking him? It had been more intense than she'd anticipated. A well of emotions she'd stuffed down for years bubbled up. Swatting away her useless hands, Puck finished buttoning her blouse. Needing to focus on a task, she combed her hair with her fingers.

"How do I look?"

His eyes flicked up to her and then returned to her buttons.

"Freshly fucked."

She punched him hard in the shoulder, but he yanked her into his chest and curled himself around her.

"Fucking beautiful," he murmured. He must've checked the clock because he said, "We have five minutes before Officer Dipshit comes back here with his nosey-ass self."

"Officer Dipshit?" She made a scoffing noise in his chest.

"I wish I could take a shower with you or lie down beside you in bed right now," he confessed. Placing a light kiss on her lips, he released her and motioned her to her seat. Her heart melting, she turned away to wipe down the saliva from the files on her desk and re-arrange her scattered pens and notepads. Anything but give way to the weak-kneed feeling their intimacy had evoked.

This is about justice for Sasha and keeping Kingpin behind bars. It wasn't about re-igniting a relationship of *any* kind with Puck. She'd do well to keep that in mind. In the meantime, it was best to shove down the tumble of feelings whirling inside her. They'd do her no good whatsoever.

"I'm going to open the door to air this place out in case Dipshit smells something." She gave him a quizzical look. "The scent of me fucking you," he expanded. "Not that I don't want to claim you in front of him and every other male on this fucking planet. Because I fucking do."

Before she could respond to that ridiculous statement, he unlocked the door and swung it open. A cool breeze swept through, and she fanned her heated cheeks, hoping her skin returned to normal before Derick arrived. How did Puck look so calm and collected after what they'd done while she sat there looking like a hot mess?

"What about Kingpin?" she whispered harshly. They hadn't gotten a chance to talk about any progress he might have made.

Leaning back and folding his arms, he smirked at her. "Guess that'll have to wait until our next *appointment*, Ms. Evans."

10

PUCK

P uck was jonesing for another session with Ava.

He couldn't wait to taste her again. She'd been so damn hot, smooth, and silky around his cock. Christ, the way she came, pulsing and milking him for all she was worth.

He'd hit pussy gold, and he wasn't giving it up for anything. The hand on the clock was inching toward three o'clock, so he moved to the table closest to the door of the unit. A few minutes before the hour, a CO came to the main entrance and called out, "Santos! O'Leary! Dupres!" and waited by the door. Why the fuck didn't she call his name?

Standing up, he approached her slowly. His size sometimes made women nervous, and he guessed that would be doubly true in the pen. "My name wasn't called. Rossi."

"Who do you see?"

"Ms. Evans."

"She called out."

"What for?" he followed up, swiftly. Was she avoiding him because he'd moved on her too fast? He'd planned to hold off, but couldn't help himself when she flared up at him. For her to run from him with Kingpin on the line, he must've fucked up bad.

He hadn't moved from his spot, and the CO narrowed her eyes like she was about to tell him to fuck off, so he quickly asked, "She okay? She's my social worker and helps me with my...stuff." His eyes pleaded for something, any fragment of information.

"She called out sick. There's been something goin' around, so I'm not surprised. Don't worry, inmate, she'll be back."

Now that he thought back, she was sniffling a little last time he saw her. Worry battled with the misery of knowing he wouldn't see her for another four days at the very least. Could be longer if she caught the flu, although he recalled hearing that prison employees were required to take the flu vaccine or something like that. His concern over her won out. Did she live alone, or was she still with her mom? If she lived alone, who would take care of her? He imagined her in bed, running a high fever with no one to make her soup, check her temperature, or feed her Tylenol.

Thanking the CO, he went straight to the pay phone and dialed the clubhouse collect. Whistle picked up, thank fuck, and conferenced him into a call with Loki.

"Hey, whattup, brother? How you doing in there?" asked Loki.

"I'm dealing. What else can I do, holed up in this fucking place? Listen, I need you to get Abby to check on someone for me."

Loki was silent for a beat. The brother was beyond protective over his old lady, especially since she was pregnant. "Tell me more."

Puck sighed. "I reconnected with someone from my past in the pen." He turned his back to the rest of the room and lowered his voice, "She's my social worker. She's also an

Agency employee who works out of the county jail a few days a week. Her name is Ava Evans. Abby will know who she is. Anyways, she's out sick, and I want Abby to go check on her. Make sure she's doing okay. Stop by the pharmacy and get medicine and shit. Whatever she needs."

More silence. He could practically hear the wheels working in Loki's head. The brother was no fucking joke. "You knew her before," Loki stated.

"Yeah, she's someone from my past."

"And you want us to check on her," he clarified, talking slowly as if piecing pieces of a puzzle together. "Make sure she's okay? That she's got everything she needs?"

"Did I stutter?"

"Huh," replied Loki. *Aww, shit. Here it comes.* "She your bitch or what?"

Cat. Out. Of. Bag.

"Yeah, she's mine. Might not be completely on board with it yet, but it's happening," he pronounced.

"What the fuck is happening in there? You losin' your mind, brother?"

"Maybe, but not about her being mine. That's a done deal. I'll lose my fuckin' mind worryin' about her if I don't know she's okay. We haven't gotten to catch up enough. I don't know if she's living alone or with her mom, but I'm guessing she's alone."

"She have a man?"

"No man," he declared resolutely.

"You sure?"

"Brother, I tunneled my cock inside that already. She was tight as fuck, yo. She's a good girl."

"Then, what in the fuck does she want with you?" he snorted.

"Could ask the same about Abby," he fired back.

"Fair enough." Another beat passed. "Gotta say, I'm surprised by your request. You know if you weren't in the fucking pen, I'd be tearing into you right now."

"Thank God for small mercies, motherfucker," he replied.

"So you say she knows Abby? That must mean I've seen her. What's her name again?"

"Ava Evans. Tell Abby to go find out where Ava lives and check up on her. I already know you're gonna go with her, but you stay outside the house. I don't want you scaring Ava. You're an ugly fucker with your scarred up face. The brothers haven't stopped betting that Abby dumps your butt-ugly ass. Considering you can't get her to marry you, I'd say they're right. I'm tryin' to win the girl, so until I do, you stay outdoors."

Ignoring Puck's string of insults, Loki mocked, "Are you for real? I'm not letting Abby walk alone into a stranger's house."

"She's a single woman who works as a social worker in the same place as Abby. There's no danger, you idiot."

"Fuck you, I'll be the one to determine that. You're the one asking for the favor. Beggars can't be choosers."

Puck gritted his teeth. "Fine, fucking talk to Abby about it, but she's the lead on this job, alright? If she wants you there, then I'll allow it. But if she doesn't, then get the hell out of Dodge, and don't think I won't find out the truth once I'm out of here. Do it today. I'll call you same time tomorrow for an update."

With that, he hung up before he slammed the receiver against his forehead. Talking to a brother like Loki sometimes did that to a man.

✳✳✳

AVA SAT up on her overstuffed sofa littered with magazines, books, and used tissues. The doorbell rang, but she wasn't expecting anyone. Praying it wasn't a door-to-door salesperson or Jehovah's Witness, she tiptoed to the front door of her small bungalow. Hugging the lapels of her blue flannel robe closed, she wiped her sniffling nose and peered out the peephole. Her forehead furrowed. *Is that...she squinted...Abby?*

Abby worked at the Agency, an organization that provided mental health and other social services to a wide swath of the Poughkeepsie community. Her expertise was helping survivors of domestic violence, while Ava worked with inmates. They chatted if they happened to be in the kitchen together, and they'd both attended the Thursday happy hours at a nearby bar, but they weren't close enough to explain why she was at Ava's doorstep in the middle of a work day.

Flinging the door open on the frigid winter air, she asked, "Abby, why are you here? Is everything okay at the Agency?"

"Hey, Ava. Sorry for bothering you. Yeah, everything's okay. Are you okay? You weren't at work yesterday or today," the younger woman replied, her shiny blond hair gleaming in the bright sunlight.

Scrunching her tissue in her hand, Ava said, "I have a cold. Do you want to come in? I don't think I'm contagious anymore, but keep a healthy distance from me."

A scary-looking biker stared at her from the window of the truck idling at the curb.

"Uhm...is that your ride? Do you want to invite him in?"

Abby waved her hand dismissively. "That's my fiancé, Loki, but he'll be fine waiting outside," she replied as she stepped inside. In the foyer, she shrugged off her red coat and draped it over the back of a chair.

Clutching her robe around herself, Ava peeked out from behind the door, inspecting Loki carefully in the cab of the truck. A biker. Like Puck. She gave a little sentimental sigh and shut the door softly.

"Would you like tea or coffee?" she asked as she turned around.

"Tea would be great," Abby replied. "Cute place you have."

Ava led her toward the kitchen. "Thanks, it's small, but I live alone, so it fits me. Please take a seat." She gestured to a small round table with a gingham tablecloth that matched the curtains hanging from the windows of the small alcove. "Black or green tea?"

"Black works for me." Abby took a seat and threaded her fingers together. "I'd like to be transparent from the beginning." She paused a beat. "Puck sent us."

Ava was reaching for a tin canister of Earl Grey tea on her tiptoes. At the sound of Puck's name, her grip on the canister slipped. Fumbling with the tin, she caught it to her chest and fell back on the heels of her feet.

"Puck sent you?" she squeaked out. *Duh, that's what the woman said, Ava.*

"Yeah. Loki and Puck are brothers in the Demon Squad. He called when you didn't show up to work and asked us to check up on you. You know, to make sure you had everything you needed." Motioning toward the front of the house, she said, "I have Tylenol, Advil, a thermometer, and cough syrup in the truck. We were more than a little surprised by his request. He, like, never does more than hook up with women. I wasn't aware you guys knew each other. Small world, right?"

"Yeah, small world," she mumbled, laughing nervously. Ava turned her back on Abby and concentrated fastidiously on scooping loose tea leaves into her favorite cast-iron Japanese teapot. *What the hell was he thinking?* Moving to the sink, she flicked on the tap water and filled the teakettle. *Is he trying to get me into trouble?* Carefully, she placed it on the stove top and lit the old-fashioned burner with a match. *Because, seriously, there's no greater sin than getting mixed up with a client.*

It was a huge no-no among social workers. Whether or not he realized how unprofessional they'd been, she wasn't about to get kicked out of her job because he was clueless. Deciding to keep her answers as short as possible, she turned to face Abby and said, "He really shouldn't have bothered you to check up on me."

"I'm a social worker, too, Ava. I know all about not getting involved with a client, but if Puck asked us to do this, that means something. I would never do anything to compromise Puck's well-being and happiness. Not only do I respect him as a person and a brother, but I'm very close to his sister."

Damn him. "He really shouldn't have made you go out of your way to visit me," Ava repeated.

"There's no way I would do anything to harm Puck or someone he cared about. You have *nothing* to worry about," Abby promised in a firm tone.

Ava puffed out a breath of exasperation. "Like you, the work I do is incredibly meaningful to me, and I wouldn't jeopardize it for anything." *Lie, lie, lie.* But she was doing it to keep Sasha's killer locked up. Still, she was fuming over the fact that Puck had cavalierly suggested to one of his brothers that there was something going on between them. There was no one to blame but herself, but she'd expected more discretion from him.

"You don't have anything to worry about. Puck didn't realize. He's a simple guy, in many ways. Doesn't have a dishonest bone in his body. Can't manipulate, pretend, or hide his feelings to save his life. He wouldn't have asked me to come here if he didn't trust me implicitly. I want to make that clear. He must've been pretty worked up about you to reach out to Loki from jail. Let's just say, Loki's not the easiest brother to approach. But Puck did it because he guessed that it wouldn't alarm you if I showed up on your doorstep. He's a worrier with the people he cares about. Sammi happens to be one of my closest friends, and I've seen how he treats her. This is *not* unusual, coming from him."

"I don't see or hear a peep from him in eight years, and after a few sessions, he has someone checking up on me?" She shook her head in disbelief. "I'm a grown woman. I've lived on my own for years."

"Welcome to my life, sister. You may be repeating that phrase a lot in the future, because that's what it's like to be with a man like Puck or Loki. They're...protective." Abby canted her head to the side, an expression of curiosity lining her face. "So you knew Puck eight years ago?"

Ava rolled her eyes.

The other woman threw up her hands. "Sorry, I'm prying, I know. We're just dying to know who captured that man's attention. I mean, Loki told me he's never had an old lady—that's our term for a wife."

"Yes, I know. My father's in the Renegades, so I'm familiar with the lifestyle."

"There you go. Well, he's never even had a girlfriend. His life had been Sammi, the club, making money, the club, Sammi, and on and on. I don't know why your relationship ended, but he's clearly smitten with you now."

"That man's no choir boy," she huffed out. "*He's* the reason our relationship ended, so don't get your hopes up." Ava realized she was speaking bluntly, but she didn't want to lead her on. She liked Abby, and God knows, it was time to expand her social circle now that her mother's cancer was in remission. But there was *nothing* between her and Puck besides sex and Kingpin. Her heart throbbed with a jolt of pain. *Shut up heart, I'm not listening.*

"Oh." Abby's shoulders slumped.

The teakettle whistled, and Ava hurried to turn off the stove. Carefully, she poured the scalding water over the tea leaves. Taking her favorite green owl-shaped timer, she turned it to the number of minutes the tea needed to steep.

Resting her hip against the counter, she expanded on her earlier statement. "I don't want you to be disappointed, but Puck broke it off between us years ago. We might've been each other's first loves, but we were young and immature. Puck wants to rekindle our relationship, but I'm not interested. I refuse to put myself at the mercy of his whims."

"Whims?" A soft peal of laughter chimed through the cozy kitchen. "He's not exactly known for being whimsical. Granted, from what I've heard, he didn't take on any leadership roles in the club until recently, but he isn't a man who acts on impulse."

"You'd be surprised," Ava muttered with a slight grimace. *Oh, he's acted on impulse more than once. Like breaking up with me or fucking me on the desk of my office. I'd say that's the definition of impulsive.* "We're working together at the moment, but I don't expect to see him after he's released or transferred to another facility."

Ava opened her fridge and pulled out a carton. "Milk?" she asked.

Abby nodded, and Ava filled a small white porcelain pitcher. The timer went off. She returned to the teapot and deposited the tea leaves in a compost bin underneath her sink. Placing the teapot, cups, saucers, spoons, and a small matching porcelain sugar bowl on a wooden tray, she brought it to the table and set the items around the table.

Despite the firm stance she'd taken, a warm gooey feeling settled in her belly at the proof of Puck's concern for her. He'd been worried enough to collect call his friend and convince him to show up at her door with his fiancée. It was a perfect example and a bittersweet reminder of what it was like to be part of Puck's life. How careful and solicitous he was with the ones he loved.

Between pitching in to raise Kat and taking care of her mother, Ava was the bedrock of her small family. It hadn't occurred to her to call her mom or Kat, and certainly not her father, to let them know she was sick. She would've only mentioned it if there was an obligation she couldn't meet or she was at death's door. Otherwise, she wouldn't want to be a bother. She was the exact opposite of that to Puck.

Sitting down across from Abby, she served the tea. Ava stared into her teacup, stirring her spoon in slow circles when Abby interrupted her musings. "If you're not interested in Puck, you should get out there. Go out, flirt, date."

With a small smile, she asked, "How do you know I don't already have a boyfriend?"

"Do you? Because I don't see Puck going after another man's woman."

"No," Ava replied, shaking her head. "I don't have the time, what with my job and the responsibilities I have with my family. Then there's the fact that the bar and club scenes aren't really my thing anymore."

"You always seem a little...sad. I don't mean to pry..." Abby trailed off.

"It's okay. You're a social worker. I understand the impulse of caring about people and wanting to help them live their best lives. Perhaps I am a little melancholic. In my late teens and early twenties, I partied hard. In fact, Puck and I partied together. Then life barged in and he broke up with me. Now, I have serious family responsibilities on top of my own career goals. I worry about my clients, and you know how that can bleed into your private life. Sometimes it's hard to leave everything at work at the end of the day. Doesn't help that I'm feeling under the weather."

"Well, you should come out with me and my friends. You should meet Sammi. You know her, right?"

"Sure, I know Sammi," Ava replied with a sad, wistful smile. Her heart leaped in her chest. They'd had begun a little tentative friendship of their own before Puck ended things. Ava had become something of a loner after Sasha's death and getting clean. Although she'd love to hang out with Abby and reconnect with Sammi, she couldn't. Once Kingpin was taken care of and Puck was out of jail, they'd part and go their separate ways.

"I bet she'd love to see you again."

"I don't think it's a good idea. Once Puck is out of my life, it wouldn't do to see him around." She swallowed around the lump in her throat. "He'll be with other women. That would be hard for me. One small mercy about our breakup was that, once it was over, we never crossed paths." *Except for when he showed up at Sasha's funeral.*

"I suppose so," Abby agreed reluctantly. She took a sip of her tea and then inquired, "Do you need anything? Like I said, I have a mini pharmacy in the truck."

"I could do with more Tylenol. I'm experiencing residual aches and pains from the fever."

Abby's face brightened. "Sure! Let me go get it."

Ava followed her to the door as she rushed to the truck and fiddled with some bags while talking to Loki. He followed Abby as she returned with a plastic bag filled with stuff. Greeting him, Ava ushered them inside. As Abby described what was in the bag, Loki inspected Ava from head to toe. Wearing only a nightgown and robe, she suddenly felt nervous. Shifting from foot to foot, she retied the belt of her robe around her waist.

Abby slapped Loki's arm. "Stop staring! You're making her nervous."

"Jealous that I'm checking out another woman?" Loki teased as he looped his arm around Abby's middle, hauled her against his side, and rubbed her small baby bump. Planting a kiss on the crown of her head, he looked down at her with so much affection that Ava felt a tinge of envy.

Abby chuckled. "Hardly."

Breaking free of his hold, she gave Ava a quick hug before she could protest about being sick, and then they were both out of her house with waves of goodbye.

Ava closed the door behind the adoring couple. Stillness, tinged with emptiness, permeated her cozy little sanctuary. No matter how comfy her home was, it couldn't make up for the absence of a loved mate.

11

PUCK

Puck may not have been able to see Ava, but his thoughts never strayed far from her.

Being cut off from his family, his brothers, his bike, and his home was unnerving. He didn't have any of his belongings. There was no privacy. Noise and chatter all the fucking time. Tack on mind-numbing boredom, and stir-crazy didn't begin to describe what he felt like.

His trial date hadn't been set, so Puck had a chunk of time on his hands. It was the thought of losing his jury trial that had him shuddering in his oversized jumper. If he was convicted, he was looking at a minimum of five years in a federal penitentiary. He could plead down to second-degree assault, but then he was guaranteed to serve over a year. What a fucking mess.

Ava was his oasis of sanity. It offset the powder keg of stress he lived with every day. At times, he had to go back to the basics, like focusing on her sultry vanilla scent. Instead of being in an enclosed musty room stinking of sour body odor, he was transported to a beach in the Florida Keys.

The following day, Puck called Loki and found out she was

home with a cold but, otherwise, doing well. Pride swelled his chest when he heard how she took the Tylenol because she'd run out. *See, what'd I tell you?* he wanted to shout out to the universe. Loki complimented him on how fine his woman was, and then ribbed him until Puck got sick of it and simply hung up on his ass.

Feeling more at peace after his call, he set out to do the job he'd promised Ava. Puck played cards, but it took a while to get in on a game with Kingpin's crew. There was one man, a kid really, who either worked for the drug dealer or was related to him. Little shit was named Jiggins. High half the time, the kid was a weak link, and Puck's way in.

Hanging around the card tables, Puck got subbed in on a card game of spades with Kingpin, Jiggins, and another guy named Poison, of all things. Jiggins must've sucked ass if Puck was teamed up with him.

"Ace high, no bags," Jiggins called out as he gave Puck a wink. What in the fuck that meant, Puck had no idea. It didn't take long to find out Kingpin had a little side hustle, managing the gambling at the card tables and taking sports bets. Enterprising man.

To gamble, the inmates used bags of chips and sodas from the commissary, a store inside the jail, where inmates purchased stuff, like snacks and hygiene products. From his dilated eyes, it was evident Jiggins was coming off a high, which meant this was gonna be a wash of a game. He ground down on his back teeth. Puck hated losing, for any reason, but it was a necessary evil to get an in with this crew.

Kingpin scratched his closely shaved head as he dealt the cards. On the other side of thirty, he had a square jaw and heavy jowls. Skinny guy with a paunch, generic tribal tats covered his biceps and neck, poking up from beneath his collar. Puck knew exactly the type of dealer he was. The chummy kind, who pretended to use alongside his customers but cut his product with God knows what behind their back. All in all, he was a viper and a coward. But, first and foremost, he was an opportunist. Being a hustler himself, that was something Puck could exploit.

Picking up his cards, Puck considered them as Jiggins bid his tricks. They went around until each player bid. The game played itself out, and Kingpin won the round with a ten of spades, the highest card. Jiggins was the next to deal.

Grabbing the deck of cards, he shuffled a few times and asked Puck, "Whatcha in for, dude? Me, I'm in for possession." It was a common question among inmates, as an icebreaker but also to get a pulse on the kind of man they were dealing with.

"Pistol-whipped a guy," he replied as he picked up his cards. "Owed me five Gs. Couldn't let that stand." The assault was true, the reason behind it was not, but he didn't much care if they believed him. He sure as hell didn't believe every damn thing an inmate told him.

"Five Gs is a lot of dough," commiserated Poison.

"Fuck yeah, it is. If you don't got the money, then you gotta pay up another way, know what I mean? I'm not from a bitch-ass club."

"I heard the Squad went clean," Kingpin murmured, studying his cards intently.

So the fucker kept tabs on other criminal enterprises in the city. The Squad had been one of the main cigarette smugglers in the region for years, until recently.

"There's clean, and then there's clean. President's old lady is a lawyer, so we had to clean up the image, know what I mean? But a brother's gotta do what a brother's gotta a do to survive, feel me?"

"True dat," piped up Jiggins.

"You've got to survive," Kingpin repeated.

What the fuck does that mean? What kind of cryptic shit is that?

"Survival's the name of the game, yo," Puck stated, watching Kingpin from the corner of his eye. Kingpin lifted his gaze from his cards and carefully studied Puck. Tapping his cards against the table, he refocused his attention and played his hand. Puck had to give it to him; he was a cool motherfucker.

"Amen," supplied Jiggins.

Each man called out his tricks and they settled down to playing their hands in silence. Puck wasn't surprised when Kingpin won game after game.

"With the luck I'm having, if I'm gonna keep playing cards, I'm gonna need cash," Puck muttered, loud enough for Jiggins to hear, but not the rest of the men milling around their table.

Jiggins's gaze shot to Puck's face. "Yeah?"

"Always ready to make money moves," replied Puck. "My brothers take care of commissary, but they're not generous enough to pay the bills pilin' up while I'm laid up in here. And playing cards? Let's just say, I can't be owing people."

"That you can't," Jiggins agreed.

"Yeah, already had one fight and got thrown in the hole. Not lookin' for a repeat."

"There might be somethin' for you to do. Always lookin' for hard-workin' men who know the score."

"That would be me, but I ain't lookin' to add time to what I already have," Puck warned. It was the God's honest truth.

Jiggins chuckled low. "No worries, brah. The COs don't give a fuck what we do as long as we don't riot. It's fucking Walmart on Black Friday up in here. I'll talk to Kingpin and see what you can do. Gonna be real small in the beginning. Test you out to see if you do what you're told."

"I can be trusted," intoned Puck. Jiggins shouldn't be running his mouth, but that wasn't his problem.

"Like I said, I'll talk to my cousin. It's for him to decide."

So Puck was right that the little shit was related to Kingpin. Nothing else made as much sense. Satisfied with having set the wheels in motion, Puck got up from the table once the game was done and paid his loss. Chips and soda were a small price to pay for entry into Kingpin's circle.

12

AVA

"You did what?"

Ava stared at Puck as they faced off in her office.

The instant the door closed and locked, they were sealed in their own world. Outside of an emergency that required him to get back in his unit for head count, no one would interrupt them during a counseling session. Besides, Puck had an ear out for anything happening outside her door.

Grinding the heels of her hands into her eye sockets, she asked, "What in God's name were you thinking? I said find out what he's doing, not get *involved*. You could get caught, and then you'll have serious drug charges on top of whatever else you have. The stakes are too high. You have to abort this plan."

"They're sneaking drugs in through the mail, glued to paper or the paper itself is soaked in heroin, ecstasy, and fentanyl. Not just letters, either. Shit like cards, Bible verses, funeral notices. Kingpin even joked about getting a Harry Potter coloring book or, as he called it, a Heroin Potter book through the mail."

Her gaze lifted to the poster illustrating the cycle of addiction on the wall facing her.

"What?" she breathed out in disbelief. "My God, it's worse than I imagined."

"Yeah, much worse. The jail is drowning in drugs. It's coming in through every fucking crack in the walls. Besides the visitors and a few corrupt COs, which I haven't yet been able to identify, it's being thrown over the wall in tennis balls and dead pigeons. Jiggins told me of drones dropping shit in the yard, for God's sake. But the majority is coming through the mail. If you wanna take him down, focus on the mail 'cause that can be traced back to him and his source on the outside. You could catch both ends."

Ava covered her eyes. "I don't want to do this. I don't even know where to start."

"I'll hook you up with my lawyer. She knows people. There's no way you can trust anyone up in here. Everyone is suspect, from the lowest employee to the warden." Taking hold of her hand, he squeezed. "Do you hear me? No one is to be trusted. If it weren't for Sasha, I'd forbid you to proceed with this. There're hundreds of thousands of dollars being made by drug dealers on the outside. Maybe cartels. Who the hell knows."

"He's as dangerous inside these walls as he is outside. I knew inmates were getting access to drugs, because they sometimes come in here high, but I can't take down a whole syndicate. I just want to get *him*. Just him," she ended in a guttural tone.

"Wherever he goes, he's gonna find a way to hustle in drugs," warned Puck.

"There's nothing to do in here, day in day out. Men get real creative when they're bored and have too much time on their hands. They'll always find a way to get the illicit substances they crave. Half the fuckers in here are high, and can you blame them? Even if they don't come in already hooked, why the hell would they wanna stay clean? Hell, I spend my day fantasizing about you to keep from going fucking insane. You're my drug, baby, so I'm not gonna cast stones."

She blinked at his admission. It twisted her insides. Dammit, he was stealing her heart again. How could she not trust a man who jeopardized his future for her sake? Puck wouldn't sabotage his chances of getting out, and leave Sammi to struggle alone, for a simple fuck. And she knew how much he despised being locked up. For a man whose life was founded on the concept of freedom, it was agonizing. No, his actions were intentional. She shifted uncomfortably in her seat. She wasn't sure she was ready to acknowledge what seemed to be right in front of her face.

He broke into her thoughts, "You have to figure out how far you want to go with this."

Ava raised her hand to his cheek and said, "Thank you. You did it. Found out more than I ever thought possible. Sure, I had my suspicions, but you discovered more than I'd imagined possible. Now, though, I need you to stay safe. Get out of it."

Taking her hand, he dropped an openmouthed kiss in the center of her palm.

"It's gonna take time. They trust me now that I'm working for them. The best way to shut it down is for me to get the hell outta here. I've been indicted, so the prosecutor has over two months to set my trial, not that it usually takes that long. The trial itself won't be more than a few days. After that, pray to fucking God I'm set free." He let out a heavy sigh that cracked her heart open even further.

A quiet settled upon them, each dwelling in their individual thoughts. Puck broke the silence first. "What are you going to do? I need to know so I can protect you." Tears welled in her eyes, and he hushed her. "I've got you, babe. You tell me what you wanna do, and I'll help you any way I can."

"I'm not going to get involved in a sting to bring down a drug ring in jail. I'm not a crusader, and that's not how I want to spend my energy. I know it's likely selfish of me, but my focus is on Kingpin. The goal is to lock him away in a maximum-security prison for a long time. He's going to prey on the weak wherever he goes, but he won't be preying on teens like Sasha. I'll have to watch him and work to dismantle whatever he rigs up, but at least I'll have more control over him if he's in prison. And he definitely deserves to be there. He's a menace."

"Fine, let's take time to think about what our next move should be."

She pressed her hands to her cheeks. "I don't know if I want you to continue, Puck. I'm serious. This is beyond dangerous."

"Worried?" he asked with a smirk in his tone. Pulling her hands off her face, he ordered, "Come here."

His gruff demand triggered a shiver down her spine. She let out a long sigh and stood up. There was no way she could deny him. Not after he went above and beyond his duty. Not after putting him in danger for her sake. Inwardly, she recoiled at the notion that she'd placed him in a risky situation. She came over to his side of her desk. Hands on her hips, she shook her head at him, but he simply tugged at her shirt until she fell into his lap.

The more time she spent with him, the more he broke through her resolve to maintain her emotional distance. Even two hours a week was enough to wreak havoc on her peace of mind. Abby's visit the other day, instigated by Puck, had battered at her defenses. After Abby and Loki left, she'd been home alone and sick, but in an odd way, she felt coddled, as if he were nearby. It put her in a giddy mood for the rest of the weekend. The fact that he'd reached outside their little bubble in jail challenged her assumption that they'd go their separate ways once he was free.

The expression on Puck's face when he entered her office hadn't disappointed, either. Beneath his stoic mask, she saw his relief and desire. Once he saw she was healthy, his slitted eyes told her that the instant they were alone, she was his.

Even as she sat on his lap—her favorite position of all time—he was in full possession of everything that was about to happen between them. Dominance oozed from his pores. His fingers ran lightly across her back, reassuring her.

"You okay, angel?" he queried, looking her over. "I was worried about you when you missed work. Thought I scared you away."

Shaking her head, her tresses fell across her face and a strand stuck to her slick bottom lip. He gently plucked it off and looped it around his index finger.

"No, just had a cold, but honestly, it didn't occur to me you'd worry," she admitted.

He pulled back from her, surprise raising his eyebrows upward. "Not worry? Seems I'm not doing a my job if you doubt me."

She shifted on his lap, his husky tone and huge body affecting her concentration. Leaning against him, she shrugged lightly and inhaled his spicy male fragrance. A warm fuzziness spread through her body, making her muscles lax with desire. She gave him a sultry look underneath her lashes.

"Do I need to show you how much I care?" His tone dropped to a low pitch. "How much I missed you? Be careful what you say. You may not like what you unleash in me."

"I didn't say anything," she countered.

"Sure about that? Questioning how much I care is like waving a red flag in front of a bull."

His cedar scent wound around her like a flame, flicking at the edges of her skin. She'd self-combust if he didn't touch her soon.

"Show me," she said simply.

He didn't answer with words. His fingers gripped her neck, and he leaned over her, his lips hovering over hers for a long moment. Then, like an explosion, he devoured her.

✳✳✳

PUCK GRIPPED her nape and pulled her in for a hot, wet kiss. Slanting his head for greater access, his tongue delved deep and deeper still. His other hand swept down to cup her butt, fingers curling to take her taut, firm ass. He slipped his hand over to her belly and unzipped her pants. Fingers explored until they found what they sought. Fuck, she was primed for him. One finger dipped inside her soaked core. Then another. Her inner walls clenched around his digits. His heartbeat pounded in his ears. Feeling her pulsing around his fingers, knowing how it would feel around his cock, was almost too much to bear. Pressing the ridge of his erection against her, he pushed in deeper. His other palm brushed down her torso, tugging at her shirt until it was free of her slacks.

"Next time, I want easy access," he demanded against her lips. Grasping her shirt, together they managed to pull it off.

Fuck him, the cups of her bra were a see-through pink. Her already pink nipples shimmered beneath the mesh fabric. Swear to God, he was going to spill in his jumpsuit. Cupping a breast in the palm of his hand, he lifted it to his open mouth and sucked on the plump flesh; his teeth scraped her diamond-hard peak. A low hiss fanned across his cheekbone.

"So fucking tasty," he praised. Using the sopping wet mesh, he rubbed her nipple. Giving it a firm pinch, he moved over to her other breast. The scent of her warm skin permeated his nostrils, whisking him away to a tropical island, far off from this jail that smelled of piss and misery. It was like scenting heaven, and he hadn't even gotten to taste her pussy yet. He gave her breast one last hard suck and then helped her up. Standing before him, his harsh breath rasped over her collarbone, and her body gave a stiff shudder.

"I need in, baby girl."

Wrangling with her pants, he worked them and her panties down to her feet. Down on his haunches, he took one pant leg off and spread her feet wide apart.

"Take off your bra. I want you naked."

She fumbled with clasp and flung it off behind her. It landed haphazardly somewhere on her desk.

"If anyone finds me like this..."

"No one will see you," he growled. The very idea drove him crazy. Ava was his. His to see and touch. His to fuck and love. All his. Besides the dinky little lock, he had an ear out for any potential problems. No way would he risk anyone seeing her or jeopardizing her job.

Standing up, he admired the contrast of her nudity to him being fully dressed. Everything was illicit. Inmate and employee. Fucking in the middle of the afternoon. The sound of people walking past, the crackling radios, the messages on the intercom speaker.

But, eyes locked on each other, they were in their own world. Looking over her shoulder, he gazed down the slope of her long spine ending in her beautiful, rounded ass. Reaching around, he grabbed hold of one of her buttocks and jiggled it. *Sexy as fuck.* Cocking his head, he listened carefully. For the moment, everything was quiet outside, so he gave her bouncy flesh a crack of his hand. A harsh breath vibrated from her parted mouth. He cupped her cunt, catching her juices in his palm, and let out a soft groan.

"Tsk, tsk, tsk, messy already. Oh, I'm gonna add to this mess," he promised with a dark chuckle as he slid his wet palm up to her tit, massaging her wetness roughly into her skin. His tongue followed an invisible line up the side of her neck.

"Please, Puck, please," she sobbed brokenly.

He unzipped his jumpsuit while landing nicks and nips along her throat. She nodded in encouragement and he said, "Brace yourself."

She scooted up on the desk, her palms slapped down on the desktop. He'd been half hard when he walked through the door. Now, as he drew her thighs wide open, seeing her glistening slit and engorged pearl, his balls felt as heavy as a pound of lead each.

"So fucking eager," he murmured as he fit his flared tip at her entrance. Inch by slow inch, he pushed into her wet heat, watching as that pink flesh wrapped around his shaft and sucked it in. His eyes almost rolled to the back of his head. His fingers cinched around her hips to keep her still because she was trying to push forward and take more of him.

"Hurry, dammit," she pleaded. "Harder."

"Listen, I'm in control of this fucking," he barked, although his movements made a liar out of him because his hips slammed hard, rooting him in rough and deep. A few more thrusts, and he bottomed out. "Christ *fuck*, that feels good."

Curled over her, he grasped her hips and pumped, moving in a blur, their wet flesh slapping at the same pace as their moans. Knowing he wasn't going to last for shit, he thrummed at her clit. She tightened and pulsed around him. His strumming turned into short, hard pinches, and she clamped down on his cock, writhing against him in a frenzy.

Her wild abandon fucked with his control because he popped off like a champagne bottle. One moment, the bubbly was inside a bottle. The next instant, his come spurt out in long ropes. Pleasure overtaking him, he pounded into her roughly. The tendons of his neck strained as he threw his head back and bared his teeth, clenching to stop the howl ripping out of his throat. He clutched her jaw and smashed his open mouth over hers, filling her with his scream while absorbing her own.

Rutting into her like an animal, he felt the shudders of her aftershocks beneath his hands as she milked him for all he was worth. She wrapped her slim legs around his hips and linked them at the base of his spine, wringing every last drop from him as his arrhythmic thrusts finally slowed.

Tearing his mouth away, he bit down on her shoulder, heaving out ragged breaths. Once he regained his breath, Puck pulled out, stumbled into the chair, and pulled Ava onto his lap. She curled into him as best she could, her long legs dangling over the side of his lap. He swiped sweat-covered strands of hair from her forehead and inhaled a sated breath.

Fuck, he didn't think he'd ever come this hard. Sure, doing something forbidden added to the thrill, but it was more than that. The energy between them had always been striking. Inexplicably, it bypassed boundaries of time and space. If anything, it'd grown in their time apart. The first time they'd fucked in her office had been a reintroduction. Today was raw passion.

He laid his hand on her belly and stroked. "That was too fast. I want to savor you. Stretch you out on a bed and lick you from top to bottom," he confessed, his voice tinged in regret. Her hand slipped down to cover her pussy, dripping with his come.

He swatted it away. "Nuh-uh, I want you to spread your legs, not close them." Greedy mofo that he was, he wanted to see his seed seeping out of her, more evidence of where he'd been. Dropping his head, he shuttered his eyes and groaned out, "Christ, what a sight."

When he got out of jail, he was going to keep her naked and covered in his seed for days. He wasn't going to let her shower, just let his come dry on her pristine skin until she smelled like him and their combined fucking.

But today he didn't have that luxury.

"Come on," he said. "Let's get you dressed." Lifting her to his feet, he tagged a few tissues and cleaned her, swiping a few extra times 'cause that's the kind of *helpful* guy he was. Once she was decent again, he dragged her back onto his lap and pressed her back against him.

"Better?"

"Yeah, thanks," she replied with a satisfied sigh. The sound reverberated through his chest. Having Ava lying against him was a heady feeling, indeed. He'd done that; he'd put that blissed-out expression on her face. He'd never felt such a deep sense of pride in bringing a woman to completion. Not that he left women hanging. Never that. But no woman brought out this side of him. He'd stand on the top of the building, beat his chest like a caveman, and shout to the world that she was his.

13

AVA

They'd worked out a routine in the past three weeks.

It had serious limitations, but whenever she was frustrated, Ava reminded herself that she had it better than every other family member with someone behind bars. They only got to see their loved ones during visitation, without a moment of privacy.

The time she spent with Puck, talking, fucking, and strategizing, brought them closer than she'd ever thought possible. Along with Sage, Ava had contacted and started collaborating with the Office of Special Investigations. The OSI had initiated a narcotics investigation. Not that she expected to be kept in the know, but she hoped the investigators would be able to intercept telephone calls from jail and JPay, the service inmates used to email and video-call with people on the outside.

Ava's days started at seven-thirty in the morning because life in prison started early. Puck's sessions were her last of the day, but it was past three o'clock, and there was still no knock on her door. The nervous hum she experienced before seeing him morphed into a tight knot.

Where is he?

She checked her clock again. Fifteen minutes after the hour. There hadn't been a lockdown or anything else to cause a change in schedule, and jail ran like clockwork. Had Puck gotten into another fight? Was he in the hole, again? Had he gotten caught doing something for Kingpin? A frisson of fear slithered down her spine.

Logging back on to her computer, she checked to find out where he was. Nothing. She did a quick search on the inmate locator database. Her spine hit the back of her chair. He'd been released at 7:57 that morning. He'd been freed hours ago but hadn't contacted her. Grabbing her work phone, she checked her voicemails, but there were no messages from either him or Sage. She opened her cell phone but only found a text from Kat.

He was gone.

Ava slumped into her seat once more, a long exhale whooshing out of her lungs.

Really, Puck? An array of conflicting emotions tore through her. Relief and happiness were closely followed by a hefty load of nerves. Had he used her? Besides their intimacy and his declarations, the risk he'd taken with Kingpin had convinced her that he was serious. But perhaps she'd served her purpose, and now that he was free, he didn't need her anymore. Because making zero attempts to contact her was *not* a show of commitment.

Ava grabbed the receiver of her work phone to call Sage, but insecurity surged through her. What if he didn't want to see or hear from her again? Even if he hadn't used her, she might not be important now that he was back in society. He was busy getting back to his life, Sammi, and his club. What if he was at his club at this very moment? She sucked in a breath. *With another woman.* The thought ignited a swell of jealousy in her. If he was at his club, he was currently surrounded by biker chicks, any of whom would be more than willing to welcome a brother home from jail.

Swallowing down the bile rising to her gullet, Ava slowly returned the receiver to its holder. Glancing at the clock, she saw that there were thirty-five minutes left of the workday. She could wait and decide what to do once she got home. Just in case, she placed Sage's contact info into her cell phone and waited out the remaining time, like a prisoner.

❊❊❊

AVA DROVE sluggishly down the tree-lined residential street toward her house. Her heart was heavy; a gloom had descended upon her. Not being in the mood to go straight home, she'd first stopped to do some grocery shopping. Dusk had already descended upon her quiet neighborhood by the time she drove up to her house.

Parking the Clementine, she popped open the trunk. An uneasy feeling pricked the hairs at the back of her neck, but she did a quick sweep of the street, and nothing was different. There were a few extra vehicles, but that was to be expected since one of her neighbors was constructing a screened-in patio. Hurrying up the path to her house, she juggled her work bag, purse, and two shopping bags in her arms when a large hand landed on her back. Her eyes flew over her shoulder, and she let out a yelp. Right behind her was Puck. She clutched her chest and cried out, "Oh my God, you scared the hell out of me!"

Grinning wide, he grabbed her bags and carried them to

the entrance to her house. Scrambling to catch up, she asked, "What happened? How are you out? Where did you go? Why are you here?"

Smirking at her flurry of questions, he replied, "Come on. Let's get into your house. I don't want my first kiss as a free man to be in front of your neighbors."

The automatic light on her front porch flicked on as they reached her front door, flooding them in light. Hand trembling, she quickly unlocked the door and stepped inside. Puck followed, and the instant the door shut behind him, he dropped the bags on the floor. A second later, his fingers speared through her hair, holding her head firmly in place as his mouth found hers.

Dumping her purse and work bag, she leaned into him and took hold of his leather biker jacket. The scent of leather and musk sifted through her senses. His hands were on her, and his tongue was exploring her mouth. A wave of relief swept through her.

He's come for me.

Melting into him, she reveled in their kiss, tongues dueling for dominance. Blindly tugging off her gloves, she dropped them on the floor, unzipped his jacket, and spread her hands over his broad chest. He slowly broke off their kiss and moved away to pick up the grocery bags. He found his way through her small one-floor home to her kitchen. She peeled off her coat, tossed it on the couch, and joined him to take the groceries out of the bags.

Once they'd put away the perishable food, he pulled her in close, murmuring against her lips, "I want you in bed. Been fucking dreaming about this for two whole months." Her heart leapt in chest.

An instant later, there was a burst of movement. Each raced to strip off their clothing as quickly as possible, leaving a trail of discarded items in the kitchen, the hallway, and on the floor of her bedroom. Neither bothered to turn on a lamp, and the blue glow of twilight streamed in through the windows. Ava glimpsed over his shoulder at a procession of low-level clouds, stained cayenne orange and magenta, edged in crimson.

Nude, Puck shifted, blocking her view. She placed her hands on his strong shoulders and swept her fingers down his chiseled chest sprinkled with dark hair, reveling in every inch of his hot, taut skin. In the past weeks, she'd reacquainted herself with his physique. Not a trace of the slimness of his youth remained in his solid frame. He was all thick bulk and muscle.

Her fingers sifted through the roughened texture of his chest hair. An electric charge ran up her arms as her hands brushed down the ridges and bumps of his pecs, ribs, and abs to his long, thick shaft and wrapped around the silky skin over hard flesh.

Yearning to taste him, she fell to her knees despite the tugs on her hair and the protests on his lips. Her own lips enveloped the crown of his cock; salt, musk, and his distinctive cedar scent filled her nostrils and coated her tongue. She moaned around his staff, and his fingers tightened around her tresses. The stringent control of this man when he was in jail, vanished. It was replaced by wildness. Without realizing it, his fingers had turned rough, tangling her hair in a twist that pulled sharply on her scalp. She relished the pinpricks of pain because it was proof of his lack of restraint.

"My dirty little angel, you want a taste of me, huh?"

She moaned her acquiescence around his sensitive flesh, and he hissed in response. "You're a bad girl, taking me into your wet mouth like this when I've dreamt about taking you to bed." A strangled groan escaped him. "Goddamn, look how beautiful you look with your lips wrapped around my cock."

Yeah, she wasn't getting on her back before he came in her mouth. Gripping the root of his shaft tightly in her grip, she sucked in deeper. Her mouth began to ride him in a slow, persistent rhythm meant to drive him crazy.

One of his hands coasted down to her breast and kneaded roughly. Tweaking one nipple was like igniting a hot wire to her pussy. Giving as good as she got, Ava dragged a finger along the seam of his balls and then cupped them, testing them in the palm of her hand.

"Fuck, baby, you're killin' me," he uttered hoarsely.

Her only reply was to give them a good massage as her tongue swirled around the crest of his cock. His body jerked. A second later, all ten of his fingers tunneled in her hair, holding her tight as he took over. "Enough with the teasing. You want me to fuck this beautiful mouth of yours? Done."

He grunted as he thrust into her mouth. She kept immobile for him to use her as he wanted. And, oh, did he use her. Deliciously so.

"Breathe through your nose, baby. I need access to that tight throat of yours."

She did as he instructed, and his thighs began to shake, curses exploding above her head. A moment later, a roar shattered her eardrums as he spilled into her mouth. Too fast for her to swallow, streams of come trickled from the corners of her mouth and dripped onto her breasts. One final thrust, and Puck withdrew, stumbling back a few steps. Bending over, he clutched his knees as harsh breaths sawed in and out of his heaving chest.

Ava settled on her haunches, hands daintily resting on her lap as she licked the corners of her lips like a satisfied cat laving cream from her chops.

Watching her from a few feet away, he huffed out, "Pretty fucking proud of yourself, aren't you?"

Her lips spread into a gloating grin. "Yes."

He chortled. "You should be. I've been rubbing one off every fucking night, and it was *nothing* compared to this gifted mouth of yours."

Her smile grew even wider. It was obvious by the way he'd needed to instruct her that she wasn't experienced in deep throating. They'd never done that before, and this was the first time her throat had truly been *taken*. Quite an experience but worth every moment of watching Puck lose himself under her direction. He had staying power, but she'd gotten him to come so fast, it'd brought him to his knees.

Rising to his full height, he approached her, his half-hard cock bobbing in front of him. *How did he do that?* He offered her his hand and led her to bed. Pulling back the covers, he gestured for her to go first. And she did, making sure to swish her ass from left to right as she crawled on all fours to the middle of her mattress. Thank goodness she'd invested in a king size, because there was a king-sized male crawling in behind her. Dragging her to him, he tucked her to his side and drew the covers over them.

Ava puffed out a contented little sigh. Sure, she was aroused, but she'd take a cuddle in bed anytime. Their couplings at work had been intense, but fast and furious. This was the first time they could luxuriate in each other's company, skin to skin. He'd come looking for her, and after the scare she'd had, that meant the world to her. Stroking the ridges of his abs, she snuggled closer.

"Tell me everything," she said in a dreamy voice. "I want to hear everything from the moment you found out you were being released."

14

____

PUCK

P uck shifted her until her thigh was lying over his, opening her up so he could rub her wetness on him.

Hmm, damn that feels good.

"Imagine my surprise when I woke up to my cellie cursing up a storm," he began. "Door unlocked, lights on, and two COs standing in our cell, ordering me to wake up and grab my shit. 'Guess what, inmate? You're being released this morning,' one of them said. I was escorted out of the unit, strip-searched—not sure why, because what in the hell was I going to take *out* of jail—and my belongings were searched. After filling out a butt-load of paperwork, I was placed in a holding cell. Then, lo and behold, the main entrance to the jailhouse swings open, and I'm taking a breath of air as a free man.

"Holy hell, the smell of air was better than anything I've ever smelled—other than your pussy, that is," he said, cupping Ava's hot and juicy cunt. "Swear to God, I opened my mouth to taste the snowflakes on my tongue. Haven't done that since I was a kid. After the stink of piss and caged men for two months, the scent of cold air was fuckin' dope. Kingdom and

Sage were waiting for me. They took me home, and there, I got the shock of my fucking life."

Puck's arms instinctually tightened around Ava. He breathed in deep, the scent of her instantly calming his rapid heartbeat. His gaze wandered around her bedroom, touching on every detail, greedy to learn everything about her. It was feminine, like her. Besides the night table with a fringed lamp on it, there was a desk and a distressed, white-painted dresser. There were a few potted plants, a couple of candles, and photos of her, Kat, and her mother. Books about social work and addiction, self-help books, and romance novels were scattered over every surface and spilling out of a low bookcase.

Exhaling slowly, he continued, "Sammi was attacked by the guy I assaulted. She also hooked up with the prosecutor on my case to help me out and ended up falling for the rich, entitled bastard. Christ, I leave for two months, and all hell breaks loose. After her attack, she moved in with him. Kingdom, Sage, Sammi. Everyone hid it from me. Needless to say, when I found out, I was *pissed*. Tore through the house. Punched a hole in a wall. It took a while before I calmed down and then more time before I convinced Kingdom to bring me to the fucker's loft. Had it out with Sammi. She must've called him 'cause the prick showed up during our argument, in the middle of the day. Man, I was heated when he tried to intervene. That man has a death wish."

Ava shuddered out a pent-up breath of air on his chest. Staring down at her, he tilted his head. "What, you thought I tossed you aside? Are you fucking kidding me? I meant to get Sage to call you and let you know I was out, but my temper got the best of me. Anger at the motherfucker who hurt Sammi, anger at myself for having gotten arrested and for sparking this mayhem."

"It wasn't your fault," she said, lifting out of his arms to glower at him. Tousled locks of hair cascaded down her bare shoulders and cherry-tipped nipples. Her puffy red lips called to him. Gripping the back of her head, he took a kiss.

Searching her eyes, he asked, "You really thought I'd left you?"

Her eyes skidded to the side, and she gave a little shrug of her shoulders. "Maybe," she replied in a dismissive tone.

"When are you going to fuckin' get it, Ava? You're my property," he declared. The words were out before he could stop them. He didn't regret his outburst, because his words were true and they felt right. His heart squeezed tight.

"I claimed you when I was nineteen and never really let you go. I compared every woman to you. I've wanted you. *Only you*. After my mom died, I took care of myself and Sammi, but it took being alone to appreciate how you'd taken care of me. You're my past, the happy past before everything went to shit. You're my present. I've spent hours in solitary or in my cell daydreaming of you. Fantasizing about you. I'm fucking warning you right now that you're gonna be my future. I love my family and my club, but there was one thing missing. I'm not fucking asking you to be my old lady; I'm *telling* you. You're more than a woman to me; you're *the* woman. You're my dirty little angel. Little angel, because that's what you are; dirty, because that's what you are with *me*. I'll do whatever it takes to keep you leashed to my side, Ava. This is for real. This is for life. Period."

"Wow. You know," she replied dryly, "some men go down on one knee with a ring in one of those little black-velvet boxes and *ask* a woman for her hand in marriage. I've heard it's a thing."

"You want a ring in a black box? I'll get you a ring in a box. You want me on my knees? I'll go down on one knee, put that ring on your finger, and lick that hot little pussy of yours after

I'm done. I will do everything in my fucking power to gratify your every wish. That satisfy you?"

"Hmm...we'll see. I haven't said yes, yet. What about Sammi? How will she feel?"

"First off, Sammi doesn't have a fucking leg to stand on, let me tell you. What the hell does Sammi have to do with anything?"

"She might have bad memories of me...abandoning her," Ava said, carefully. "I disappeared right after your mother died. We went out shopping at the mall. On her thirteenth birthday, I took her out to get her first mani-pedi. We developed our own little relationship, but I didn't have the guts to say goodbye to her, because I knew I would've begged you to take me back, and I was too proud for that."

"Sammi isn't one to hold grudges. We get into fights on the regular, but we let it go and move on. Otherwise, we'd never be able to share the same house. By the way, I'm letting you know I'm not going back to that house. They cleaned up the place after her attack, but I can't stay there." He gazed down on her. "I came here right after I was done putting that new boyfriend of hers in his place. Stanton fucking Prescott, the prosecutor on my case." He shuttered his eyes, still processing the fact that his little sis was fucking a man older than he was. "Christ."

"I'm sure he's not that bad," she replied with a laugh.

Puck shook his head, a dark expression on his face. "Whatever. It's out of my hands now. I'm not tryin' to pressure you or anything, but I can't go back there. Not yet. If you don't want me to stay, I can go to the clubhouse. They'll make space for me to crash, or I'll double up in a room of one of the brothers."

Her gaze drifted away from his nervously but quickly snapped back to his. "No way," she said with a vehemence that had his eyebrows rising high on his forehead. "I know biker bitches. They'll be all over you."

He smirked internally. Possessive little thing. There was no way in hell he was sticking his dick in another woman. That wasn't happening...ever, but he liked seeing her little claws come out. He still hadn't banged her tight pussy the way he wanted. With her legs bent and high in the air. With her screaming his fucking name until her throat was hoarse. He wanted to keep her screaming all night long. Throw in a little discipline. Hear the smack of his hand on her ass, nice and fucking loud. No holding back. No interruptions. No time limits. He couldn't wait to do everything they couldn't do in her office. Christ, just being here...lying on a real mattress with a thick downy comforter and fluffy pillows under his head. His arm wrapped around the luscious curves of a naked Ava, her hair smelling so fucking sweet. He'd about died and gone to heaven.

Kingdom and Sage had taken him out to the Squad Bar, where he had a big-ass steak and a draft beer. Best meal of his life, but he couldn't wait to cook and eat with Ava. Incarceration had taught him to savor every moment of his life. It had been a pretty damn good life before Ava, but he was ready to be domesticated.

He had a long list of things to do, from picking up the pieces of his life to getting into the Squad Bar and figuring out how to make it profitable. At that moment, his only desire was to lounge around the house with Ava, eat meals with her, spend time getting to know every damn thing about her. Oh, and fuck her for days. She wasn't going to get much sleep tonight, and he didn't feel an ounce of guilt about it.

"Alright, then. We'll go to my house, and I'll pack up some shit. I don't want to go back there for at least a few days. The place has been violated. I get mad when I think about what happened, and then I get mad at myself for not having been there to protect her. What in the fuck was I thinking?"

"Is she happy?" Ava asked, laying a hand over his heart.

His eyelids blinked a few times, and he let out a long breath. "Yeah," he admitted. "She says she is. She looks happy, and the attack wasn't that long ago. The bastard she's with is protective of her, I'll grant him that much. The instant I made a move toward her, I was up against the wall with an arm to my throat. That led to a little scuffle, but he backed down when Sammi got upset. He seems to care for her...and I trust Kingdom. He wouldn't have let Sammi go with the fucker if he didn't trust the guy to take care of her. That girl is spoiled. The irony of all this is that he's Sage's ex-fiancé." Puck gripped his temple. "Thinking about this is giving me a fucking headache."

Ava's hand came and gently moved his out of the way. She settled on top of him and massaged his temples. That, along with her hot, wet pussy rubbing on his belly went a long way toward relaxing him. *This, here, is fucking heaven.* Never would he take anything for granted again, but especially not her. One good thing had come from his incarceration, and that was reuniting with Ava. His hands slid up her flanks. She was so fucking gorgeous. Her perky tits were bouncing near his face, and he was about to lean forward and take a little pink bud in his mouth when she asked, "How did you get released, Puck?"

His broad palm slipped over her breast, and he cupped it lightly, enjoying the weight of her feminine flesh in his hand. *What's the question again? Oh, yeah.* "There was one other reason I allowed that bastard who's sharing Sammi's bed to keep breathing. He's the reason I'm free. Turns out, the cops pumped me for information when they shouldn't have been talking to me 'cause I asked for my lawyer. I was high on the rush of having beat down that cocksucker, and I sang like a fucking bird. It was captured on the dashcam in the police car. Come to find out, Stanton remembered something I said in court. Sounded fishy to him, and he checked the dashcam video. In the end, my confession was thrown out of court. Not sure what happened, and truthfully, I don't care about the details other than the fact that Sage got me released. Without a confession and without a witness to testify, there isn't much of a case."

"Wow," she breathed. "I can't believe it was that easy."

"Easy?" he scoffed. "Not easy. It was a combination of sheer fucking luck, a kick-ass and devoted lawyer, and knowing powerful people like the prosecutor Sammi's currently fucking. If not for that, I'd be rotting in Duchess County like every other bastard in there." Planting his hands on her waist, he growled. "Enough. Right now, I'm hungry."

"Oh! What do you want to eat? Pasta? I have pizza dough waiting. I took it out while we were putting away the groceries. I can make you a homemade pizza. I'll make anything you want."

"Anything?"

"Of course."

"Then, I want this." He cupped her pussy. "Hot and juicy just how I like it," he said as he flipped her on her back and moved on top of her, bracing himself on his forearms.

She smacked him lightly on the shoulder. "Be serious," she chided him.

"I'm dead fuckin' serious. After I devour you and swallow down your cream, then I'll take a pizza."

15

AVA

I t was past eight o'clock before Puck allowed her out of the bed.

Not that she was in any rush to leave the cozy, sex-saturated scent of her bedroom or the hard, warm body that spooned hers after a marathon session of fucking.

Sitting up, the blanket fell off her, and cool air puckered her nipples. Puck's hand reached for her. Starting at her collarbone, his touch skimmed down her breast and flicked a nipple lightly before taking a handful of her bottom.

She squirmed a little because he'd given her butt a little talking to with the flat of his hand earlier. Naturally, in the most delicious way possible. His soothing touch rubbed away any residual ache, but it set off an altogether different kind of ache in her core.

"You must be starving. We need to eat," she said.

"Hmm...don't mention hunger, because given the choice, I'm gonna choose your pussy over food every time."

A soft giggle flew out of her mouth. "You had my pussy in jail, but you didn't have enough good food."

"I'll never get enough of your pussy," he answered soberly,

his dark eyes taking on a glittery sheen. She caressed the large, rounded muscle of his shoulder then dipped her hand into his chest hair, twisting a little with her fingers. A rumble from deep in his chest vibrated through her hand. Dark eyes flashed up to hers. "You teasing me, angel? You don't wanna know what I do to cock-teasing little girls."

"Maybe," she replied, but dodged his hand and scrambled off the bed. If she didn't initiate it, they'd never leave the bed, and Ava had a profound desire to cook for him. To feed and take care of him. She grabbed her robe from a nearby armchair. It was old and raggedy on the ends, but it was made of fleece, and she'd gotten into the habit of wearing it when she puttered around the house. *Not exactly sexy...unless you count the fact that I have no clothes on underneath, that is.*

Like any girly girl, she had a drawer full of sexy underwear, but Puck would have to learn to take her as she was, which was quite different from the hipster she'd been when they first hooked up. As Kat constantly teased, she was now washed.

Not that Puck seemed to mind, because he soon padded into the kitchen after her, wearing only a pair of boxer briefs. Throwing the pizza dough down on a wooden cutting board, she scraped her bottom lip. How in the world was she going to concentrate with those gorgeous muscles of his graphically on display? She wanted to lick every last one of them.

Turning her attention to her task before she jumped him, she called out, "Would you please put the oven on at 425 degrees?"

An instant later, his hot breath was warming the curve of her ear. "I fucking love to hear you say *pleuse* in that prim teacher–social worker voice of yours." His chest was a wall of heat at her back. He palmed her ass and grunted when he got only a handful of cloth. Flipping her robe up, he grabbed a butt cheek and commanded, "Say it again."

"Please," she obeyed, her voice a low rasp. Her breaths were coming out short and fast. Puck untied her belt and slipped his arms around her waist as she did her best to focus on kneading the pizza dough. His fingers skidded down her belly and played with her small patch of hair. She pressed her lips tightly to thwart a moan that was desperate to escape.

"Your skin is like silk. I can't stop touching you, and I can't stop fucking you." His chin settled on the dip of her shoulder as his middle finger stroked into the cleft of her pussy. "You sore?"

"A little," she mumbled through her front teeth, clenching her lower lip. She might be a little sore, but that did nothing to prevent wetness from seeping out and coating the finger that breached her. She clamped her hand over his, strings of dough dripping off. "Let me finish. It won't take much time."

"How long?"

His teasing finger was clouding her brain. A notch furrowed between her eyebrows. "How long what?"

"How many minutes will it take you to make the pizza?" he inquired.

"Uhm... I've never timed myself before... Maybe seven minutes."

"Seven minutes it is," he declared as he stepped away from her. "You got a timer?"

"Yes, in the top drawer over there," she said, gesturing toward the stove.

He prowled over, yanked it open, and rummaged around until he found her green owl-shaped timer. "I suggest you hurry up 'cause every extra second will be a smack to your ass before I fuck you."

"What?" she exclaimed. "I'm not *exactly* sure that it's seven minutes."

"Then, make *exactly* sure it's seven minutes 'cause that's the amount of punishment-free time you've got. If I were you, I wouldn't stand there and argue. I'd get crackin'."

Her eyes flew to the clock and then back to his face. His eyes had turned a flat steely black. He wasn't joking. She ran around the kitchen like a whirling dervish, grabbing the round pizza dish, spreading the dough, and then throwing the fridge open to grab the pizza sauce and mozzarella. After shredding the mozzarella and spreading the sauce, Ava was about to spread the cheese when the ringer sounded loudly throughout the kitchen.

"Dammit," she cursed out.

Chuckling low, he counseled, "Hurry up. The clock isn't stopping."

Narrowing her eyes at him, she finished spreading the cheese, grabbed the large wooden pizza peel, flung the oven door open, and thrust it inside. Slamming it closed, she leaned against it and folded her arms over her chest, a disgruntled moue on her lips.

"Not bad. Only twenty-seven seconds over. C'mere," he ordered with a crook of his finger.

Grrr. She hate-loved when he said that and crooked his finger at her like she was a wayward child. It pissed her off and turned her on at the same time. Gritting her teeth, she adjusted her folded arms over her breasts and protested, "No."

"No? That word shouldn't be in your vocabulary when it comes to responding to an order." His baritone dropped a sexy octave as he promised, "I'll make sure you have the climax of your life after you take your punishment like a good girl." Then it turned harder as he finished, "But, if you get salty on me, you'll get the wallops without the coming."

Ava curled her lip at him. "Fuck you, Puck."

"It's not the first time I've slapped your ass," he noted as he took a step closer to her, cocking his head to the side as he watched her curiously. "You never complained before."

"Those were a few slaps in the middle of having sex. Not twenty-seven smacks without a guaranteed climax afterward. There's nothing in it for me, and I'm not doing it," she concluded with a stomp of her foot.

He scowled at her. "You've refused long enough, so no orgasm for you. One thing you better learn is that you're my property, Ava. My old lady. I'm a biker, and sometimes, being an old lady means answering directives without question. We've got enemies. Could be the difference between life and death. More than that, you've got to trust me enough to turn your ass over to me. It's mine, to do with what I want."

What had started out as a fun game had veered into a lesson in obedience. "That's not fair! I didn't do anything wrong."

"There are smacks and then there are smacks. I was gonna make your punishment so damn good you were guaranteed a climax, but your stubbornness changed this into discipline. We didn't get to this point when I was in jail. Didn't have enough time to do much more than have a conversation and a fuck. But I'm out now, and we're building a life together. That's gonna require a little molding from me, I see."

Okay, his words were doing a whiplash on her emotions. She almost curled up to rub on him when he talked about building a life together so casually, like it was a done deal. But the idiot had to mess it up with his last comment, which had her seeing red. Ava didn't lose her temper often, but when she did, logic and rationality were swapped out with dogged obstinacy. He wanted to get to her ass? Yeah, well he was going to have to catch her first.

Her chin raised an inch.

"Make me," she snarled low.

"Oh, angel, you don't know what you're askin' for." He barked out a laugh. "You wanna play? Game. Fucking. On."

Stalking her, his hand stretched out to grab her, but she backed out of his reach, twirled around, and raced out the kitchen door. Down the corridor and into the living room she went, with Puck in hot pursuit. Panting out a staccato of breaths, she circled the low coffee table. His hands swiped for her, but she dodged his grasping fingers. Little giggles escaped as she bobbed and weaved. She was impressed with herself, considering he outweighed her by almost a hundred pounds. Whirling around, she broke for a run and fled back into the kitchen. Hot on her heels, he almost caught her robe, but she'd escaped around the corner of the kitchen, down the corridor and out into the living room. His footsteps pounded behind her, and panicking, she sprinted past the couch and coffee table to the far end of the room. Where she promptly realized her mistake. There was nowhere to go but behind a compact swivel armchair.

Cornered.

She rounded it swiftly, holding on to the back of the chair like a shield. Out of breath, she stared Puck down as he prowled toward her slowly, wearing a shit-eating grin that made her want to smack him. His bare chest distracted her for a moment, but she snapped back to attention when he grasped the arms of the chair dramatically. Scooting the chair backward, he effectively shoved her into the corner of the room.

"Hmm, looks like my naughty angel got trapped like a little birdie. You need to get your wings clipped, and I'm the owner who's gonna do it," he gloated.

"Fuck you," she spat out, doubly mad because it'd taken

him only five minutes to catch her and the chase had turned her on. Meanwhile, he hadn't even broken a sweat.

He might be shaking his head as if disappointed, but he looked a tad too gleeful for her liking. "That mouth is going to cost you. Come on out. Every second you stay there is another smack tacked onto your punishment."

"What does it matter after what I have coming for me with no pleasure at the end of it," she gritted out as she smacked her palms against the top of the chair.

"You do have a point there, but I can't have my woman losing her temper. You're gonna have to earn your way to getting your pussy tapped good and hard the way you like it. Now, don't make it any harder on yourself," he counseled. "Come on out of there. Like a good girl."

"No," she bit out. Her thighs were quivering with want, but she pressed them together.

He grabbed her by the scruff of her robe and dragged her out from behind the chair. Furious at how easy it was for him, she fought him, pulling at his firm grip and digging in her heels to stop his forward movement. Stripping out of the robe he was holding by the collar, she almost got away. Finally losing his patience, he simply hauled her up against his chest and carried her to the sofa. With a huff, he dropped onto the couch and maneuvered her over his spread thighs.

Nose twitching, she smelled the pizza in the oven. "The pizza! It's going to burn. Let me go. I have to take it out of the oven."

His hand stilled on her lower back as he turned his head in the direction of the kitchen, scenting the air. "Hell no, I'm not letting you go. We go in together; I tie you up and take care of the pizza. Then we continue with the lesson."

She groaned, curling her hands into fists.

"Either that or the pizza burns," he warned.

"Fine," she snapped, eyes flashing. He'd better tie her up because she had zero intention of making it easy for him.

He helped her stand and held up her robe. She peevishly thrust her hands into the armholes then she was instantly tucked to his side before she had a chance to escape. By chance, her gaze swept down and landed on his crotch. She smirked up at him. The thick, defined line of his cock bulged against the stretchy fabric of his boxer briefs. At least she wasn't the only one aroused by their little cat-and-mouse game.

Once in the kitchen, he used the belt of her favorite robe to tie her to a chair. Not having bothered to close the flap, her breasts were bare, pebbled nipples proudly on display.

After checking the tautness of her ties, Puck carefully pulled out the pizza and let it cool on a rack.

"You better hurry up and get this over with because I'm ready to eat," she griped.

He arched one eyebrow. "You ordering me around? At this rate, you'll be lucky to sit on that fine ass of yours until next week without being reminded of the marks of my hand."

"Asshole," she grumbled under her breath.

Ignoring her, he untied her and hauled her back into the living room. Man-spreading his legs, he released her and pointed to the rug. "First position."

She shifted from foot to foot, considering her options. She didn't have many. He was stronger, faster, and more bull-headed. She glanced at the hallway leading toward the bathroom. Even if she managed to lock herself in the bathroom or bedroom, he'd stand guard through the night to catch her the instant she unlocked the door. Then she'd be in bigger trouble. While there was a part of her that wanted to test him—because, dammit, he was irritating as hell—she knew what she had to do.

Jaw tight, she slowly dropped to her knees. Instantly, his legs closed, corralling her with his knees. His hand fell to the crown of her head, and he repeatedly stroked her hair, like she was a fucking pet. A flurry of conflicting feelings pulsated in her chest. Pissed but also aroused. He had control and wielded it oh-so well. His caress called to her soul, and no matter how irate she was, she couldn't help but lean into his touch. Seriously, there was nothing like it. It was magic—comforting, thrilling, and drugging at the same time. Tucking her legs beneath her, she bowed her head, giving him silent directions of where to stroke.

He broke the silence. "Time to get this over with."

She glanced up at him with a pout and pleading eyes. "We don't really have to do this, you know. I lost my temper a little, but I'm calm now. I can even apologize."

He grinned. "You sorry?"

Her eyes skittered away from his, and she chewed her lips for a few moments. "Not really," she replied candidly.

He let out a guffaw. "You will be after this." Looking down at her curiously, he said, "This has always been part of our relationship. What's different about this punishment?"

She shifted on her calves, and her fingers fidgeted on her knees. Focusing on the corner of the rug, she answered, "*Punishment* would be the key word. You've only ever smacked my butt while we were having sex. I haven't done this kind of stuff with others. Sure, I've dated, and I had a couple of relationships that lasted several months, but they've never...you know..."

"Given you a spanking," he finished for her.

She glowered up at him. "Yes. Anyway, you were an asshole today for not calling me."

"I already explained. Didn't get out of there till after ten o'clock in the morning. By the time I was over my rage about Sammi, I figured it'd be easier to show up at your door."

"It was thoughtless, Puck. You want me to be your old lady, but I was torn up when you didn't show up for your appointment. I had no idea where you were. It was only once I searched the database that I came to find out that you were released, and you didn't bother giving me a call. You've already ripped my heart out once..." she finished with a firm shake of her head.

"Fucking Sage warned me you'd me pissed," he mumbled.

She glared at him. "She told you to call me, and you still didn't?"

"She didn't tell me shit. No one tells me what to do. She warned me you might be upset, but I was eating the first fucking real meal since being out. You don't know what it's like, your first day out of jail. It's disorientating as fuck. And then Sammi's bullshit was on top of that."

Her shoulders slumped, her eyes trailing down as he talked. Was this how it was going to be? The club, Sammi... everything but her came first. He placed his index finger under her chin and lifted her head up. "I'll do better."

"I'm scared. Little things that normally wouldn't bother me trigger me. I'm waiting for the other shoe to drop. What if you leave me—"

His fingers pinched her chin, and he shook it slightly. "Hey, that's not fucking happening. A biker can be married multiple times, but he chooses only one old lady, feel me? On my end, I gotta know that you can trust me when it comes to this."

He was talking about domestic discipline, of course. Now that he was asking like a civilized person, and not acting like a brute—granted a sexy brute—she was calm enough to carefully consider it. She didn't mind being spanked in certain situations. Oftentimes, it was the final push she needed to climax. Since she'd only ever orgasmed with Puck, she had to admit that whatever he did, worked for her. And he clearly wanted to take their relationship to the next level; he wouldn't have brought it up unless it was important to him. What *exactly* that entailed, she didn't quite know. Hadn't thought about it before this moment. "Do you know what you're doing?" she asked, eyeing him carefully.

"You asking me if I've been with another woman like this before? Yeah, a good number of them."

She shuffled on her knees to back out of his legs, but he pressed them inward, and his hand slid down to take hold of the back of her neck. "I like to see you get possessive 'cause it's hot and it shows me how much you care, but I mentioned them to prove that I know what I'm doing. I didn't have a fit earlier when you mentioned dating men, though the thought of it makes me want to lay into that ass of yours. That wouldn't be right. We've been apart for eight years. I didn't live the life of a monk, and I'm sure you weren't a nun. Point is, we're together now. It's part of who I am, but we wouldn't be a perfect fit if I had any doubts that it'd work for you, too. I don't have to check to know what makes you wet, angel. Now, come on. I need to clip those wings of yours because I'm getting hungry. The pizza looked fucking tasty as hell." He patted his lap. "Up you go."

Dragging her feet, she inched up and crawled over his thighs. He placed a hand on her spine and applied pressure until she hung over his lap. She heard the rustle of her robe as it was rucked up, and with a final huff, she laid her cheek on the couch. Goose bumps pricked her skin as the cold air hit her exposed skin. She had a view of the bookshelf and the window, with the shades still up. Silently, she prayed that her house was situated far enough back from the sidewalk that no one walking by would see her.

"Now for the spanking."

"Puck!" she lamented. He was enjoying this far too much.

A chuckle gusted over her bare flesh, causing her to jerk her hips nervously. The anticipation, along with the smooth glide of his hand over her buttocks and his hard quad muscles flexing beneath her, fueled a heat in her core that she really wished would disappear. If the slickness at the juncture of her thighs was glaringly obvious to her, it was only a matter of time before he noticed. She gave an inward groan. What was it about Puck and his dominance that made her clit ring like a little bell when he took full control? She was like a cat in heat, wanting to rub her wet pussy all over his thighs. If she had her way, she'd pull off his briefs and ride him bare. Just his hot flesh parting hers as she bore down on his cock.

Her reverie was cut bluntly short the instant his hand came down, catching the outer flank of her thigh.

"Ow!"

"Better hold those in 'cause there's a lot more where they came from. That was one. Count them off, Ava," he commanded as a hard swat landed on her buttock.

"Mmffm," she said between sealed lips, as she fought to stifle her cry.

"Two. That's the last one, Ava. They'll only count toward the total if you count off," he warned before another landed on her ass.

"Three!" she screeched.

"Good girl," he replied. He may have called her a good girl, but he wasn't treating her like one by giving her a break. At first, she writhed over his lap until he sharply told her to settle down. Instead of taking it easy, he pursued a punishing pace.

She was forced to call out every time the flat of his hand connected with a section of her body. He didn't restrict himself to her butt, either, but swatted her thighs and on the sides of her bottom. His smacks built on top of one another. The blistering fire of his paddling shot electricity right between her legs. Pleasure and pain danced a tango in her body. Head hanging down in delirium, she let out a low, carnal moan.

"Christ, the noises you make could bring a weaker man to his knees." He bent forward and took his teeth to the spot where her neck met her shoulder. Only, after sucking long enough to guarantee a bruise—*on purpose?*—he lapped it better. By now, her nerve endings were whirring.

He spread his thighs, widening a gap between her own legs. They were only halfway through her punishment, but he was definitely intent on torturing her, because while rubbing her abused flesh, his fingers dipped between her thighs. Her secret was out. He could feel how saturated she was. One finger circled her swollen little clit.

"Dirty little angel, not only can I feel it but I can smell how much you need to get fucked. How bad do you need it, girlie?" He added another finger to her core.

She pressed her lips firmly closed but circled her hips, clenching her inner walls to suck in his fingers. He pulled away, purposely keeping his touch light. *Sadistic bastard.*

"Don't wanna talk? Alright, that must mean you want me to return to the task at hand." With that, he withdrew his touch completely. She almost whimpered, but bit down at the last moment. She'd prove to him she could take anything he threw her way.

They returned to the spanking, blood rushing back to the places where his hand fell. By the time Ava counted out a final thirty-five, her thighs quivered and both her buttocks were on fire, but she was also wetter than ever. He'd found just the right pressure and rhythm to morph that pain into searing pleasure.

Puck eased her up to her hands and knees and then sat her down on his lap. Ava was in hell. Her pussy was throbbing for release while her stinging bottom was pulsating with pain.

With a well-placed kiss on her cheek, he suggested, "Let's eat that pizza. Then you can earn your way back into my good graces and get the fuck you need."

Her jaw clenched. How was she going to eat when she wanted to kill him?

***

"Die, motherfucker, die!"

Ava struggled out of sleep. A rough, animalistic sound coming from beside her shattered the stillness of her bedroom. She bolted up, shaking the cotton out of her head until she got her bearings. The hairs on the back of her neck went stiff. Blinking her eyes, she adjusted to the darkness and turned to find Puck twisted into contortions, his face scowling and grunting. A few more curses flew out of him.

He jackknifed up and bellowed out, "I'm gonna kill you!" and then fell back down on his back.

She jerked at his outburst, her hand clutching her racing heart. Night terrors. Leaning over, she checked the digital clock on her nightstand. It was 2:47 a.m. He was in his REM sleep cycle, for sure. While she yearned to give him relief, there was only one option.

Wait it out.

Hands clenched around the edge of the bedsheet and

blanket; his head swiveled from side to side on the pillow. Moonlight streamed through the windows, falling on the sweat dotting his forehead and the strands of soaked hair along his hairline. He must have been suffering for a while.

Fearing to touch him in his agitated state, Ave laid on her side, facing him, and sang the first thing that came to mind. *"Rock-a-bye baby on the treetop, when the wind blows the cradle will rock."* Her voice was soft and raspy, but she sang until her voice was too hoarse to go on. She continued humming the silly nursery rhyme until, finally, he settled into quiet sleep.

Ever so slowly, she crept off the bed, rushed to the bathroom for a washcloth and returned to gently pat him dry. Flinging the cloth on the floor, she returned to bed and cuddled against his side. As if sensing that she'd left and returned, he rolled over and gathered her close into his arms. Using his bicep as a pillow for her head, Ava inhaled the woodsy scent of him. His large chest rose and fell in a steady rhythm.

He'd been fast asleep through the entire episode. She'd seen it often enough to recognize that he suffered from Post-Incarceration Syndrome, a common problem, especially for those who'd been recently released. Perhaps he was reliving a fight he'd been in, but the very fact of being imprisoned could trigger PIS. Tomorrow, he'd wake up without a clue of what had transpired in the middle of the night. It was his mind's way of coping with whatever trauma he'd experienced. Uncomfortable conversations were a part of her work, but she wasn't looking forward to this one.

She gently brushed the sweat-laden hair off his forehead, traced the bold line of his nose, and outlined the top of his lips. Something had shifted in her after their disciplinary session. Although he'd left her unsatisfied, it had blasted through the final walls she'd unwittingly retained between them. Despite his release, she'd kept a part of herself in reserve. When he'd made her his old lady and said they'd get married, she hadn't verbally agreed. Puck didn't comment on her lack of reciprocity, but the fact remained that his declaration had been one-sided.

Tonight he'd blown through her remaining reservations. Perhaps her brain was scrambled, because after he was done with his punitive session, her spirit felt lighter. Freer. The doors to her heart had swung wide open for him to saunter in and stake his claim. They might both be a little twisted, but that didn't take away from the reality that their twistedness fit together in perfect harmony. These night terrors proved that he needed her as well because this was her specialty, and she intended to help him any way she could.

Ava lifted herself a bit and pressed a kiss against his lips. Yup, it was official. Broken or not, she'd fallen for him.

16

PUCK

Since moving in with Ava, it'd been four blissful and fuck-filled days for Puck.

The day after his release, he went to the Squad Bar to check things out, confer with Whistle, and get the place into shape. The bar was most definitely a long-term project. First off, most of the waitresses were shit. Several of the Squad's biker bitches helped out as a favor, but they had to be replaced with a professional waitstaff, pronto.

After the shit show he'd witnessed his first day back, he was ready to fire the lot of them. Whistle had convinced him to keep one waitress, the one he was obviously fucking. Puck promised to keep her as long as she wasn't the thief giving away or selling off their inventory behind their back.

Accompanied by Sage, he'd personally met with the investigator from the Office of Special Investigations. He broke everything down in detail, like the places where they stashed the drugs Kingpin got through the mail. Even the contraband cell phone that was concealed in an electric typewriter Puck had happened to see when he walked into Kingpin's cell once. They seemed particularly excited by the cell phone.

Sage explained that a phone gave them the opportunity to wiretap and listen in on conversations. Ava had testified against Kingpin at his recent parole hearing, which drove him fucking crazy because it was too dangerous. They'd fought about it. Puck had argued that with an investigation underway, Kingpin would be kept in jail long enough to bust him. It was totally unnecessary to expose herself to potential trouble, but she held strong, and ultimately he'd relented. Her guilt ran so deep that she couldn't let go of an unnecessary risk. Whatever. They'd made up, and he got to paddle her ass for it. Christ, she was so eager he had to wonder if it remotely counted as a punishment.

After a long day at the bar, Puck wanted to be lounging in bed with his woman, better yet, *inside* his woman. Instead, his ass was at a clubhouse party in honor of his release. He should be grateful—seeing as brothers from neighboring cities had come in to celebrate his return—but the loud music was grating on his nerves, and he was getting itchy.

The brothers weren't helping on that front, either. Christ, the bastards were like sharks at the first scent of blood. What had gotten them riled up? *Seeing me come in through the clubhouse door with my arm around a woman.* Payback was a bitch, and the brothers were making sure Puck felt what a bad bitch she was. All the times he'd mocked, pranked, or downright insulted them were coming back to him tenfold. Didn't make it any easier to survive, though. Here he was, with one arm hooked around Ava's waist, gritting his teeth as he sucked up a ton of bullshit thrown his way.

Understandably, Cutter was taking the lead. Puck had been audaciously rude to him when he was trying to lasso in that wildcat, Greta, he now called his old lady.

Pawing at Ava's shoulder, Cutter said, "Who do we have here? Been a long time—oh, wait, that would be never—since

I saw Puck hangin' onto a woman. What's your name, sweetheart?"

"Av—" began Ava.

Back teeth grinding, Puck cut her off, "None of your damn business, you fucker. And take your hand off my woman."

His eyes pinched together in pain. Fuck, had he just claimed her in a room full of assholes?

Cutter's eyebrows hit his hairline. "Your wo—*what*? Did you call her your *woman*, brother?"

A low whistle came from behind Cutter. "Hey, aren't you the social worker back at Duchess jail?" piped up Whistle.

Cutter's head swerved to the side and then back to Puck. "You met up in jail? Damn, and I thought I was dirty. What'd guys do up in there? You've been a bad boy, Puck."

"Yeah, every inmate wished they had a drug problem so they could have appointments with Ms. Evans," divulged Whistle. Ava's cheeks flushed a pretty shade of pink. "Even overheard the COs talking about her. Sayin' how sexy she is."

That was a fucking given. Even Puck had heard them talk. Yet another reason he loathed Officer Dipshit. Bringing Ava tighter into his side, Puck growled, "It's not like that. I've known Ava since we were kids. Happened to see each other again in there, is all. Don't make a mountain out of a molehill."

"Had me checking up on her from jail, though, so it's a big-ass molehill if you ask me," interjected Loki, unprompted.

"Didn't I tell you not to say anything?" snipped Puck.

"Oops," replied Loki with a wide, mischievous grin. Smacking his lips, he made lewd kissing noises at Puck. "My bad."

"Gonna get you back for that one," Puck warned. "And it's gonna motherfucking hurt."

"Not scared of you, scrub," Loki fired back. "It's worth every damn moment to see you squirm like a little bitch."

"After the shit he talked when I hooked up with Greta, he finally bites the dust," mused Cutter.

Ava's eyes were round as saucers, and her head was probably dizzy from snapping from man to man. His muscles tightened. It was all in good fun, or maybe dirty fun, but he didn't want his woman thinking badly of him or his brothers. She'd been around the Renegades, but they were a bunch of rich old men who rode on the weekends. The Squad was an entirely different animal, and she was getting a crash course on what a real club was like. Of course, she was used to roughness, working among inmates, but he didn't want her view of him to change somehow. Fact was, he was feeling edgy. The loud music, the hollering and shouting, the jostling of people. Add a crew of foulmouthed smart-asses, and his nerves were pulled taut.

"Damn, had no idea you were gettin' it on with Ms. Evans," Whistle noted.

Puck cuffed him on his head. "Shut the fuck up, prospect." Whistle hadn't been a prospect in a while, but he'd been in the most recent batch of brothers to patch in. Hurt flashed briefly over his face. The brothers commonly insulted Whistle, but Puck protected him. Guilt settled uncomfortably in his chest, but he couldn't apologize in front of fuckers like Cutter or Loki. Plus, the boy had to learn to shut his damn mouth.

"AHHH!" came a scream so loud it almost popped Puck's eardrums. He shut his eyes and took in a bracing breath of air. He knew that sound anywhere.

Opening his eyes, he saw Sammi flying toward them and slam into Ava. Wrapping her arms around his woman, his little sister jumped up and down, chanting, "Omigod, omigod, omigooooood. It's true!"

"I told you it was true," gloated Abby from behind them. Loki immediately hooked his arm around Abby's neck and drew her in to him.

Stanton stormed in right behind Sammi, looking harried. As he should. Fucker. Puck narrowed his eyes at the bastard who'd deflowered his baby sister. Not deflowered, in truth, but she was a baby. A fuckin' baby, and the man had somehow weaseled his way into her heart. Granted, he'd ultimately gotten Puck released for Sammi's sake. Goddamn, his head was splitting from veering from hatred to gratitude and back to hatred again. He was a simple man, who wanted a simple life, where things were black and fuckin' white. None of this gray shit.

"Ava, look at you. You're even more gorgeous than I remember!" his sister screeched as she held Ava at arm's length to take a good look at her. "Puck! I can't believe you guys are back together. You didn't mention *any* of this when I saw you last." That's because he was moments away from decimating her fiancé, that's why. Stanton stepped in closer to Sammi, causing Puck to growl under his breath.

"I had other things on my mind," he grumbled, giving Stanton the stink eye again. Pondering on how to sabotage his relationship, he watched carefully as Stanton unhooked Sammi from Ava and dragged her into his arms. Hmm, not possible. Sammi tilted her head and beamed up at Stanton. *Aww, fuck.* Despite his bouts of denial, she was in love with the guy, and one thing he'd never do is mess with his sister's happiness. His gaze dropped to Stanton's hand smoothing over Sammi's flat belly. Not that he'd ever get used to the rich prick mauling his sister in public.

"Can we cool it with the PDA, maybe," he snapped. Sammi turned stricken eyes at him. Even Ava sucked in a breath and smacked him in the arm. Cutter barked out a laugh.

"Or not," he backpedaled. PDA was a given in biker culture. Pulling Ava into his embrace, he buried his face in her hair and inhaled her comforting scent.

"Ignore him," Ava huffed out, although she didn't fight him when he tightened his arms around her. The number of people surrounding him, the music, the noise was bringing on a migraine, and, like in jail, he returned to his lodestone. Ava.

"How are you, Sammi? It's so good to see you," Ava began. "Is this Stanton?"

Puck let out a low sound of disapproval for her ears only. She responded by pressing back into him and rubbing her fine ass against his groin in a way that distracted him from his anger. Fine, he'd back down and let her handle this for him. And so she did. She got caught up with Sammi's life, teasing her lightly about Stanton in a way that made Sammi blush. Fuckin' blush. But it was with pleasure, so he couldn't be anything but pleased that his woman was getting along with his sister and soothing the rough waters.

Noticing her bottle of beer was empty, Puck murmured that he'd get another from the bar. Casting a dubious eye at the crowd, he dropped a kiss on her head before diving into the crush of people to get to the bar. When he returned, he found that Skull, a wiseass from the Albany chapter, had sidled up to Ava and inserted himself in their conversation. Audacious bastard.

Ava was his goddamn prize, and he didn't appreciate a brother gettin' up in her space. She wasn't wearing his jacket, so...brother or no, she wasn't advertised as his. The God's honest truth was that he was getting mighty pissed as he listened to Skull asking her questions like whether she'd been around bikers before. Dark energy filled him, like thunderclouds rolling in on clear skies, turning everything an ugly shade of gray.

"When am I gonna see a jacket on her ass? Or hear wedding bells?" Loki cut into his ruminations loud enough for everyone to hear. That brother had his back, making it plain to Skull who Ava belonged to. Not that Puck was going to thank him for his help.

Returning to Ava's side, he looped an arm around her shoulder and replied, "Not everyone is obsessed with weddings like you. Oh, wait, that's 'cause you can't lock your woman down."

Loki guffawed. "True that. One fuckin' mistake, and the bitch is giving me a run for my money. No worries, though. I'll get her to the alter eventually. Specially since she's carrying my kid."

It was a sign of how good things were between Loki and Abby that he could crack a joke like that. The man hadn't smiled for years after his brother killed himself. Puck relaxed a little. He may have come out of jail, but men like Loki had it harder than he did.

"You paddle her ass yet?" piped up Cutter. "It ain't legit until you paddle her ass."

"Not every woman's crazy-ass wild like yours," drawled Puck. "Some are good girls." He gave Cutter a wicked grin and a sly wink at Ava, whose eyes had narrowed dangerously. His hand dropped to the bubble of her ass and gave it a long caress. Remembering their session from the other night got him wanting out of there more than ever.

Skull grabbed Ava's hand and cajoled, "Come on, Ava, you can't say you've been to a Squad party if you haven't danced, and it's a damn fact that Puck doesn't dance. Ain't that right, Puck?" Puck grunted. "This ain't no Renegades party. This is a real biker party. Come on."

Ava threw her head back and gave a throaty laugh that got Puck's cock on the high alert. "It's true, he's not big on dancing.

Never has been." Being his good girl, she gazed up at him and asked, "May I?"

Fuuuck, when she talked all prim and fucking proper with the "please" and the "may," he turned into a fucking pussy. Without hesitation, he nodded his acquiescence. Skull scooped her out of his grasp and guided her toward the makeshift dance floor.

Whistle turned toward him and began to talk about the problems at the bar. He'd finished going through the inventory and discovered another theft. At least that got the brothers turning their attention away from Puck. Half listening, his keen eyes skated across the clubhouse floor in search of Ava. Narrowing his eyes, he spotted unusual movement at the edge of the dance floor, near the offices.

It was Skull, tugging at Ava's arm. Talking into her ear, he seemed to be half-dragging her toward the darkened hallway.

Mother*fucker*. Red suffused Puck's vision. Everything faded away—the room, the brothers, the noise. Through tunnel vision, he saw his woman being towed away. Roaring at the top of his lungs, Puck shot off and bum-rushed through the writhing masses of dancing figures. Bile rose to his throat. Shouldering through people bumping into him, Puck reached the far end of the dance floor. After a quick side-glance to make sure Ava was unharmed, he tackled Skull like a raging beast. Locked in a destructive embrace, they toppled to the ground.

Skull landed on his back, Puck on top of him. The biker writhed under him to get away. Jerking his head back, Puck slammed his forehead into the bridge of Skull's nose. There was the sick crunching sound and blood sprayed into Puck's eyes, momentarily blinding him.

The other biker screeched in pain, releasing Puck to grab

hold of his broken nose. "What the fuck was that for?" he bellowed out.

By then, Loki and Kingdom were grabbing at Puck's shoulders. After a brief struggle, they had him in a choke hold. Doing his best to break their lock, he thundered out, "Lemme at him! Let me get a piece of that motherfucker!"

"Puck, calm your ass down," Kingdom barked above him. They'd brought him facedown on the ground, arms cinched behind him. The red rage morphed into something dark and deadly.

"Let me up, asshole!" he threatened. Kingdom repeated for him to chill out, but the longer he was in a helpless prone state, the more he struggled. Gnashing his teeth, he began to slam his temple against the ground. *Thump, thump, thump.* Jolts of pain assailed the side of his head. A pressure the size of a boulder squeezed the oxygen out of every tiny air sac in his lungs. Pain circulated over his chest cavity, and his breaths came out short and choppy.

"Let me go!" he snarled on repeat.

Suddenly, Ava's knees were in his line of sight. Throwing herself over him, she cried out, "Let him go! You're hurting him. He can't breathe!"

The distress in her voice penetrated through the fog of rage. Loki and Kingdom commanded her to get off him. No other man ordered his woman around. Adrenaline pumped through his veins.

"Leave her alone," Puck howled around the agony searing his head. Her voice sounded far off and muddled, but abruptly, he was hauled to his feet. Warm liquid, most likely blood, flowed from his temple. Opening his mouth, he hauled in a gulp full of air. He did it again but choked on the next one. His vision got fuzzy and dark. Stumbling, he dropped to his knees.

17

PUCK

Tender fingers caressed the side of his head as a gentle voice counseled, "Slow down, Puck. Slow down your breaths, or you're going to hyperventilate again."

Ava.

He was being guided with a soft nudge, and his legs were moving him somewhere. Vision still hazy, he followed that touch and voice like a meek child, allowing himself to be led somewhere quiet. Gradually, the dark tunnel receded, and his circle of vision grew until he found himself on the leather couch in Kingdom's office. Puck heaved in a huge breath of air. The booming bass of music from outside reverberated under his feet, but otherwise, everything was quiet. Near the open door, Whistle hung back, shifting on the balls of his feet.

Ava's face hovered in front of him. Lifting a finger in the center of his eyeline, she urged, "Follow my finger, Puck." She swiped left, back to the center, and then right. Several times she passed her pointer finger in front of him.

Expelling a sigh of relief, she fell back against the couch, beside him, and said, "I don't think you have a concussion."

His lungs still burned, and a steel band wrapped around his chest, but at least he could breathe. Expanding his chest cavity nice and full, his hand crept along the leather surface of the couch until it found Ava's. He gripped it, and their fingers tangled together.

Twisting around to face her, his hand curled over her shoulders, and his mouth crashed down on hers, lips bruising hers in his ravishment. A small whimper vibrated up her throat. He felt it in the kiss and responded with a satisfied rumbling of his own. His anger was dissipating. Either that, or she'd converted the dark energy swirling inside him into white-hot desire. The woman had the power to sway his mood in an instant.

Fingers slid up his chest, flexing and clenching against the hard planes of his abs and pecs.

Breaking off, he pressed his nose against the side of her throat, scenting her. Inhaling deeply of her natural perfume seemed to calm his raging pulse. He yearned for more, and he knew where to get it. The source. His hands came down and wrapped around her waist.

Through the thickness of his throat, he rasped out, "Fuck, baby, I need you."

Ava arched into his touch. "Yes," she replied in simple confirmation. The need for her tenderness clawed at him.

Without breaking his focus on her, he commanded, "Whistle, leave us."

There was the rustling sound of jeans, the scuffing of boot heels on the concrete floor, then the whishing sound of the door closing, and they were alone. Blessed silence. A breath shuddered out of him as he scrunched the hem of the figure-hugging sweater she wore and yanked it up her torso to expose her luscious tits.

Groaning at the sight, he nipped at the outside curve of

her breast. Dragging down the thin mesh and satin of her black bra, her breast popped out. He did the same to the other. His tongue flicked and teased her beaded nipples until Ava squirmed beneath him.

"Shhh," he said against her plump, fragrant flesh, cupping her mons over her skirt. "Sit still."

By the time he got to addressing her other breast, her breath was coming out in short pants. He got down to business, coaxing the nipple with laves of his tongue, little nips, and long sucks. He pulled back and examined his artistry. There were bite and sucking marks scattered over her neck and tits; no man would doubt who she belonged to now.

Pulling up her skirt, he commanded, "Lift up."

She immediately complied, making the corners of his lips quirk against her silky skin. He scraped the bristles of his five o'clock shadow against the underside of her breast, inciting a sharp breath. The little noises she made were porn-worthy. Those tiny moans and whimpers, interspersed with little grunts, turned him into a beast ready to fuck.

His hand rooted inside her panties until he found the hot, tight hole he was seeking. Soaked, just the way he liked it. His fingers inched in, deeper and deeper. Moving them in and out, they set off more slickness. Curling his fingers inward, he hit a spot that almost triggered an orgasm, but he pulled away at the last moment.

There was a ripping sound, and he glanced down to find he'd torn her panties off her in his eagerness. No matter. Kneeling on the ground, his shoulders shrugged a few times to prompt her thighs to open, and then his tongue replaced his fingers. The hit of her taste on his tongue triggered a heady buzz.

He didn't coax or play with her. Not tonight. There was no cajoling or teasing in his movements. He fucked her pussy, the thick muscle of his tongue brutally commanding surrender. Her fingers twined in the longer locks of his hair, tugging and yanking, sometimes clawing and tearing, depending on what his tongue was doing to her. Like Morse code, those fingers of hers divulged how close she was. And by the way they were snatching at his hair, she was skating on the razor's edge.

"Puck, Puck, Puck." She chanted his name like a mantra. He fucking loved listening to her breathy voice when she was so damn close to losing control. It brought him back to his core—to the calm, steely crux of his soul. Fucking finally, after the debacle outside, he felt whole again. How he had called himself alive in the years they were apart, he had no idea. He couldn't imagine living another day without her, much less a month or a year. She was like the air in his lungs, the light that hit his pupils, the sweetness lacing his taste buds.

His mouth moved to suckle her clit, and she arched off the couch. A scream rang out, hair twisting between her clasping fingers. Her cream flowed, dripping down his chin as she came over his face. He licked and lapped at her, staying with her as little aftershocks shuddered through her body in tiny waves.

There was nothing in the world like bringing this woman to completion. It had become his obsession. She bared her soul in the way she turned herself over to his ministrations and directives.

Bright multi-colored eyes cracked open and focused on him. An auburn sheen danced across the long mahogany tresses falling across her face. Her lips spread into a glorious smile, and he swore it was like the roof had cracked open and rays of sunlight fell on him through a tar-pitch blackened sky.

"I can tell you're doing good, my dirty little angel."

"Can you? Hmm," she murmured as the back of her hand tested the temperature of her cheeks. "I suppose my skin is flushed. Everyone's going to know what happened in here when we walk back out there."

"Good. I want them to know," he growled. A frown creased his forehead, remembering the fight.

Her fingertips lightly touched his temple and caressed down the outline of his cheekbone. Concern darkened her irises to a whiskey color. "You were bleeding. What happened, Puck?"

"He was going to take you somewhere. Hurt you. He was dragging you toward the offices."

Puck was still positioned between her open legs, her juices slathered along the lower half of his face. Her discarded skirt was somewhere on the floor of the office, and her destroyed panties were caught under the toe of his boot.

Her knuckles softly followed the line of his jaw. "There were dozens of people around us. He was joking, messing with me to follow him. I wasn't in any danger."

"You don't know that for sure," he snapped. "He could've forced you into an empty office and hurt you."

"A Squad brother? I highly doubt that. If there's one thing I've learned is that bikers live by a code. I may not have been wearing a jacket with your name on it, but he knew I was with you. He was just playing around. You misread the situation."

Puck's gaze flicked away. Had he? From his position, it had looked like Skull was yanking at her arm. "Didn't look like a joke to me," he grumbled.

She continued with her caresses, keeping him calm under her touch. "You know what else?" she asked, a bit too casually.

His gaze swung back to her suspiciously. "Why do I feel like that's a trick question?"

"You had night terrors last night." Her fingers paused. Then she simply added, "Bad ones."

Puck pulled back from her and broke off their connection. "The fuck?"

"You were fighting in them. Shouting that you're going to kill some motherfucker."

Horror struck his chest. "Why didn't you wake me up? Fuck, if I'm cursing and shouting in bed you need to wake me up."

"From what I've read, it's not a good idea to wake someone up when they're having a night terror. It's disorientating. Don't worry about me. I wasn't in any danger. More importantly, what you need to understand is that it's a common sign of PTSD or, in your case, PIS." Sympathy poured from her eyes, but he was already shaking his head in denial. "Post-Incarceration Syndrome."

Icy-cold tendrils wrapped around his heart. There was no way he could be crazy. That was weak, and he didn't do weak. He was always, and he meant *always*, the strong one. It's what he'd always been, especially after his mom died. Despite his tendency to joke around, he prided himself on his stability. The woman he was crazy about would look at him like he was a fucking rabid dog.

"What are you sayin'? Spit it out. You think the pen made me crazy? You think I'm a fucking psycho because I was locked up?"

"I don't think anything of the sort," she replied with a calmness that made him want to punch a wall. "It's a common phenomenon, especially for people who've been in solitary like you were."

"It wasn't even a full week. Hell, there are guys who've lived in solitary for months. *Years.*"

"That's true, but that doesn't take away from the probability that you have it. In Duchess County, you got into a fight, but even if you hadn't experienced violence or the deprivation of solitary, being incarcerated has a set of built-in stressors. The lack of activities, the rules, the correction officers, the physical restraint of being in a cell for seventeen or more hours a day. It's a strain on the strongest of people, both men and women. It's quite normal," she concluded.

Puck tagged the knitted wool skirt off the dirty floor and handed it to her. The mood was broken and the tranquility that had fallen over him, gone. Ava stood up and got herself dressed. Sitting back down on the couch, she tucked her legs beneath her as he paced the small office from wall to wall in an unending circle. Hands folded tidily on her lap, she waited him out. Puck stalked the length of the room a few more times. A riot of emotions exploded like shrapnel in his chest. His throat clogged with the urge to scream out his frustration and beat his chest. Besides feeling vexed, he was struck with fear. The dread that she'd reject him. Even if she didn't do it outright, she might still look at him as damaged and pathetic. He couldn't stand it if she felt sorry for him. He'd always been the strong one in his family, the reliable one in the club. No way he could be anything less in her eyes. His gaze flicked up to hers. There was no outright pity in her expression. Only understanding.

"You're not broken, you know?" she said, finally breaking the silence. "I bet you think you're messed up. You're not. It's simply the body and mind's response to a select number of unique stress factors." Her tone was matter-of-fact, almost scientific.

He gave a noncommittal grunt, but his lungs stretched and took in a long breath that eased the tightness in his chest by a fraction.

"It's true," she said, her tone turning vehement as she leaned forward. Then she released her suddenly clenched hands and leaned back. Cool once again, she continued,

"You're one of the strongest, most demanding men I know. This isn't about who you are at your core. It's about your body and mind reacting to a specific set of circumstances that have created temporary triggers." She raised her hands in a so-what gesture. "Eventually, it'll pass. Just out of curiosity, how was the noise level for you out there?"

His eyes were drawn to the office door. Booming music filtered in from down the long hallway and through the thick wooden door. The bounce of the heavy bass shook under his boots.

His gaze returned to hers.

"Not good," he admitted.

Although he'd been at the bar with music playing or the TVs on, he'd worked during the day. Tonight was the first time he was in a place with a seriously high-decibel sound level.

"The crowds? Did it bother you being around so many people?"

"Yeah," he conceded grudgingly.

"And did you have trouble breathing at any point?"

"You know it," he replied with a baleful look.

"I don't know anything for certain. These are common symptoms, but everyone is different and there's a range of triggers."

"So you think I'm fucked in the head?" The muscles of his shoulders tensed as he waited out her answer.

"Absolutely not. Why are you being so harsh with yourself?"

"You said it was temporary. If that's the case, then it'll go away on its own."

"I *do* believe it's temporary, because you weren't in jail for an excessive amount of time, but I can't say how long it will last. What I can tell you is that there are steps you can take to get better quicker."

He squinted at her suspiciously. "What's your suggestion?"

"It would be a good idea to see someone," she replied, her eyes lighting up with hope.

"You mean like a shrink? Oh, hell no," he replied definitively.

"Only be for a short period of time. Long enough to figure out what your symptoms and triggers are, get pointers on how to relieve the stress, and check in on your progress. That's it."

"No, no, and no," Puck denied flatly. He returned to pacing, passing her a few times before pausing in front of her, hands on hips. "Anyways, you're a social worker. Hell, that's like being a shrink. You can do it for me."

"I really can't. Believe me, it's not that I don't want to. I'm not a qualified therapist, and it's not my area of expertise. I can help you if you're in the middle of a panic attack, like what happened earlier, but I'm not the best person to help you overall."

"Christ, why you gotta be so difficult?" he spat out.

Ava suppressed a small smile. "Your reaction isn't surprising, but I know what I'm talking about. Let me ask you this. If something's wrong with your bike, who's the best brother at fixing bikes?"

"Cutter. He's a certified mechanic."

"If he tells you how to fix it, would you follow his advice?"

"Fuck, I'm not a kid. Of course I'm going to follow what he tells me to do."

"Imagine me as Cutter in this scenario. I'm telling you how best to fix the problem." She arched a single brow at him. "Are you going to follow me?"

His hammering pulse had slowed down and the band around his chest had loosened significantly, but his nostrils flared at her last question. The last thing he wanted to do on this God-given earth was go see a shrink, but his momma didn't bring up no fool, and he sure as hell wasn't looking for a repeat of what he'd gone through. Nor did he want to accidentally hurt Ava. What if he lashed out at her during an attack in the middle of the night? He hoped she'd smack him awake, but he'd never forgive himself if he hurt her. It was his job to protect her.

If nothing else, his image would be shot to hell if he had another panic attack in public. Sammi already worried about him. It was natural for her to stress out while he'd been behind bars, but shit was legitimately messed up if his little sister had to worry about him outside of the pen.

Lucky for him, Skull had a reputation for being an all-around dumbass. Brothers would automatically assume he was in the wrong. An apology should do the trick to get the Albany brothers off his back. Considering he'd busted up Skull's nose, he'd make amends. What a clusterfuck. He speared his fingers through his hair. Just when he thought life was going his way, he was facing another pain-in-the-ass problem.

Taking a seat on the couch, he scented her fragrance, and it evened out his breathing. Dropping the back of his head against the couch, he stared up at the ceiling and said, "Yeah, alright. I'll do it but," he tilted his head in her direction, "you owe me. You realize that, right? Every day I show up at an appointment with a motherfucking shrink, I'm coming home to a woman who will do whatever I want. All fucking night. That's the deal."

"You with your deals." She chuckled, shaking her head. "And what exactly will I be getting from all of this?"

"An old man who's not insane?"

"Not funny," she chided.

His hand reached for hers, his eyes burning into hers.

"Don't worry, baby girl. I'll always make sure you're taken care of."

"And I you, Puck, and I you," she responded. "I'm proud of you, you know? It takes a strong person to do what you're doing."

His fingers twined with hers. "Would you leave me in peace if I didn't do it?"

Ava threw her head back and laughed. "Probably not."

Puck smirked. "There's your answer, then."

"I love you, babe," she whispered. Puck's heart burst. More than relief filled his chest at her admission. It was pure fulfillment. He'd worked hard to gain her trust. It was no joke after the way he'd broken her heart, but he was one lucky bastard. He'd do anything for this woman. *Any*thing.

AVA

Ava gathered her hair in her hand and cast a look over her shoulder, a furrow lodged between her brows.

The hairs of her nape stood on end, and a small shiver coursed down her spine. Shifting on her stool at the counter of the small burger joint where she waited for Abby to meet her for lunch, Ava couldn't find anything out of the ordinary. She should feel safe in the middle of a restaurant packed with the lunch crowd.

The place was a hole in the wall, with one narrow aisle lined with small tables on either side and a counter in the back. At a table near her, a man rustled the newspaper in his hands. The upper corner of the paper flopped forward. Her eyebrows arched as she recognized the top half of the face behind the paper. It took a moment for his eyes to flicker up and focus on her. Derick's serious eyes remained on her as he slowly folded the newspaper and tucked it beneath the empty plate on the table.

Getting up, he slid into the seat she'd been holding for Abby.

"Hey Derick, how are you?" she asked with a smile. It had been a while since he'd stopped by her office during his coffee break. Too wrapped up in Puck, she hadn't realized until now that she hadn't seen him in some weeks.

He gave her a grin. "Been a while," he said, his gaze moving down her figure. An eyebrow curved up as he deliberately paused on her bare thigh, exposed from the high slit of her dress. Since Puck moved in, she'd been dressing differently on the days when she worked from the Agency office. Not that it was by any means provocative, but she loved the way Puck's eyes followed her in the mornings as she got dressed. How he grabbed her butt, gave her a searing kiss, and told her to behave herself just before she left for work.

"Wow, gotta say I like how you dress when you're not working at Duchess County."

Laughing nervously, she covered her thigh with the clingy material of her dress. "Yeah, I'd never dress like this at the jail." She gave a little shrug. "It's different when I'm at the Agency."

"Sure is," he replied, his gaze dipping down one more time before crawling back up to her face. "Never thought you dressed like this. Period."

"Trying to change things up a little bit. Can't let life get too dull, you know?"

Derick chuckled lightly. "Sure thing."

"What are you doing here?" she asked curiously.

"Oh." His eyes darted through the large window behind her and then back to her. "Had a doctor's appointment and came to grab lunch afterward."

"Is everything okay?"

"Yeah, yeah," he replied with a small, sheepish chuckle. "Annual exam. My sister's always pressuring me to go get checked out. My mom was diagnosed with diabetes a few months back, and she's been hounding me. You know the kind. *You have a stable job with health insurance, and if you knew what was good for you, you'd use it,*" he said in a nasal voice. "Older sisters," he mocked with a roll of his eyes.

Ava laughed. "Oh, I know all about older sisters since I am one. Definitely always listen to your older sister."

"You have a younger sister?"

"Yes, much younger than I am. I practically raised her," she replied with pride. It struck her that Derick didn't know her that well if he didn't know about Kat.

"Didn't see you come in. I was focused on the paper someone left on the table when I ordered. You here with someone?"

"Actually, a work friend is supposed to meet me any minute now." As if summoned, Abby pushed through the front door, Loki following close behind. Pointing, Ava said, "Oh, there she is. With her boyfriend."

Derick's posture stiffened as he took in Loki, who pressed Abby behind him to pave a path through the busy aisle leading toward the counter.

"Hey, Ava," greeted Loki. Abby poked out from behind him and jabbed him with her elbow until he moved far enough for her to get in front of him.

"Bossy," she huffed out in irritation.

"I was trying to help. Anyone could bump into you and hurt the baby, Pixie," he explained.

"God forbid. Loki, it's a pregnancy, not a handicap, but I'll *handicap* you if you keep up with the pushy attitude," she snapped. Shaking her head, she gave Ava a hug. Derick got out of his seat and gestured toward the empty stool. Abby looked at him and then at Ava.

"This is a colleague from Duchess County. Derick, this is my friend Abby and her boyfriend—" Loki coughed out,

"Husband," in his fist, and Ava adjusted, "I mean, her fiancé, Loki."

Derick moved back suddenly and bumped into the waiter, who shoved past him with a scowl. Loki inspected Derick carefully and gave him a silent chin lift.

"I've got to get back to work. See you tomorrow, Ava. Nice to meet you," he muttered without casting a look at Loki and backed away.

"Oh...okay. You're not taking the day off?" she asked politely to ease Derick's nervous energy. Eyeing Loki, she figured he might seem threatening with the nasty scar on his face, but it's not like Derick was one to cower in front of rough-looking men.

"Nah, with our shortage of COs, we can't take full days off unless we're sick or something," he mumbled. With another goodbye, he gave Loki a silent nod and hustled through the narrow aisle toward the exit.

Watching his retreating back, Loki noted, "Strange guy. Nervous."

"Yeah, it's you, Loki. It's not the first time you've scared someone off with your broodiness," huffed Abby.

Loki's eyebrows slanted downward. "So be it, Pixie. I don't like strange men around you anyway, even law enforcement."

"You do realize there's such a thing as *over*protective?" she taunted.

One side of his mouth lifted in a smirk. "Is that right?" he drawled. "Never heard that theory before." He let out a grunt. "Sure as hell not gonna follow it."

Slipping into the empty stool, Abby tapped her fingers on the countertop and narrowed her eyes at him. "Are you staying, or did you just follow me because you're insane?"

He dipped his head and dropped a kiss on her nose. "Could be I missed you."

Abby's eyes melted. Her face went slack and tears gathered at the corners of her eyes. "Darn these pregnancy hormones."

He gathered her into his arms and rocked her. "Enjoy your lunch with Ava, and I'll see you tonight, alright?" Looking at Ava, he said, "I'm not a stalker. I had business in the area, so I stopped by to check out how my woman was doing. Is that a crime?"

"Not by me," piped up Ava.

"God forbid anything happens to you, Ava, because Puck will be just as bad."

Picking up the greasy menu that had been left by the waiter on the countertop, Ava looked at it and mused, "I highly doubt either of those things would happen. This is your special hell."

"Tell me about it," Abby grumbled.

"You're dreaming if you think Puck will be any better," Loki warned Ava. He loitered beside Abby until she threw her hands up in exasperation and gave him the kiss he was waiting for. Raising her eyebrows, Ava was surprised the building hadn't scorched down to the ground from the heat coming off them.

Loki wished them a good lunch and left. The waiter stopped at their end of the counter, mechanically scribbled down their order, and rushed off.

"It should be here soon," said Ava with a pat to her friend's hand.

"Thank God, I'm so hungry. I think that's why I was short with Loki. Eating for two is not as fun as it seems." Leaning against the back of her stool, she asked, "Who was the guy? He seemed into you."

"Derick? No, I don't...well, maybe. He's a CO at Duchess County and used to stop by my office during his coffee break a few times a week, but he stopped coming around." She shrugged. "He actually asked me out at one point, but then backpedaled, which is for the best now that Puck and I are together."

"Speaking of Puck, how are things?" she asked with a saucy wink.

Ava ducked her head. "Good," she mumbled, suddenly a little shy. "Great. Better than the first time around, honestly." She cleared her throat. "He...uhm...he kind of moved in with me."

Abby's lips spread into a bright smile and she grabbed Ava's hand. "Welcome to the club, Ava. I knew that time we stopped by your house when you were sick that he was serious. He's never been interested in a woman to the point where he went out of his way for them."

"You were right. I didn't want to acknowledge it at the time, but we've come a long way."

Two plates with burgers surrounded by the shop's famous hand-cut french fries slid in front of them.

"Mmm, time to eat," declared Abby, and they dug into their meals.

19

AVA

va should've realized that, despite Puck's promise to seek help, it wouldn't be as easy as she'd anticipated.

Weeks passed without him contacting someone on the list of therapists she'd texted him after the incident at the clubhouse party. Each time she brought it up, he blew her off with an excuse that he was too busy with the bar or hadn't had time to call. *Blah, blah, blah.*

Sunday morning rolled around, and they were lounging in bed, eating waffles she'd made with an old cast-iron waffle maker she'd picked up at a yard sale. Puck insisted on feeding her himself. She was licking maple syrup off his forefinger while trying to think of a way to broach the subject one last time, when her eyes fell on the front page of the Poughkeepsie Journal that Puck had picked up from her front stoop. The headline news stated: "Inmates Run Major Heroin Fentanyl Ring out of Duchess County Jail."

A roar flooded Ava's eardrums. She surged over the plates and cutlery on the bed, leaving a clattering of china in her wake. With trembling hands, she rattled the newsprint open and read aloud, "Inmates are running a drug ring out of Duchess County Jail in the City of Poughkeepsie, selling crystal methamphetamine, heroine, and fentanyl supplied by ex-convicts, according to the Department of Corrections, Office of Special Investigations."

Her eyes glanced through the rest of the article, and she read out the details of the bust and the drugs they found hidden in Kingpin's cell. Raising her eyes at Puck, a smile tugged at her lips. "You did it."

"*We* did it," he amended, grinning at her.

Shaking her head, she said, "No, it's you. I've been trying to keep him in jail for the past three years, but you did it. He's going to be put away in a federal prison. Probably Green Haven Correctional Facility, since that's the maximum-security prison closest to here. This wasn't a little slap on the wrist for a simple possession charge. This is a bust. We're talking about conspiracy to distribute. If it's drug trafficking, it's a felony. Hopefully more than one."

Throwing the paper to the side, she flung her arms around Puck's neck and tackled him to the bed.

"The plates. The maple syrup," he said with a laugh as she straddled him and pinned his arms to the bed.

"I don't care. We can clean that up later. I want to celebrate."

A twinkle entered his eyes. "Yeah? How you gonna congratulate me? All those hours spent kissing that bastard's ass..." He gave her an exaggerated pout and fake sniffed. "It was so hard on my soul."

"Oh, yeah? That's not the only thing that's hard," she teased as she ground herself on his thickening cock. She leaned over, rubbing her hard nipples against his chest when there was a ring at the door.

Puck glanced past her to the door of the bedroom.

"Expecting someone? If an old boyfriend has the guts to show up at our doorstep on Sunday morning, expect me to kick his ass."

With a chuckle, she replied, "Oh, hush." Scrambling out of bed, Ava grabbed her robe and threw it on.

"Yeah, and your ass is going to get a paddling after the ambulance takes him away," he shouted behind her as she hurried out of the bedroom door.

Peeking out of the peephole, she saw Abby standing on her doorstep, lilting over to one side as she maneuvered a big plastic carrier in her grip. Loki was stomping up the walkway behind her. In the past few weeks, they'd spent much more time together. Ava even joined Sammi and her for "brunch" last Sunday. Although it had turned out to be more about Abby plying Sammi and Ava with drinks since she couldn't have any because of her pregnancy.

Flinging the door open, Ava greeted her friend. "Hey! What's going on?"

"Hiya," Abby replied with a sheepish smile on her face. "I'm assuming you didn't get my texts from last night. Should've figured you were living the honeymoon phase of a new relationship."

Waving her and Loki inside the house, Ava admitted, "Sorry, I haven't checked my phone since I left the office yesterday. What's going on?"

"Well, I found a new furry friend after dinner last night. I don't know what kind of karma I have hanging around me, but I have a knack for finding abandoned animals."

"A knack, or you go behind the dumpsters of every damn restaurant we visit to see if there are animals living out of cardboard boxes?" Loki teased.

Abby gave him the stink eye. "It's not my fault if I worry about helpless baby animals exposed in the wild."

Loki snorted. "Poughkeepsie is not the wild. It's not the Serengeti up in here." His hand draped over Abby's shoulder as he looked down at her fondly. "I see you, Pixie. You can't stand to have any living being suffer."

"Hell, you must be feeling her fo' sure if you're gracing my doorstep at ten fucking a.m. on a weekend. What in the hell is wrong with you?" boomed out Puck from behind Ava.

Ava's hand flew out to her side and smacked Puck in the belly.

"Oww! Fuck, I'm just telling the truth," he groused from behind her. "Loki would be taking out his knives if I showed up at his house this damn early in the morning." He eyed Loki with a smirk and went on, "Oh, wait, I forgot. You're living the life of an old married man now, even if you can't lock her down. You're so washed, you probably don't fuck in the morning no more."

"Puck!" Both Ava and Abby exclaimed at the same time. Only Loki chuckled in response.

"Sorry for bothering you guys so early, but Ginger isn't happy with this little one in the apartment. The scent of another cat was driving her crazy, and it was too painful to watch her get stressed out. She's very sensitive."

"Don't apologize to that asshole," Loki ordered. "We're here, so we might as well leave the thing with him."

Puck held up his hands, palm out in a halting gesture. "Whoa, people, hold the fuck up. What exactly do you think you're leaving here? This ain't your place. This is our place. Our home. We didn't ask for savage animals to be thrown on us."

Abby bent down and opened the animal carrier. Out hopped the smallest, cutest little calico kitten.

"Oh my God!" Ava shrieked as she dropped to her knees and scooped up the tiny animal. The little sociable thing wasn't scared at all. She cuddled into the crook of Ava's arm and began purring instantaneously.

"Aww, fuck. Look what you've done, you useless motherfucker?" Puck spat out at Loki as he stared him down with a death glare. "Why you gotta do me like this?"

"If you really gotta ask, then you're dumber than I thought," Loki shot back at him.

Ava looked up at Puck with glistening eyes and pleaded, "Please, Puck, can we keep her? She's adorable."

"Ava." He growled in a low authoritative pitch. "Be serious, we're always working. The thing will tear this house apart, alone all day. You know we're never home."

"That's not true! Outside of work, we're always home," she argued. It was so sweet and cuddly...and it could help him. Holding up the little kitten in the palms of her cupped hands, she thrust it toward Puck's face. "Look at her, baby. Please," she said in a low, husky voice. The kind she knew incinerated his resolve.

"No," Puck repeated, turning a cold, narrow-eyed gaze on Loki. "This is your fault. I don't know what kind of payback this is, but you best believe I will get you for this. You'll be crying like a little bitch by the time I'm done with you," he vowed.

Ava sighed. Puck's stubborn streak was coming out. She hated when he dug his feet in. Inhaling deeply, she drew on her reserve of patience.

"Go ahead, do your worst, asshole. You think you can scare me? Oh, fuck no. You can't make me 'cry like a little bitch,'" Loki mocked in a high-pitched voice.

Ava bent down and covered up her laugh in the little kitten's fur. "What's her name, Abby?"

"She's like a patchwork quilt of colors, so I called her

Patchy. If you don't like it, you can change it to whatever name you think fits her best."

"Patchy," Ava rolled the word on her tongue. "That sounds—"

"Fuck no. No cutesy name like that. Nah, that's a biker cat, and a biker cat ain't gonna be called Patchy. The cat should be something like Stryker or Rider or…or…"

"Patchy?" Abby finished for him. Ava hid another giggle in the kitten's fur. "I was thinking that Patchy works for a biker as well because it's a derivative of the word 'patch,' like when a biker patches into his club," she quickly improvised.

Puck observed her askance, but Ava knew he didn't stand a chance when she blinked up at him with her wide-eyed doll-like innocence. Cocking his head to the side, he inspected the kitten. Then his squinty eyes rapidly jetted back to Abby as if trying to catch her in a less guiltless expression. But she still held the same wide, open look on her face.

Patchy elegantly sprang out of Ava's embrace, hopped over to Puck, and rubbed between his jean-clad legs, her tail swishing back and forth.

"She can help with the panic attacks. Did you know that petting a cat or dog can lower your blood pressure?" Ava said casually. A soft, cuddly little fur ball like Patchy could calm him down right away, should he get riled up.

Puck's face paled, and his eyes bulged out. She groaned inwardly. Shit, she'd outed him. Biting down on her bottom lip, she held her breath.

"You get panic attacks? Since when?" cut in Loki, his eyes sharped on Puck. "Wait, was that what happened at the club party the other night?"

"No, asshat, I don't have fucking panic attacks," Puck snarled. "Don't jump to conclusions. This isn't a Chopper situation."

Chopper situation?

As if hearing her silent question, Abby turned to her and explained, "Since you're practically family, you might as well know about Chopper. He was Loki's younger brother, who came back from Iraq with PTSD. He killed himself a few years ago." Reaching for Loki, she tucked herself under his arm and squeezed his waist. "It's not a secret, but..."

"It's a sensitive subject," finished Ava. She caught the stricken expression on Puck's face before he covered it. "I understand."

"Why do I not believe you, Puck?" Loki hissed. "You know what letting shit fester does to you. To your family. If you think I'm not going to get in your face about it, think again. Already let one good brother die. Not gonna happen again. Not on my watch."

"Christ, Loki, back the fuck off." Turning to Ava, he declared, "And you. You need to learn to keep your mouth closed."

"Puck—"

He slashed his hand in the air. "Baby girl, we're not airing our dirty laundry right now." Sending Loki a warning look, he went on, "Yeah, alright, I admit I've been on edge since getting out, but I'm dealing with it. Ava gave me a list of people that I can go see and," he swallowed before biting out, "talk about this. Satisfied, *Dad*?"

Loki gave him a long look and then turned to scrutinize Ava. "Alright," he accepted with a slow nod of his head, "but to get me off your back, you gotta take the cat." He cracked a grin. "To seal the deal, you know?" Angling his head, he gave a chin lift to the cat snuggling in the crook of Puck's arm. "God knows fucking why, but she's taken a liking to you. She must have a thing for assholes."

"'Course she likes me. What pussy doesn't?" he huffed out.

Ava rolled her eyes.

Giving Patchy's spine a long stroke down, he grudgingly acknowledged, "I suppose that'll work. Anything to get you off my fuckin' jock."

Ava let out a breath of relief.

Clapping her hands together, Abby yelled out, "Yay! This is so happening! I'm so excited."

Puck pointed at Ava and warned, "Don't think you're out of the woods yet. Haven't begun dealing with you yet."

Ava happened to glance at Abby and caught her quick little wink, which had luckily gone unnoticed by Puck.

"Great!" said Abby. "I had a feeling this would work out, so we stopped by and got kitty litter, food, and a bunch of toys before coming here."

Puck turned to Loki. "Is this what your life is like every fucking day? Being steamrolled by someone half your size?"

"Yup," Loki replied proudly, hooking his thumbs in the front pockets of his black jeans.

"So pussy-whipped," Puck muttered under his breath as he dropped on a bench near the front door and pulled up his boots.

"Heard that, motherfucker," Loki said, his hand on the door handle. "Wait and see. That shit's gonna happen to you soon."

"No it won't," Puck volleyed back.

"Yeah, right. Don't make promises you can't keep 'cause you're gonna look like more of a fool the day she hands you your ass while you're on your goddamn knees beggin' for forgiveness. Can't wait for that day," he finished with a hint of glee in his tone.

Ava commiserated with Loki's sentiment. Even she sometimes wanted to see him brought down a peg or two. Abby waved Ava over as she moved toward the kitchen. "Come on, let's have coffee while these guys set everything up. Knowing them, it'll take them a while to figure out how to put the litter box together."

"I heard that," hollered Loki from outside the open door.

Abby rolled her eyes as she walked toward the kitchen. "It's not like I was trying to keep my voice down."

Ava gave Puck a sidelong look. Catching the frown on his face, she hurried behind Abby. Anything to get out of his way because she had no doubt they were going to have it out once Loki and Abby were gone. He was going to blister her ass for this one.

Abby stopped and linked her arm in Ava's and murmured, "Don't feel bad about it, Ava. You're a social worker. We're more comfortable talking about these kinds of things. It's Puck's hang-up, not yours."

Her shoulders drooped. "I know, but I spoke without thinking. I can sympathize that he might be upset. He's the guy who went to jail. He doesn't want to be known as the guy who came *out* of jail with a problem. It slipped out."

"Sure, it did. You're comfortable around us, and I'm a social worker, too. At work, we talk about clients all the time to bounce off ideas and get feedback."

"I rarely make mistakes like that, though. I'm so careful with my clients."

"Well, he's not a client. Not anymore. He's your old man, and it's your right to worry about him," she replied firmly.

"Yeah, I wish you could remind him of that on your way out," she joked, casting a last worried glance at Puck before turning the corner into the kitchen.

20

AVA

va watched as Puck and Whistle pushed through the double glass doors of her father's shop to meet her and Kat for dinner.

Kat was bouncing off the walls in her excitement, although she stopped in her tracks the moment her eyes fell on Whistle. Even Ava had to admit that Whistle was exceptionally handsome. He could have easily been a fashion model with a square jaw that sported the perfect amount of scruff and a pair of brilliant, unusually colored eyes. They were turquoise, framed by long, tar-black eyelashes. His matching black curls were perfectly tousled.

Of course, she much preferred the warmth of Puck's chocolate irises. Especially when they turned black obsidian, like when he was aroused. She instinctively rubbed her bottom in memory of the fight and makeup session they'd had yesterday after Abby and Loki left.

As they sauntered toward the counter, Ava sensed Kat's nervousness. "These are Squad brothers," Kat hissed beside her. "They're...like...wow," she ended, at a loss for words. "I'm glad you came early, so I wouldn't have to face them alone."

"Leaving you speechless, eh?" she teased.

That got her a whack on her arm. "Don't you dare embarrass me," Kay threatened in a deadly tone, eyes glued on their approach.

"Who me? I would never," she retorted with a small chuckle.

As per his usual inconvenient timing, her father chose that moment to come out from his back office. Stumbling slightly when he saw Puck and Whistle, his shoulders squared back. His eyes went from Puck's face to the patch on his cut and back to his eyes. *Guess he recognizes Puck.* His back stiffened, but he pasted on a professional smile. Ava frowned at his reaction.

Puck scooped Ava up in his arms and planted a smoldering kiss on her lips that screamed ownership. Ava melted in his arms and also cringed internally because it was in front of her father. As he dropped her gently back down on the ground, Ava had a little trouble on her rubbery legs, but he kept an arm hooked possessively around her waist. She glanced over her shoulder and found her father glowering at them.

Leaning down, Puck murmured in the curve of her ear, "Missed you, babe. How you doin'?"

She smiled up at him, loving how he took a moment to check in with her. "Good. A little tired. You know how it is at the jail. I wake up early, and those days tend to run me ragged."

With an understanding nod, he murmured low, "I'll take care of you when we get home. Promise."

A flush of heat swept over her cheeks. By God, he knew how to make her ache for him. Shaking off the lust, she introduced Puck to her family. "Puck, you may not recognize Kat after so many years, but this is my little sister," she said as she tried breaking away.

He tightened his hold for an instant before letting her go. "Sure don't recognize her after all these years, but you've grown into a beauty," Puck said kindly.

Kat flushed at the compliment, ducking her head in embarrassed pleasure. Squeezing Kat's shoulders, Ava said, "And this is Whistle, Puck's right-hand man. Whistle, this is my little sister Kat."

"Whattup?" he replied with a chin lift.

From under her lashes, she returned his greeting. Whistle's eyes didn't linger, which Ava was grateful for. At fifteen, Kat was still a girl to a man like Whistle. At least, for now.

Ava's father, Grant, put forth his hand and introduced himself. "Hey Damien, I'm Grant. Been a long time since I heard about you."

Puck carefully laid his palm in Grant's, and they had a little wrangling handshake standoff. "Glad to meet you, sir. I go by Puck now," he replied respectfully, breaking off the handshake.

Grant's face was set in a cold expression. Ava pressed her lips together to stop herself from jumping in. No good would come from her interference. Puck hadn't formally met her father the first time they dated. It was during one of the rougher patches with her dad, when she refused to talk to him.

She wasn't sure if that was the reason behind the antagonizing ripples coming off him, or if he didn't like that she was dating a member of the Squad. He'd never commented on the men she dated in the past. She didn't think the issue was about Puck being a biker, because he'd dropped enough hints of setting her up with a Renegades member. Either he didn't like the Squad, or he was feeling protective of Ava because Puck had ended their relationship. She'd find out soon enough. While their relationship was one of reserve, her father wasn't one to pull any punches.

"Hey, Kat," her father said. "Why don't you show Puck and Whistle around the shop. I'm having trouble with my computer and need Ava's help."

Kat glanced at her father quizzically. "Uhm...sure...yeah." Directing Puck and Whistle toward a row of bikes near the front of the shop, she said, "Let me show you the new arrivals. They're dope." Although only fifteen years old, Kat practically lived in the shop and already worked there part-time.

Puck glanced back at her, but she gave him a reassuring nod.

Once they were out of earshot, she looked over at her father, who waved her toward his office.

Shutting the door behind her, she took a seat near his desk. "What's going on?" He'd never once asked her for help with his computer. The man was a whiz with them.

"He's the boy who dumped you in a hot fucking minute eight years ago," he declared, leaning his back against the glass door, effectively blocking her view to the outside. "Kat told me you hooked up with him again. But to bring him here? To introduce him and his brother to Kat? What the hell are you thinking, Ava?"

Her eyelashes fluttered in surprise. She jerked back at his presumption. Who was he to comment on who she chose to be with?

"Where is this coming from?" Ava asked, social-work mode kicking in. Her father didn't mince words, but what he said was out of left field, and he was coming at her hard. "I mean, I've been an adult for quite some time, and you've never gotten bent out of shape over anyone I've dated before."

"That's because you've never brought a man around before and you've certainly never dated a biker like *him* before."

"Okay...so I'm bringing a Squad brother around. Do you have a problem with that?"

"The question is, why don't you?" he asked, his eyes flaring with incredulity. "His track record isn't spanking clean. He's a fucking dirty biker is what he is. One who broke your heart before. Look at you!" He flung out his arm at her. "You're a gorgeous, smart woman. Can't you find anyone better than that asshole? Hell, I'll find you someone better, if that's the case."

Ava's head tipped back at his vitriol. Her temples started throbbing with pain, and her heart beat fast against her ribs. *What the hell...?*

Lowering his tone, he continued, "You've got a lot going for you, Ava. If you like bikers, I can set you up with Turbo. He's a biker, but he's a stand-up guy, a businessman. What does Puck have to offer you?"

Shaking her head to clear her mind, she stammered out, "Uhm...his heart."

"Pfft. Come on, be serious," he scoffed.

"I have to admit I'm surprised by your reaction. You've never gotten involved in my choices, or really much of anything in my life," Ava noted, as she crossed her arms and rubbed them nervously.

"Ava," he said, as his jaw flexed with tension. "I've been there when it counted, and I've shown up when you asked me for something. The big things. I know you still resent me, and so I try to back off, but this is too serious for me to let slide. Let's face the facts; you're pushing thirty." *Wow. Just wow. He's bringing up my age now?*

"The guy you choose now is the guy who's gonna give me grandbabies. Kat loves everything about bikes, bikers, and the biker lifestyle. In that way, she's followed in her mother's foot-steps. You're the only one I can count on to make a *normal* choice. Plus," he jutted his thumb toward the outside, "I don't trust that guy. The Squad has a reputation for smuggling. They're a bunch of wild jackasses."

He pushed off the door and took the seat beside her. Ava simply watched, stunned, as he took her hand in his and said, "Look, I know you can't forgive me for what happened between me and your mother. I've made my share of mistakes, and I know what it is to hurt someone I love. To live with that mistake. Knowing that I damaged my relationship with my firstborn. He's hurt you once before. Can you trust him not to do it again? With the biker bitches and hangers-on in that club of his? Hell, Squad brothers makes the Renegades look like a bunch of Boy Scouts."

Ava slumped into her seat. "This...is quite a speech."

Her father fiddled with her fingers. It was the most phys-ical contact they'd had in years. Normally, she was prickly when he came too close. They'd lived in a routine for the past several years. It was a delicate little dance they hadn't strayed from. By bursting through the invisible fourth wall, he'd created a unique space of honesty. The courage to do that deserved a candid response from her.

"There's no denying that I've resented you. It's lessened since Kat's mom left and I got closer to Kat. The way you stepped up to raise her helped change my image of you, which was pretty low."

"Like I said, I regret hurting you and your mother. Neither of you deserved to be treated like that. I see myself in Puck, you know? The entitled asshole who doesn't see past his immediate desires."

"No." She shook her head because there was a world of difference between her father and Puck. She had to make him see that. Truthfully, she was a bit offended by his harsh judgment and tried to maintain her equilibrium. "That's where you're wrong, Dad. Puck may come off like a bad boy, but that's not who he is on the inside. He's extremely attentive and caring toward me."

"Humph," her father replied.

"He's not at the clubhouse, partying away every night. He works at the bar and then comes home to me." Ava hesitated to bring up Puck's arrest and incarceration, but she wasn't ashamed of Puck's stint in jail. After all, his case had been dismissed, and he didn't have a criminal record. "When he was arrested—"

"What?" her father shouted, dropping her hands, and shooting to his feet.

"If you'd let me finish—"

His face slackened with shock. "Hell no. Not my daughter. Not happening."

"Dad! Dad, will you calm down and listen to me? His case was thrown out of court, and he'd gotten arrested for protecting a woman from her abusive husband."

"Forget the fact that his case was thrown out. He shouldn't be engaging in behavior that will get him thrown in jail. Proves my point that he's a criminal...or a borderline criminal. Whatever. The point is he's not a regular, honest, hardworking man." Raising his hands in a pleading gesture, he said, "I want what's best for you. You could have any man you want. You have so much to offer. You should have the best, not some two-bit criminal biker."

"You're being unfair," she said with a slight tremor in her voice. He was fast wearing on her patience.

"I'm being real. I'm a man and I know men, specially men like him and his friend. They're more than rough around the edges. They're criminals. The Squad has been one of the largest cigarette smugglers up and down the East Coast. Try asking him about it, although I wouldn't trust what he says, because he'll probably deny any involvement. Why can't you find a nice boy...someone you work with or...or...anyone," he pleaded.

She was a bit rattled by his revelation about the smuggling. She didn't know about any smuggling. Was the Squad involved in illegal activities? She'd never considered it. The Renegades weren't those kinds of bikers. It hadn't crossed her mind, especially since Puck's conversation only revolved around the Squad Bar and the Box. She'd ask Puck about it later. What truly concerned her was her father's admission that he saw himself in Puck. Now, that was worrisome. Her father had never overstepped before, so he must feel strongly about it to broach the subject.

Ava rose and took his hands in hers. She happened to glance out the door and saw that Puck, Whistle, and Kat were back at the counter. Puck's eyes ticked up and fused with hers. He knew something was up.

Breaking eye contact, Ava's gaze returned to her father. "I appreciate your concern, but I have to go with my gut on this one, Dad. I will find out about the smuggling. That's concerning because I don't want Puck to spend another day in jail. Look, they're waiting for me, and I need to go. We can talk about this another time."

Griping her forearms, he shook her slightly. "Be careful. Don't give your heart to a player. That man out there isn't serious."

Her jaw tightened, and she gritted out, "You don't know him."

"I know men, especially players. Remember? I was one once. Settled down too young. Wasn't ready to get married and have a kid. Came to bite me in the ass, along with hurting you and your mom. Don't let the same thing happen to you," he warned somberly.

His tone sent a shiver down her spine. She definitely didn't want a repeat of what she'd experienced when her father left or when Puck had ended their relationship. No thank you to that level of heartbreak.

"I'll take your advice into consideration, Dad, but I've got to go."

Her gaze flickered to Puck, whose gaze was intent on her. He pushed off the counter with a determined expression on his face, coming for her. Ava broke away from her father, kissed him on the cheek, and murmured, "Don't worry about me, Dad."

She was out the door and meeting Puck with a hand on his chest. Grasping her elbows, his gaze bored into her. "You okay, angel?"

"Yeah," she breathed out. His touch stabilized the commotion her father had stirred up inside her chest. Puck's dark eyes scrutinized her, drilling in as if he could comb through the layers of her soul.

"Come on, let's go get something to eat. I'm starving," she said.

Ripping his gaze from her, he raised his eyes over the crown of her head, probably latching them onto her father. Tugging on his jacket, she moved in front of him and dragged him away by his sleeve.

"Don't like that fucker botherin' my woman," he grumbled under his breath from behind her.

"Hush now, that's my father you're speaking about," she replied with a suppressed smile.

"He doesn't like me," Puck declared.

Her eyes slid sideways toward him. "How do you know?"

"Doesn't take much to put two and two together. Kat

looked surprised when he asked for your help, so I know that was a ruse to get you alone. And me being the first man you brought around the shop, at the age of twenty-nine—"

"That's not true," she cut in, although it was a total lie.

"Alright, but I'm the first biker. That much I do know. Either way, I mean something to you if you're introducing me to your sister. I know that, and so does he. He's threatened by me."

"Yeah, baby, he's jealous of your swag," she teased, giving him a peck on the cheek. Puck let out one of his little quirky grunts. They'd reached Whistle and Kat, who had migrated toward the front door. Glancing over her shoulder, Ava found her father by the register, watching them intently.

Kat ran to give him a hug and then bounced back to the front door, and they left the store. Checking over her shoulder, she caught her father's grim expression still following them. Ava stifled a sigh. Her father's words tumbled around in her head. Smuggling. Player. She couldn't let another person's doubts—doubts based on assumptions and judgments, not on facts—affect her feelings toward Puck. But she would get to the bottom of what the Squad did, more specifically, what Puck did for a living. As for the rest, she had to trust him. She did, didn't she? A flurry of fear flapped in her belly, and she didn't like it. Not one bit.

21

PUCK

Puck emerged from the back office to tend to the bar during the afternoon lull, right before happy hour, during the turnover of the waitresses.

He was behind the bar, wiping down the top, when a stranger came through the front entrance. Puck's senses automatically went on alert. He was a big man, looked like a bouncer at a club, with a crooked nose that had obviously been busted up numerous times.

But he was dressed mighty fine for a mere bouncer, sporting a cashmere coat and a silk scarf. Taking a seat on a stool, he placed his hands on the bar top. The sleeves of his coat pulled up and showed wrists decorated with curb-chain bracelets that looked made of eighteen-carat gold. Mafia, by the looks of him.

"You know where I can find a man named Puck."

Puck looked him over, meticulously memorizing every feature of his face, from his flat steel-gray eyes to the scar crossing his left eyebrow.

"You found him," he replied simply, putting away the clean

glasses that had been washed and left to dry beneath the counter.

It was the man's turn to inspect Puck.

"What do you want?" Puck asked. He didn't like this stranger nor the way he was being scrutinized.

"I'm an *associate* of Kingpin," he declared. He paused for a beat. "Remember him?"

"Yeah, I remember him. I remember he's in County Jail and I'm not. I remember I left his ass behind and went back to my life."

"Funny thing about jail. The friends you make in the pen, specially if they're a boss...that association can follow you outta jail."

Puck barked out a laugh. "You don't know shit about me, son. Did what I had to do while I was holed up in there, but I'm out now. I don't own nothin' to nobody. Men walk out of jail every single fuckin' day of the year."

"Yeah? Difference is that you left a void."

"A void that can be replaced by the next sucker who comes along. Workers are replaceable. You know that as much as I do. Hell, that's true in the real world. Kingpin and I didn't have a discussion, much less an understanding, that I'd continue working for him."

"Maybe you were such a good worker that he wants to keep the job going."

"The job's done, yo. I'm out. I got a job right fuckin' here. I'm not lookin' to make extra cash, but if the need comes up, I'll reach out to Kingpin myself. You've got balls, man. You come in here and don't even introduce yourself. What's your fuckin' name, anyway?"

"I go by Nikki. Funny thing, but a couple weeks after you left, his life got a helluva lot harder. He thinks you might have something to do with that."

Puck's face hardened, and he crossed his arms over his broad chest. "I haven't heard shit from him or about him. If his situation went south after I left, I fuckin' guarantee you that has nothing to do with me. First you tell me I'm indebted to him in some way and I gotta continue working for him. Now, you're fucking insinuating I was involved in fucking with his shit when I don't know nothing about it. You know what?" Puck said as he bent over the bar top and thrust his face in the fucker's space. "You can go fuck yourself."

He'd kept his voice low, but Whistle appeared behind him in the blink of an eye. Yanking a bottle off the shelf, Whistle smashed it, and liquor gushed everywhere. Puck inwardly cringed, hoping it wasn't one of the more expensive bottles. That could've been two hundred dollars down the fucking drain. They were both carrying, so it wasn't a matter of actual power. It was a symbol. Wielding a jagged-edged broken bottle was a show of strength.

"What the fuck is this Russian Bratva doin' here?" Whistle sneered.

Puck's gaze cut to Whistle.

The man named Nikki chuckled darkly. "Little shit knows nothing. I'm not Bratva," he snarled.

"Whatever the fuck you are doesn't matter. I'm not in the goddamn slammer no more, so Kingpin has no power over me, you hear? I did my fucking time. Did what I had to do to survive, but I don't owe no one nothing. Don't know how tough he thinks he is, but I'm a member of the Demon Squad. Unless you wanna start a war, get the hell out of my bar before my *associate* here stabs that fucking broke-down bottle in your motherfucking eye."

Puck backed down and spat on the floor.

Nikki gave him the evil eye. "You fuckin' spit at me? You

must not know what that means where I come from, but I fucking guarantee you it's nothing pretty."

Puck almost laughed in his face. He wasn't going to be intimidated by some two-bit mafioso criminal. Once a fucker thinks he's a Made Man, he likes to go *Soprano* on people, but he wasn't living out a fucking HBO special. "Unless you've got something else to say, I suggest you turn your ass around and get the fuck outta here."

The man didn't move. Puck arched an eyebrow while Whistle snapped his gum behind him, waving the bottle around a little. With one last vicious look thrown his way, the asshole stomped out of the bar and slammed the door behind him.

"What the fuck was that about?" inquired Whistle. "Been in and out of Duchess County half a dozen times, and no one's come after me on the outside."

Puck grunted as he marched over the broken glass that crunched under his boots. He skirted the bar and checked which direction the man had gone, but there was no trace of him. Luckily, the waitresses were gabbing in the backroom and had missed the drama. Coming back around the bar, he explained, "Had to do some things when I was in Duchess County that I wouldn't normally do. For Ava."

Whistle's eyebrows jumped up. "No shit."

"Yeah, and I don't know if he wants more of me or if he's onto the fact that I snitched on him."

"Fuckin' hell," Whistle muttered.

"Had to help my woman, Whistle. One day you'll understand what that means. Kingpin is a bad mofo, and he had to be put down. He might suspect me, but that bastard could be shaking down any number of men. I wasn't the only one working for him, and he's a rat, so he has enemies. After I left, he got caught with contraband. Don't know exactly what Kingpin wants, but if he's associating with mobsters, that could be a problem in itself. I wasn't aware of every one of his contacts."

"Christ, Puck."

"I had no choice. Ava wanted something bad, and I did what I had to do to get it for her. I knew the risks, and I was willing to take them. True, I didn't expect them to follow me out of jail, but he's a coldhearted piss-ass pussy. He'll be on trial soon, and there's no doubt he'll be convicted. Then he's off to Green Haven maximum-security prison, where he'll have to start over, build new contacts, and find creative ways to smuggle his drugs into prison. There's no stopping a man like that. All we did was keep him off the streets."

"Does Kingdom know about this?"

"Yeah," Puck replied wearily. It hadn't been an easy conversation to have, but in the end, he got Kingdom to admit he would've done the same thing in Puck's shoes. "I'm not naïve, but I didn't expect that fuckwad to sic some dirty mafioso on my ass. You thought he was Russian?"

"He's not be Russian, but he's from the old country. I can tell by the way he speaks, the way he moves." He blew out a breath. "Not good, brother. Take it from me, those fuckers are animals. Think he'll be back?"

"No fuckin' idea, *brah*. No fuckin' idea," Puck answered, his eyes glued to the empty street outside the bar.

✳✳✳

After his visitor the other day, Puck wasn't especially surprised to find the bar's front door busted open, swinging wide in the gusty wind. Didn't make the bitter pill any easier to swallow when he surveyed the extent of the damage.

"Motherfucker," he cursed aloud. The place had been trashed. Some of it was legit destruction for the sake of destruction. Besides the splintered pieces of broken stools strewn all over the ground, the cushions of the booth seats were slashed, stuffing spilling out like disemboweled carcasses. Half the liquor bottles on the shelves behind the bar were gone. He guessed they were lying broken on the floor beneath. TV screens had been pried off the walls and thrown across the space. It was like a tornado had passed through.

His fists instinctively balled at his sides. Fucking hell. Rage and an excruciating sense of helplessness battled for dominance in his chest. The bar had just started to turn around and make a profit. All gone to hell. The financial hit of the attack was going to be felt by the club, but it was the hit to their pride that stung the most.

Gently nudging pieces of a broken table with his boot to pave the path ahead, Puck made his way to the back rooms. The storeroom had been emptied of everything that wasn't bolted down to the ground. They'd had a delivery the day before, so this attack was meant to hit them where it'd hurt the most. Either it was an inside job, or there was a lookout casing the bar, but either way, it was a professional job. Chances were high that it was Kingpin, but the Squad couldn't start a war with a dealer and the mob without proof.

There were cameras, but he doubted they'd find anything worthwhile. He'd get Flicker to comb through the footage. For real proof, though, he'd need Cutter. Cutter was the tracker of the club. Opening the walk-in cooler, Puck stopped in his tracks. *Christ, they even took the kegs.* He hit dial on his phone and waited for Kingdom to pick up.

"Whattup?" Kingdom began.

Without a greeting, Puck broke the news. "The bar got busted up."

There was silence. "Come again."

"The bar got trashed. It's a professional job. They did the maximum amount of damage possible. Someone wanted to send us a message. I need Cutter down here to get any clues of who did it."

"Fuck!" Kingdom bellowed so loud that Puck had to pull the phone away from his ear. Putting his president on speaker-phone, he went through the bar, describing everything as he'd found it. If this was Kingpin, if Puck was the reason behind this clusterfuck, then he'd decimate that motherfucker. Shame burned a hole in his gut. He was the fixer, not the fuckup who brought trouble to his club.

"This could be Kingpin, though it seems like a bit much," suggested Puck. "It's not like I owed him money or any product. It doesn't make sense, Kingdom. Someone wants to fuck with us, or me, but I can't figure out a good enough reason why."

"I'll be right over. Get ahold of Cutter and tell him to meet us down there. Don't clean or move a thing before we get there. We'll go through the place together with a fine-tooth comb. I'm going to contact the brothers and call Church. This needs to be addressed today. No one fucks with the Squad and gets away with it," he vowed before hanging up.

The die had been cast. It was just a matter of figuring out who'd cast it, but someone out there was in for a whole world of pain, and Puck would be first in line to inflict it. Like Kingdom said, no one fucked with the Squad.

※※※

Puck spent the morning talking to the police and insurance company but made it in time for Church as the brothers filed into the meeting room at the clubhouse for their gathering. After going through the perfunctory opening motions, Kingdom updated everyone on the situation and announced, "We believe it's the Renegades."

"What?" Puck jolted off his seat onto his feet. His head pounded like a jackhammer was trying to puncture a hole in his cranium from the inside out. "What the fuck are you talking about?"

"Cutter found this," he said grimly and threw the remnant of a patch across the table at Puck. Catching it in his hand, he inspected it carefully. It was a corner of a bottom rocker that had been torn off, but there was enough of a skull left to recognize it as the Renegades MC. "Where'd you find this?" he asked as he fell back into his seat and passed the evidence to the brother sitting beside him.

"Near the back door. Probably came off one of their cuts when they were hauling the kegs out of the bar. The footage from the cameras show a few men with vests, but they didn't have patches on them," explained Cutter. "Must have cut them off, but for this piece that hung on, and then got ripped off when they were wrecking shit." He grimaced as if he'd sucked on a lemon. "Sloppy."

"It doesn't make sense. The Renegades are a bunch of old weekend warriors. Ava's father is a long-time member. At least fifteen years."

Kingdom straightened and gave Puck a sharp look. "Yeah. What's he like?"

"Met him one time. What I do know is that he doesn't like me, but that doesn't mean much. I'm the dirty biker that's fucking his little girl."

"Doesn't it, though? If he's been a biker that long, he can't have a problem with you being one. That wouldn't make sense. What would make sense is that he doesn't like you fucking his precious daughter. And you know any biker, even his kind, can go mad dog on you," declared Kingdom.

"He know about your past with Ava?" queried Loki.

"Yeah, and she told me he was pissed when he found out I'd come out of jail. The guy definitely doesn't like me. But to go this far?"

"It was the Renegades," Cutter said with finality. "Don't matter the reason behind it. The proof points to them, and the way to hit them hardest is at their shop, like they've done to us. Tit for tat. 'Cause right now, it's our liquor they're guzzling down their throat."

The thought had Puck's head about to explode. No one touched what was the Squad's. It riled him up like nothing else. He'd poured blood and sweat into the bar, been there every minute of every fucking day he wasn't with Ava, and even then, he'd duck out of her house to check on the bar.

It made no damn sense for the Renegades to fuck around like this with another, stronger club on their home turf, but there was no denying the anger rolling off Ava's father when Puck met him. Later that night, she'd told him what her father said about him, and he sensed she was holding back in a misguided attempt to spare his feelings. He hadn't enlightened her to the fact that he didn't give two fucks what her father thought of him. The man hadn't even been in her life during phase one of their relationship.

The Renegades had a rep for being waxers—bros who'd rather wax their bikes than ride them. On the other hand, bikers were bikers, and who the fuck knew what could set them off. No kind of biker should be underestimated, whatever colors they wore. Maybe it was revenge 'cause he was corrupting the man's little girl. Maybe it was something else.

As Cutter said, the reasons didn't matter as much as the

reality, and that reality now included revenge. After Loki stepped down, Puck became the sergeant at arms, which meant it fell to him to plan the attack on the Renegades.

"Hit them where it hurts. The Harley shop. You know that's were their money comes from," revealed Flicker. "I checked their finances. Ava's father is the primary owner, but there's a consortium of Renegade members as investors."

"What about Ava?" asked Kingdom.

"I'll take care of Ava," Puck replied in a bleak tone. He swallowed. Christ, he prayed he was right. This could put a wedge between them. Shit could get ugly fast in a fight between clubs, even a fake one like the Renegades. But she wasn't a member of the Renegades. Although this affected her family, she wasn't exactly close to her father. He had to trust that if it came down to choosing between him and her father, she'd choose him. He squeezed his eyes shut. Christ, he hoped he was right.

Loki turned to him, "You sure you want to do this, brother? After all, this is your old lady's father. We can handle this without your involvement. Maybe even find another way."

"This is the best way. I'm the sergeant at arms, so I've got to be involved. This is happening because of me. The least I can do is take a lead to right the wrong. Either Ava understands, or she doesn't. Nah, I got this."

"Suit yourself," replied Loki with a skeptical expression on his face.

Kingdom slapped his palm on the tabletop. "Time to vote on what we're gonna do. Everyone for revenge, say 'aye.'"

22

PUCK

It was already past seven o'clock and Puck was dragging his feet about heading home.

After Church, he'd gone back to the bar with several of the brothers to clean up. He'd been ignoring Ava's texts throughout the day. Couldn't pretend something monumental hadn't happened but wasn't ready to disclose what had transpired, either. The cell phone in his back pocket buzzed. Ava would worry, this late in the day. Tearing off his work gloves, he pulled out his cell and shot off a text that he'd be home soon.

"I'm heading out," he said as he handed his gloves to Whistle and shrugged on his leather jacket. Fifteen minutes later, he was rolling down Ava's street. With a heavy sigh, he turned off the engine and sat for a moment, inhaling the crisp, cold air into his lungs. *Here goes nothing.*

The door swung open before he was halfway up the path to her house. Ava was wrapped in her cute little robe, the one that showed off her curves. Her hair was mussed up like she'd been lounging on the sofa, reading a book or her e-reader. Lit from behind, her hair was a halo fashioned out of burnished mahogany.

Stomping up the pathway, he took her into his arms, breathing in her comforting tropical fragrance. Her fingers unzipped his leather jacket and burrowed their way around his waist to the small of his back. Her warm lithe body snuggled up to his; the simple gesture tilting his world on its axis. A balmy languidness swept over him after surviving the stress and frustration of the day.

"What happened today? I could feel something was wrong. Then you didn't reply to my texts," she chided softly, although it came out muffled against his chest. His muscles tensed, and a weight the size of an elephant settled on his chest. He didn't want to distress her. He'd sworn to protect her, but here he was, once again, torn between two allegiances.

"I'll tell you. Let's go inside."

They walked in together, and he stripped off his jacket before following her sexy, sashaying ass into the kitchen. Pressing him down into a seat, she asked, "Are you hungry? I made lasagna."

"That'd be perfect."

She refused to let him when he raised up to help her. Shooing him back down, she flittered about the kitchen, making his plate, and retrieving a bottle of beer from the fridge. Once everything was settled in front of him, she took a seat.

"I'd rather be eating you out, right now," he said in full disclosure. He was kind of hungry, but the stress weighing on him suppressed his appetite. He was dead serious about where he'd rather be at that instant.

"You need to eat," she prodded. "Go on, eat my lasagna. I've gotten much better at it over the years. Perfected my grandma's recipe."

"Alright," he said and did his best to dig into the meal she'd prepared. "You crushed it, baby girl. It's fucking delicious," he commented. Ava's cheeks blushed in a pretty way that made him want to snatch her up and carry her off into the bedroom. Once he was halfway through, he placed his knife and fork down against the porcelain lip of the plate and dove into what happened. "The bar got trashed."

"What?" she replied in genuine alarm. "Was anyone hurt?"

"No, the place was empty when it happened. I found it a fucked-up mess this morning. It was a crazy-ass day, angel. Busy trying to figure out who did it, getting on the phone with the police, filing a police report for the insurance company. I was on the phone for hours with an insurance agent. Then there was the club. We had emergency Church. It was stressful as fuck, to say the least."

"Oh my God," she breathed out, her hand covering her mouth. "Who would do such a thing?" Her hand moved over the expanse of the table and grabbed his. Yeah, she understood how invested he was in the bar, how many hours he'd poured into trying to make it a success. Besides running the damn place, he'd set up social media accounts and strategized on other marketing projects.

"That's the thing. Ava." He paused and ran a hand through his hair. "It was the Renegades."

"W-what?" she stuttered, and her eyes blinked rapidly. Her finely arched brows slashed downward. "You're kidding, right? The Renegades aren't those kinds of bikers. They're neither violent nor vengeful. They're a bunch of middle-aged men who spend more time looking at their bikes than riding them."

"Yeah, that's what I thought...at first." Staring straight into her eyes so she understood how serious he was, he stressed, "We have proof. Undeniable proof. It's them, Ava."

Her breath hitched.

"My father?" she squeaked out.

Puck's hands yanked at his hair again. "We don't have enough details, yet. No idea if he was involved, but I know for sure he wasn't there. I checked the footage from the cameras myself to make sure. The men were covered and masked, but no one had his body type or moved like him. I can rule him out on that end."

A pent-up breath blew out of Ava. "*Oof*, what a relief."

"I don't know about that. Your father is the only link between the Squad and the Renegades."

Ava's hand slipped off his and tucked into her lap. "What are you saying?"

The *crackle, pop,* and *bang* of the old-fashioned radiators hissed and popped in the tension that descended as Ava waited for his response. There was no sugarcoating what he had to say. "This is club business." He gave her a hard look. "Normally, I don't talk club business, but in this case, I was given the go-ahead to tell you the Squad will retaliate."

"Retaliate how?" Her voice rose a few octaves, eyes wide with alarm.

Puck gave a small one-shouldered shrug. "Cutter said it best: tit for tat. We're gonna hit the Harley store."

Ava inhaled sharply. "No, not the store," she breathed out. Shaking her head forcefully, she pleaded, "The store means everything to him. And to Kat. Especially to Kat. She doesn't only work there part-time; she practically lives and breathes that store and those bikes. That would crush her little heart." Her hand jerked out and gripped his. "Puck, you can't let this happen. Please, you need to stop this. People are going to get hurt, and I can't have my father and Kat mixed up in this somehow."

"The decision has already been made. The best thing you can do is make sure that neither of them are in the store when we come in to wreck it. Doubt anyone will be on the premises that late at the night, other than guards. At this point, it's the only thing you have power over."

"No, no, no," she said on repeat, her voice inching towards hysteria. "This is my family. You can't do this." Her eyes bulged out with panic. "What if I told you I was planning to sabotage Sammi's business? What if I was going to do something that would hurt the Squad? You wouldn't stand for that. The difference is that I would never put you in that position in the first place."

The strain and tightness surrounding his head pressed in harder, the pounding more intense than ever. He didn't answer. None of her questions were worth answering, because they both knew he'd never allow anyone to touch his family. And, yeah, she was right when she declared she'd never put him in an indefensible position. That was the difference between them. He'd pledged his loyalty and life to the Squad. Outside of Sammi, *that* was his family. Like a good soldier, he followed orders. Only now, looking across the table at her glistening eyes bleeding fear mixed with disappointment, he realized he might've made a misstep.

He was reluctant to admit it, but it hadn't occurred to him how this would affect Kat. Ava was upset about her father, for sure, but this mess touched Kat, and that was no fucking joke. Kat was to Ava what Sammi was to him. By taking on Ava, he'd taken on Kat. Only he'd forgotten about her, and there was the rub. By not taking up for Kat, he wasn't taking care of Ava. Without thinking, he'd simply gone along with the rules of engagement as defined by club. The wheels had been set in motion, and he couldn't see a way to derail them.

Ava broke into his thoughts. "Puck, you have to do something. Go back and talk to Kingdom and the brothers. Figure out another solution. Maybe the Renegades can pay for the damages to the bar. I know they have money."

It was Puck's turn to shake his head in denial. "Too late. Shit is already in the works. There's no stopping them now."

"You could try," she countered, a bitter expression on her beautiful face.

He remained silent, the answer to her statement.

A high-pitched screech echoed through the kitchen as Ava scraped her chair back. Slowly, she got to her feet. Standing tall, she stared at him, hands trembling by her sides.

"You're choosing them over me. *Again*. After your promises of never letting it happen again... you're putting me second," she whispered. "The fact that you won't even consider changing their minds for me—" The rest of her sentence was choked off.

"Don't be naïve. You know that's not how the world works. You start something, you gotta finish it. Those are the fucking rules, Ava. When the Renegades broke into the bar and busted everything up, that was an act of war. I can't go back to my brothers like a fuckin' pussy. The Squad can't appear weak in this town. Once our reputation slips, everything else goes to hell."

His heart was slamming against his chest bone, black fuzziness eating up the edges of his vision. The deed was fucking done. Why couldn't she understand that? Yeah, he got that he could've fought for her at Church, and that was on him, but the time to negotiate was done. There were rules—specifically, rules of engagement. Only weak-ass clubs went back on their word.

"We voted in Church. We don't go back on a vote," he attempted to explain again.

The band around his chest cinched hard; he was having trouble pulling enough oxygen into his lungs.

"I call bullshit," Ava said, a tremor in her voice.

Aww, Christ, her temper was rearing its ugly head. He had to get out of there before everything went to shit. Nor could he hit rock bottom in front of her, because all signs pointed to an oncoming attack. Grinding his teeth and curling his hands into fists, he held on tight. The panic was bum-rushing him at full speed, like a marauding bull, but he had to keep his shit together until he was out the door.

"I gotta go," he muttered as he pushed his plate away and stumbled to his feet. His head felt like it was in a vice, getting tighter and tighter until it popped. Patchy jumped on the table, circling between them, and mewled pitifully. Fuck, even the cat was upset.

"What do you mean you've got to *go*? We're in the middle of a serious discussion," Ava snapped. *Whack, whack, whack. Jesus, my head.* "You can't just leave. It's bad enough that you didn't call me when you found the bar in disarray. You called Kingdom and your brothers, but not me. You attended Church and voted on something that directly impacts my life and the people I love, without a thought to what it'd do to me." *Is she talking really loud, or is it me?* "Instead of confiding in me, you avoided me. Didn't answer any of my texts. Here I was, fretting about you being overworked and cooked lasagna, baked a cake." Her hand flung in the direction of an iced chocolate cake on the center of her countertop. He tried following the direction of her hand, but his head was swimming and his vision was shaky. "Did you consider my peace of mind? Or did you just go full speed ahead the way you usually do? Are we a couple, or are we not? Because this is *not* how couples communicate."

"I can't handle this bullshit right now," he declared, gripping his temples.

"I see." She cocked her hip and slammed a hand down on the table. "This is bullshit to you. When it comes to my life and the safety of my family, you're just going to walk out? Run out on me like you ran out on your PSI? Are you planning to avoid me like you avoid treatment?"

Her questions assaulted him like a flock of vultures, each one pecking away at his patience and self-restraint.

"Fuck this, I'm out," he declared in a tight voice. It felt like a bullet had blown a hole into his head as stabbing pain swarmed over him.

Shoulders back, Ava lifted her chin in a stubborn tilt as she cautioned, "If you walk out that door, you better never come back, Puck. I won't be abandoned a second time. I'm warning you, I won't tolerate it."

"And I don't take kindly to ultimatums," he shot back, practically blind with pain.

Eyes fluttering with unshed tears, her voice cracked as she asked in a small voice, "Are you really leaving?"

"Sure fuckin' looks like it," he snapped.

"Don't do it," she implored, but he was too far gone. He could barely talk through the screaming agony in his head, much less admit he was having an attack and needed to get a grip before he could say another word.

It was too much. Too much. Clawing at his throat, he pushed away from the table and propelled himself out of the kitchen. Stalking across the living room, he flung the door open and pounded the sidewalk.

He couldn't think straight as he sprinted down the street and turned the corner. He could barely see more than a few feet of sidewalk in front of him as he pumped his arms and put more distance between himself and Ava. By the time he stopped, he was many blocks away from her. Crouching down on his haunches, forearms on knees, he heaved in gusts of air, sweeping his head from side to side until his vision returned.

Burying his head in his hands, he shuddered. *Christ, what the hell did I do?*

23

AVA

Oh. My. God.

Puck rushed out of her home like a bat flying out of hell. Ava stared at his back as he stomped out of the kitchen. She followed him as he threw the door open and stormed out. Unbelievable. Reflexively, she closed the door behind him, pieces of her heart breaking off and falling to the ground as she stiffly made her way back into the kitchen.

The first real argument they had, and he walked out on her. Dumped her again. Yes, she had given him an ultimatum. He was correct in that assessment, and maybe that hadn't been the right tactic to take, but her anger was justifiable. Who deserted someone after they got upset over something legitimately upsetting?

He'd threatened to hurt the shop. The shop her father slaved over. Granted, her relationship with him wasn't close, but that didn't mean she'd step aside and let the Squad wreck it. Kat loved the shop with her entire fragile teen heart. They'd be devastated, and not only because of the financial cost, although that would surely be great. Did she not do enough to explain what that shop meant to her family?

No. She hardened her heart. She would've never put Puck in such a position. Ever. It was unconscionable. He hadn't fought for her at Church. He wasn't willing to go back and seek a compromise. He'd avoided her the entire day. The one text he'd sent came off as obligatory. Usually, he responded to her promptly. Sometimes it was immediate, as if he were checking his phone for her texts.

Ava picked up his half-eaten plate of food and walked numbly to the garbage can. The tip of her foot pressed on the pedal. Unseeing, she scrapped the uneaten food into the garbage. He'd ditched her, same as he had eight years ago. *Fool me once, shame on him. Fool me twice, shame on me.* Yup, that about summed it up. Ava deposited the dirty dish and silverware in the sink and pulled on her gloves. Twisting the faucet roughly, she scrubbed dishes mercilessly and then deposited them in the dishwasher even though they were clean.

Unlike the first breakup, there was no excuse for his behavior this time. She wasn't a flighty party girl anymore. Staring down at her robe, Ava huffed out a little laugh of disbelief. If anything, she couldn't be more boring if she tried. Her eyes welled up with tears, but she tightened her entire body to prevent them from falling. No, she refused to cry over that man, even if the chances of her having an orgasm with another human being had fallen to zero.

After cleaning up, she dragged herself to the bathroom. She was in the middle of brushing her teeth when she swore she heard the pipes of Puck's bike. That couldn't be right. She slammed her hands down on the sides of the sink and gripped tightly, fighting off the urge to check. Ultimately, she failed and hurried to the living room to look outside, but there was nothing outside her window. Great, now her mind was playing tricks on her. Overwrought, she ridiculously imagined that he'd come back to her on his hands and knees. She was such a fool. Disappointment morphed into cold fury. Fuck that, she wouldn't take him back. Time to put this hellish day behind her.

Returning to the bathroom, she finished getting ready, but everywhere she looked, her gaze landed on Puck's stuff. His toothbrush, his razor, his aftershave. Grabbing a tote from the hallway closet, she stuffed it with his clothing and personal belongings and dropped it near the front door.

Back in her bedroom, she paused as she lifted the covers back. Should she change the sheets? Ava looked up at the ceiling, considering. On one hand, it'd be the best thing to do. On the other hand, she could give herself a break tonight and revel in his scent one last time. Patchy hopped onto the bed, circled twice, and curled up on her pillow. That, on top of her emotional exhaustion and an oncoming wave of depression, settled it for her.

Scooting Patchy off to the side, Ava fell into bed. She tossed and turned for a while until she finally rolled over to Puck's side of the bed. Pressing his pillow into her nose, she greedily drew in his scent. Plumping it up, she carefully laid her head down on top, inhaling deeply for several minutes until her eyelids drooped closed.

In the middle of the night, she woke abruptly. Jackknifing up, reality rushed in to dispel Ava's dream of Puck and her entwined together, kissing passionately. Falling back on her back with an *oomph*, she twisted her face into his pillow, dragging her nose up and down, her breath hitching as she pinched her eyes shut to stop the tears from falling. She felt Patchy leap onto the bed and push her muzzle into Ava until she made space for the little kitten beside her chest. This time, it took a long time before she fell back asleep.

※※※

PUCK PULLED himself together and got off the pavement. In the darkness of the quiet suburban streets, it took him a moment to orient himself and find his way back to Ava's house. A wind chime hanging from the awning of the porch let off little peals in the evening gusts. Standing near his bike, he stared up at her house, willing her to open the door for him as she had earlier that night before everything had gone to hell.

He'd fucked up.

He'd known it while it was happening, but he couldn't do anything about it at the time. He was so used to being self-sufficient that he didn't know how to be vulnerable. *Be real, you don't like to come off as anything but strong and in control.* It was his way. Everything he did, he did with power and determination. That was the secret sauce to his success. Even with Ava, he'd come on strong. That was how he'd gotten her back. She was right when she said he didn't share himself with her. He was pissed when he'd walked into the bar in the wake of disaster. The last thing he'd wanted to do was take out his cell and talk to her. Only once it was handled could he be around her. That behavior wasn't good for a relationship, though. Especially one with Ava. She was all about communication. Hightailing it out of there was the worst thing he could've done.

Punching his balled fist into the palm of his hand, he blew out a breath. *What are you waiting for, you fucking idiot? Waiting for her to open that door and invite you in with open arms?* Not gonna happen. Wiping his sweat-lined brow, he plunked his helmet on his head, straddled his bike, and powered it up. He listened for any sign of life from the house as he let the motor roar to life. Nothing. There was no way she couldn't hear him out there. His pipes were loud as fuck.

Turning his bike, he rode away wearily with a heart loaded with regret. He circled aimlessly for a while and then headed for his house. Jiggling the key in the lock, he pushed with his shoulder to force the door open. He hadn't been there in weeks, and it showed.

Cold. It was cold as hell in the house. Checking the thermostat, he saw that some idiot had brought it down to forty degrees. He was surprised a pipe hadn't burst and flooded the place. That would've been fitting, at least. But more than cold, it was bare and empty of people...of Ava. Her scent was nowhere to be found, unlike in her home, where she was everywhere. Even when she wasn't home, he enjoyed her little house. It was comfy with her shit organized everywhere. She was a tidy little thing, and every nook and cranny of her place was perfectly arranged. Here, half of the space was empty since Sammi had permanently moved in with that asshole boyfriend of hers. After raising the thermostat, he roamed around the house, lost. Images of Sammi's attack flooded his mind. He couldn't stay here. Grabbing a duffel bag, he randomly stuffed clothing in it and left.

Ten minutes later, he was at Loki's place, pressing his fingertip on the doorbell.

"The fuck," Loki said as the door opened. Puck shoved past him without a word and dropped his duffle bag on the ground.

Shutting the door, Loki leaned back against it and crossed his arms over his massive chest. "She kick you out?"

"Worse. I left. She gave me an ultimatum, telling me that if I left, I shouldn't come back. Since I'm a dumbass, I left."

Loki made a waving motion, and Puck peered over his

shoulder to find a half-dressed Abby scurrying behind the wall.

Shaking her head at Loki, she said, "Ava's my friend, so I'm staying."

"Yeah? Then, you better make sure you're dressed, or you'll find yourself face down on the bed with your pretty little ass up in the air."

With a string of complaints, Abby disappeared. Puck heard a few stomps on the wooden floor, and a door slammed shut.

Loki made a sound in the back of his throat and then turned his attention back to Puck. "Why'd you leave, again?"

"'Cause I don't do ultimatums." He strategically refrained from mentioning the panic attack.

"You do now. Don't know her that well, but from what I've seen of Ava, she's not one to do shit without a reason."

"She has a temper," he replied defensively.

"Mmm-hmm," Loki replied in disbelief.

"She does." That much was true, although she had every right to be mad at him.

Loki walked past Puck and motioned him to follow him into the kitchen. Pointing at a chair, he ordered, "Sit, and start from the beginning."

Puck slinked down into the chair. He was fucking exhausted after the day, the fight with Ava, and then having to battle a panic attack alone on some random empty street. Not that the last two weren't his fault. He knew that; he wasn't that much of an idiot. As best he could, he replayed the argument to Loki, including the panic attack.

"Hmm, guess she does have a little temper, but nothing you couldn't handle. On a normal day. You would've done better if you'd admitted why you needed space before busting out of there."

"What can I say, hindsight is a bitch."

"You got that right," muttered Loki, placing a drink of whiskey in front of Puck. "You know, Ava's your future, brother. Sammi's got a man. She's bonded now."

"Should've never let her watch that dumbass show, *Sex and the City*. Used to even watch a few episodes with her to connect with her, you know? Look where it got me. Losing my little sister to a rich bastard."

Pulling out the chair next to Puck, Loki sat down with his own drink. "*Sex and the City* or not, she would've moved out eventually. You can't make decisions like the one you made earlier without speaking to your woman, brother. Getting her feedback."

He looked askance at Loki. "When do you ever do that?"

"When do you see me making a decision on the fly?" He paused for Puck's response. Not receiving one, he went on, "You don't. I wait to talk to Abby about anything that comes up, specially if it's going to impact her. Including how I'm gonna vote." They both took a long sip from their glasses. "It was something I learned the hard way, and apparently, you need to learn it that way, too. Your woman comes first. The Squad is a brotherhood, but no brother's gonna warm up your bed like Ava will. And I'm not talking about sex. If she's your old lady, then she's your other half. Your better half. You don't make a goddamn move without passing it by her."

"That's a ball and chain, man."

"True, but it's a ball and chain I can't live without. It's not like Abby hadn't suffered before meeting me, what with the loss of her mother when she was just a kid. She'd already lived through heartache before me, yet I managed to hurt her like no one else. Vowed I'd never let that happen again. If that means involving her in my decision-making process, weighing her mental and physical health in everything I do, I'm good with that. My responsibility is toward her, first and foremost. Any club worth its colors understands that. It's not any different for Kingdom and Cutter."

Puck knew about what Abby had gone through and how it had torn Loki apart with guilt and remorse. The man had been a fucking wreck when she lost their baby in an attack by a rival club, a vengeful act meant to hurt him. What he hadn't been aware of was the extent to which Loki went to watch over and protect Abby. Loki was a private, keep-to-yourself kind of brother, so he wasn't surprised to be hearing this for the first time. But Kingdom? *Cutter?*

"What about the club? The Renegades?"

"Kingdom shifted the Squad away from the smuggling side of our business when he and Sage were trying for a baby."

"Yeah, might've forgotten about that," he admitted begrudgingly. Christ, he had. He really had forgotten how much they'd changed as a club. He was a solider who followed orders. Of course, he knew it was about Sage. Guess, it hadn't crossed his mind that it might apply to him.

"The club's got to fit the needs of its members, and its members need their women. You've done your part for the club. Allow the club to repay the favor. That's what the term 'having your back' means. You don't have to jump in and fix every problem that arises for the club or Sammi. Sammi, 'cause she's got a man who's usurped you—"

"Alright already," Puck grumbled.

"And the club, 'cause we're a unit of men who are there to protect and back one another up. The Squad Bar isn't *your* bar; it's the Squad's bar. You may be in charge of it, but it's *our* responsibility."

"It's because of me that it was trashed, though," he reminded Loki, although the cinched belt around his chest was starting to loosen a bit. Plus, the alcohol was starting to kick in.

"That might be true, but it doesn't negate the fact that you're an integral part of the Squad. You've paid your dues tenfold, motherfucker. Why can't you stand down for once and let the brothers take care of you? We're a family, and we would've taken a different path if you'd told us what you needed."

He appreciated the reminder. Forgetting about Kat, he'd underestimated how it would affect Ava, though she was more upset than he'd anticipated. She may not be close to her father, but she was loyal to a fault. That man had helped her on more than one occasion, and with her reticence to ask for help, she'd never forget anything he did for her. Puck was so used to putting Sammi and the club first, he'd automatically shoved Ava's needs into second place. But Ava and he were one, so Ava's needs were automatically his. A lesson he'd take to the grave.

Pulling in a long draught of his whiskey, his gaze cut to Loki. "What the fuck am I going to do?"

"You're going to get Kingdom to call for Church, and we'll figure this shit out. Then you're gonna go and get your woman back."

AVA

va's eyes flew up as Abby swung the door of her office open so quickly it slapped and bounced off the wall.

Flinging herself over the desk, she brought Ava in for a fierce embrace. "Ohmigod, what an asshole!" she cried out.

Ava's stoic veneer toppled, and she deflated in her friend's arms.

"What is it with these bikers? Seriously, they have nothing between their ears. They see a good woman. They say they want to be with that woman, and then they turn around and mess it up the first chance they get. It's unbelievable," Abby rattled on.

Drawing her strength around her like an old coat, Ava squeezed Abby one last time before releasing her. "I'm at a loss for words, Abby. Didn't I do everything in my power to make it work between us?" Her eyes went to the far wall, her vision getting blurry with unshed tears. Pressing her lips together, she furrowed her brow in confusion. "How do you know that we broke up? It just happened last night."

"Hold that thought," she said as she pulled out her phone, dialed it, and put in on speaker.

The phone rang and Sammi got on. "What the fuck! My brother's an idiot, Ava, and I'm tracking him down as we speak to do what, Abby? What am I going to do to him when I get hold of that moron?"

Abby rolled her eyes. "Kick his ass."

"That's right!" Sammi screeched. "He loves you, Ava. I'm telling you he loves you. He doesn't deserve you, but I know he loves you."

Ava pressed her lips together to stop a hysterical giggle from escaping. This was so insane. Sammi was adorable and loving. Ava wished she was in her office as well, so that she could reach out and hug the girl.

"Don't mean to interrupt, Sammi, but I was catching Ava up on how I found out about what he did," said Abby.

"Go right ahead. Tell her what happened," Sammi replied, with a dramatic huff.

"Well," began Abby, "Puck came over to our house. Got drunk and stayed up half the night with Loki. Ended up crashing on our air mattress. You know, the one Loki fought me to buy because he said he didn't want any of the brothers sleeping over. He ate those words up real fast. I mean, Puck would've ended up on the sofa, but Loki says it's not comfortable," she concluded with a shrug.

"Wait, Loki sleeps on the sofa? Like when you get mad at him?" asked Ava. This was a shocker. Their relationship seemed so solid.

"Oh, no," Sammi piped up. "When they broke up, he bullied his way back into Abby's life under the guise of protecting her after the attack. She told you about the attack, right?"

"Of course. I hadn't heard that part of the story, though."

"Oh, yes, he had to crawl his way back into her favor because he'd acted like a real ass right before her attack," finished Sammi.

"Afterward, I wanted nothing to do with him. I was very strict on that point," Abby tacked on with a somber nod.

Ava gave her a disbelieving look. "You're the most forgiving person I know. I can't imagine you being tough on him."

She gave a tiny self-deprecating shrug. "I'd miscarried, and I don't know, I was torn up inside. Struggling with a range of emotions and fluctuating hormones. I was a hot mess. Anyway," she waved her hand, "we're getting off topic. Luckily, they were talking loud enough that I didn't have to eavesdrop. Loki gave Puck a dressing down. Called him an idiot for the way he treated you. Told him he was wrong on every front. On not talking to you before Church, on not figuring out a solution that protected you and your family, on not letting you know he was on the cusp of having a panic attack."

Ava's mouth parted. She opened and closed it several times. *He was what?* "Whoa there, what did you say?"

"You mean the panic attack he pretended he wasn't having? The one he needed to rush out of your house for, so you wouldn't notice? Yeah, that one." She looked at Ava with a mixture of commiseration and pity. For a social worker, it felt like a travesty when a loved one refused to communicate or confide in them. Ava swallowed down the pain of such a failure as tears pricked behind her eyeballs and her nostrils burned.

Her spine smacked the back of her chair. Memories of yesterday flittered to the forefront of her mind; Puck insisting he had to leave and clutching the sides of his head. Evident signs of distress—of a possible attack coming on—that she'd completely missed. This only proved their relationship was a farce. She wouldn't have looked down on him. He *knew* that.

She would've stopped everything, even in the middle of an argument, to support him in any way she could have. He knew that, too. And yet he'd continued to hold back, just as he had when he stepped into the Squad Bar and found it was wrecked. Instead of reaching for her in his time of need, he'd distanced himself. Like when his mother had died. Ava had no idea if it was something about her, if it was their dynamic, or what. Regardless, it was a moot point.

"Yet another reason I need to kick his ass," Sammi persisted. "I can't believe he kept this from me. I mean, I can believe it, but I'm mighty pissed about it. He can't keep treating me like I'm thirteen years old. He's such a macho dumbass. In the middle of a fight, he didn't want to look weak, so he ran away. I'm sure he came back and waited outside your house, mentally shouting out, 'Open the door, Ava! Ava!' as if you could hear in all that silence. Like I said, i-d-iot."

Ava barked out a laugh of disbelief. "I-I don't even know what to say. Hearing that just makes it worse," she confessed.

Abby inclined her head to one side. "How so? Loki talked to him. He's twisted Puck's head back on straight. Got his priorities in line."

"His priorities should've been in line all along. I should've been at the top of those priorities. Is he going to run away from me and knock on Loki's door for advice every time something comes up? He's uberprotective of everyone in his orbit." Her shoulders sloped inward. "Except me."

She swallowed around the lump in her throat. "Face it, actions speak louder than words, and his actions are screaming that he doesn't care. At least not enough to put me first...when it counts."

"But, he's going back to the Squad for another emergency Church meeting to propose a solution," Abby insisted.

"Whatever. If this were the first time, I could justify it. The first time around, I was a liability. I've changed, but he still chose another obligation over me. I'm not asking to be number one in every decision, but to not even include me in the equation? For someone who's so concerned about the people who matter to him, he has a blind spot when it comes to me. It didn't even occur to him to fight for me. No, I'm simply supposed to step aside and let him walk over me and my family," she finished in a tight voice. Again, she forced herself to look away and concentrate on the far wall to get her emotions under control.

"Don't say that, Ava. It's not true." Sammi's tinny voice came through the phone. "This is breaking my heart."

Ava's eyes fell on the phone. She leaned in closer and rasped out, "How do you know it's not true, Sammi? He would've never put your business in jeopardy. It's your heart and soul, just like the bike shop is Kat's. Let's assume that Loki helped him come to his senses. It will happen again because it's clearly a pattern."

"Oh, sweetheart..." Abby crooned, coming around Ava's desk and wrapping her arm around Ava's shoulders.

"I already had my heart crushed once. I have to protect myself because he clearly doesn't have the sense to take care of me," she concluded. Sniffling, she twisted her face in Abby's shoulder and burst into tears. *Dammit!* She'd battled not to cry over him, but this talk on top of her sleepless night, she could no longer hold back. Abby tightened her arms around her, making cooing and shushing sounds through her sobfest.

Blindly, she patted her desk until she felt the corner of the cardboard box of tissues and shook a tissue loose. Shoulders slumped, Ava blew her nose and released a defeated breath.

"My father was right, damn him. He had several concerns. First, he told me the Squad was smuggling illegal goods across state lines—"

"Not anymore," Sammi interjected.

"Yes, I know. I brought it up with Puck, and he explained the changes that were made to the Squad and why. But my father also brought up his fear that Puck wasn't capable of being serious. He was thinking in terms of cheating, because that's where his mind goes first when it comes to betrayal. He may not have been right on that front, but he was right in essence, because Puck hasn't proven he sees me as a partner. That he sees us a couple, sharing our lives together. You can't pick and choose. Either you're all in, or you're not."

Abby looked down on her with concern, but she said nothing. Nor did she bring up another argument. That, in and of itself, spoke louder than words.

"I agree, Ava," Sammi said, firmly. "All I ask is that, after I leave a mark from my stiletto heel on his face, you'll give him another chance."

Ava's spine bent forward. Flattening her lips, she replied, "I don't think I can do that. It's time for you to accept the same thing I have to accept. It's over, Sammi."

25

———

PUCK

va refused to pick up his calls or reply to his texts, leaving Puck with no choice but to go to her house.

It had started to fucking blizzard outside, a match for the bleakness in his soul after Abby told him about her conversation with Ava earlier in the day. Shivering in the cold, he hunkered down and waited. Too preoccupied to check the weather and needing an outlet, he'd ridden his bike to Ava's house before the snow began to fall. If she didn't let him in, he was going to have to call Whistle to pick him up in a cage.

The sleet—hail, whatever the hell it was lashing down on him—was like miniature knives cutting into his face. He poked away on his cell for an hour as he waited, allowing cold, wet snow to settle in the gap between his nape and his collar. Another hour passed, and his fingers were too numb to mess with his phone. Tucking his freezing hands into the pockets of his jacket, he continued his watch. Worry began clawing at his throat. Where in the fuck was she?

About a half an hour later, her car came rolling slowly through the haze of falling snow. *Fucking finally.* Hurrying up the walkway to her front entrance, she hitched her tote bag higher up her shoulder and glanced sideways at him before passing by as if he didn't exist. Alright, he deserved that. Muscles stiff, he got off his bike and made his way to her. She was about to close the door in his face, but he jammed his boot in the gap and planted a hand on her door.

"What do you want, Puck?" she asked in a dejected tone. Her gaze darted to the side. "Oh." Two large bags spilling with clothing were thrust at him. "Here you go. This is what you came for."

Ignoring the bags, he said, "I didn't come for my stuff."

"Take it anyway." She shoved the bags at him again.

"Can't. Won't fit on the bike."

"Fine, I'll drop it off at your place once this blizzard is over," she replied in a harried tone. "Go home. It's setting in."

"I'm not leaving until we talk."

"Go away, Puck. We have nothing to talk about." Her face was drawn and her eyes red-rimmed.

Christ, it felt like steel claws were tearing into his chest and shredding his heart. He was a fucking asshole to make a girl like her cry. "Baby girl—"

"No, don't *baby girl* me. Go away, I don't want to see you," she countered and shoved him hard in the chest. He stumbled back a step, dislodging his boot from her door, and before he could say another word, she'd slammed it in his face. Tipping his head forward, his forehead thumped the door. He was freezing his ass off, his head began pounding again, and melted snow dripped down his nape.

Pivoting around, he stalked back to his bike. Sleet hacked at his uncovered head and face, needling his skin until it was numb with cold. Shivering, he crouched down on his bike and waited, the wind chime the only thing keeping him cold company. Close to an hour passed, and every so often, the curtain of her front window flickered. Good, she was checking on him. Darkness encapsulated him. The wind howled in his ears, and they got so cold he had to cup his hands over them to keep them from freezing. His jaw went tight as he braced against another cold gust of air.

He didn't know how much time had passed, because he was too cold to yank off his gloves and check his cell, but eventually, the light of her porch turned on and the front door swung open. Stepping into the lamplight, she called out, "Go home."

A shiver shook his entire body. He yelled back, "I can't. It's too slippery to ride out, and my phone's dead. I can't call anyone to get me."

Her eyelids sank down for a moment. Hauling in a belabored breath, her eyes snapped open and she glared at him. "Fine, come in and use my phone. No funny business, Puck. I'm not joking."

Slowly, he peeled himself off his bike and made his way toward her. His upper body was soaked to the bone. He stomped on her snowflake-themed welcome mat and shook his iced hair with his gloved hands before stepping into the warm glow of her home.

Through the chatter of his teeth, he said, "Th-thanks."

Staring at him angrily with her fists on her hips, she accused, "You're frozen and wet. What were you thinking, coming out here on your bike? You'll catch your death of cold." Not being able to help herself, she tugged at his open jacket and helped him strip it off. Striding toward the kitchen, she called out, "I'm going to hang your jacket to dry. Go grab clothes in the bag by the door. I'm going to run you a bath. You need to warm up."

He didn't want to appear eager, but he was thanking God above that his ruse had worked and gotten him access. His eyes glided across the furniture and objects he'd become accustomed to in the weeks he'd lived there. Being in the warmth and comfort of Ava's home transferred the ache from his bones straight to his heart.

Ava poked her head into the living room. "But don't think you're staying. Who do you want me to call? I want to make sure someone's here to take you away the moment you're done with your bath."

"Loki," he croaked out. Loki was working tonight, so he'd have to get someone else to come get him. *Fucking sue me if I try to snatch what time I can.*

"I'll call Abby to tell him," she said, and then the door to her bedroom slammed shut.

Puck slowly toed off his boots and peeled the frozen, wet clothing off his shivering body. He might be a big man, but it had to be around thirty degrees out there. Add sleet on top of the low temperature, and he was clenching his teeth to keep them from clattering against each other. Scooping up his clothes, he walked to the bathroom buck naked.

He breathed in a sigh of relief the moment he stepped inside the steaming heat of the bathroom. A full-body shudder overtook him. His frozen toes wiggled in the soft strands of the fluffy bath mat beneath his feet. After dumping his clothes into the dirty hamper, he lowered himself into the bathtub with excruciating slowness. He gave a hiss at the first contact of his red, chapped skin with the hot water. Bit by bit, he dipped in until he was able to submerse his entire body. Twiddling his toes, he worked to get feeling back into his numb feet.

Sagging back against the lip of the old-fashioned claw-foot bathtub, his eyes drooped in the bliss of being in the hot bath, of being in his woman's house. His eyes drifted over everything that was hers, the bottles of shampoo and other beauty products, along with a large shell filled with bath bombs on one end of the tub. She'd corrupted him, dammit, because he no longer felt comfortable anywhere else. Not his house, not the clubhouse, not Loki's apartment. This was his home, and he damn well knew it was because of her. A slight moan slipped out of his parted lips. It was going to be a fight to get her back. The anger he could handle. It was the look of hurt and dejection that drove him to the brink. Sitting in the steaming, blazing-hot water, the depth of his loss settled in his gut. She should be in here with him now, lifting and impaling herself on his hard cock.

After Loki's rant last night, Puck had called Kingdom and given him the rundown of what had happened. In an unprecedented move for the Squad, who had a rep for reacting first and getting answers later, Kingdom had made a unilateral decision to abort their plan and set up contact with the president of the mother chapter of the Renegades. After a few hours, the president came back with a statement that it wasn't the Renegades who'd busted up the bar. Proof was yet forthcoming, but whatever the president had said to Kingdom was enough to convince him. The Renegades' president was cooperating fully to figure out what the hell happened. On the upside, Ava's family and the Harley dealership were safe. That was one of the things he'd wanted to tell her. On the flip side, it gave her more ammunition to keep his ass kicked to the curb.

The door to the bathroom creaked open, and two fluffy white bath towels materialized on the stool beside the sink. Patchy had slipped through the crack of the open door and jumped on the towels. Fuck, he even missed the flea-bitten cat. He had every intention of exploiting Ava's natural good-heartedness and sympathy, but it was her stubbornness that concerned him. After he was warm enough, he washed himself down and stepped out of the tub. The warmth, along with the scent of her and her home, had pushed his looming migraine away. But with the relaxation came stimulation, and he was currently sporting a hard-on. Not just any hard-on either, because his erection was for the woman he couldn't simply sweep up into his arms and carry into the bedroom to fuck to his heart's content. The ache of knowing she was beyond his reach kicked him in the gut again.

Finally dressed, he padded into the living room in his socks. Ava was sitting primly on the edge of the couch, her arms folded over her chest, one leg crossed over the other. He took in the sight of her, looking soft in a red sweater dress that hugged her shape and showed off her creamy skin. Damn, her skin was begging to be blemished by his tongue and teeth. Standing before her, he took his time to memorize her features.

"It seems like everyone's too busy to pick you up right away." She narrowed her eyes at him. "Did you do this on purpose?"

"'Course not," he replied gruffly. *Hell yeah, I did.* "I'd never pull shit like that." *I'll do it again in a hot second to get you under me.* "What kind of man do you take me for?" *The kind who'll do whatever it takes to get you back.*

Her slitted eyes tracked him suspiciously as he sat down beside her. "Puh-lease, do you think I was born yesterday, Puck?" *You've used blackmail before, or have you forgotten?*

"I don't have to do shit like that anymore. I'm not in jail." *Hell, I don't need to re-use the same tools.* He leaned in and tucked a lock of hair behind her ear. "How you doin', baby?"

Her chest lifted and fell in response to his touch. He knew the effect he had on her. Fuck, he didn't need his hard cock choking in his boxer briefs to tell him it was mutual.

Between pinched lips, she warned, "Don't call me that." Smart woman that she was, she moved away from him.

"Ava, I called it off," he started. "You don't have to worry about your father and sister. About the shop."

Her shoulders fell, and she unconsciously let out a puff of breath. "Good."

"We're good, then?" he asked.

She barked out a bitter laugh. "No, Puck, we're not good. We'll never be *good* again."

"Damn, woman," he replied, riffling his hair in frustration.

"Don't act as if you don't have something to do with that. You walked away, for the second time. You bullied your way back in my life, and I allowed it to happen, but you won't get a third opportunity to hurt me again. Anything else?"

Scrubbing his hand over his face, he let out a heavy sigh. "I want you back. I made a mistake. Realized it when it was happening, but I wasn't in the right state of mind to do anything about it. I'm back now to repair whatever I did wrong."

"Yeah? And what did you do wrong, Puck? Spell it out for me. Prove to me that you know, because I'm not sure you're aware of it."

"Don't talk to me like I'm a kid or one of your clients. I damn well know I didn't come to you when everything went down. I didn't fight for you, and I put you in a fucked-up position. Instead of putting you first, like I should have, I got caught up in my responsibilities to the club. I'm a solider, and it was my knee-jerk reaction. I was fueled by guilt that I was responsible for what happened. It pushed me to rush and fix the problem ASAP, without thinking about the repercussions for you or your family."

Her shoulders slumped forward into a hunched posture of

defeat. "It's obvious you have a blind spot when it comes to me. I understood eight years ago. But now? There's no excuse."

Incredulous, he replied, "You think I have a *blind spot* when it comes to you? That's goddamn bullshit."

She gave him a brittle smile, all pressed lips and no teeth. "No, it's not. It's a pattern. You've done it once, twice. You think I'm foolish enough to allow this to occur a third, fourth, fifth time?" A deep notch furrowed between her brows. "That's not going to happen."

"I don't have a blind spot," he growled in frustration. Of all the things she could come up with, that one was ludicrous.

"Sure about that? Because you didn't factor me into your decisions," she finished, swallowing a sob. She looked so small and vulnerable, her chest caving in, that he wanted to grab her and cradle her in his arms. Caress her hair and murmur in her ear how much he loved her.

"I was riddled with guilt, and...and I was...I was out of it. I was fighting off a panic attack throughout the day."

She jabbed a finger in his direction. "Ah-ha! So you admit it finally. God, you couldn't even tell me about it. I had to hear it from Abby. Do you know how humiliating that was? But it wasn't as painful as knowing you didn't feel safe enough to tell me. I don't even understand why. I wouldn't judge you. I was pushing you to find help—"

"I couldn't look weak," he shouted. Rising to his feet, he paced the small living room, yanking at strands of his hair. His lungs felt like a belt had been tightened around them. He stopped, his back to her. Closing his eyes, he breathed in slowly and confessed, "Happy? Now you know. I can't appear weak. Not to anyone. Most of all, not to you. Eight years ago, you looked up to me. I can't have you look at me any differently, especially since we met while I was incarcerated like a fucking asswipe of a criminal. Your sympathy makes it worse, not better. You look at me with pity, and I can't fuckin' stand it." He clenched his teeth and seethed out, "No one looks at me with pity." Whipping around, he turned to face her. "Lust, I want. Love, I need. But pity? No, I won't have it."

Ava's mouth parted in shock. His erratic heaving breaths were the only sounds in the silence that hung between them. She swallowed and opened her mouth to speak—

The doorbell rang.

Christ *fuck*, right in the middle of a discussion. His gaze cut to her. Jabbing his index finger toward the entrance, he swore. "I'm going to be waiting right outside that door every day when you get home."

Grasping her elbows in a hug, she moved to the door. With a hand twisting the doorknob, she retorted, "Be my guest, but we're not getting back together."

On the other side of the entrance stood Whistle. Good, dependable Whistle. Puck put on his cold-ass boots. By the time he was done, Ava had thrust his jacket in his face. He shrugged it on and stepped into her space. Her eyes dilated. His head swam in her fragrance, but he restrained himself from hauling her against him like he wanted to. There'd be time for that later.

Tipping his head down, he gave her a smug grin and vowed, "We'll see who wins this fight. If it's a prizefight you want, then we've just finished round one. Eleven more to go."

He turned on his heel and joined Whistle.

"Puck," came his name behind him. Refusing to turn around, he paused and held his breath. "Don't forget your bags."

Biting back a retort, he marched out and closed the door behind him. He'd be damned before he took his stuff out of her house.

26

Puck's broad frame, bent over his bike in the cold, greeted her every evening as she strode up the walkway to her house.

Every evening, she passed him without acknowledging his presence and slammed the front door. After checking a few times, she'd eventually swing the door open and walk back inside. He'd amble into the house, pull off his gloves and leave them on a little side table by the door, shrug off his jacket, and hang it up in her closet. Then he'd join her for dinner.

He'd attempt to start a conversation, but she wasn't having it. She may be too softhearted to leave him in the miserable cold, but she wasn't about to go belly-up and take the chance of him gutting her again. Or wheedling his way into her heart like he did at Duchess County.

Over the following days, they settled into a strange routine. He'd talk, she'd listen. He'd ask questions about her day, her job, her clients, and she'd refuse to answer, so he would continue with the one-sided conversation until their meal was over.

Puck could be an obstinate mule, and so could she, but she

couldn't deny that it somewhat mollified her bruised pride to see him at her doorstep every evening. After dinner, she'd hand him his jacket. He'd put it on, drop a kiss on her forehead that had her gritting her teeth, and saunter out the door. If they were fighting it out in a boxing match, like he'd labeled it the night of the snowstorm, then they'd passed the twelve rounds without a clear winner.

About two weeks into their standoff, Derick stopped by Ava's office on his coffee break. A week or so after the collapse of her relationship with Puck, he'd reinstated his old habit of visiting her during his breaks a few times a week.

Derick popped his head inside her office and asked, "You up for company?"

Ava glanced up from her computer and nodded for him to come in as she put finishing touches on her report. After saving the document, she gratefully reached for the Styrofoam coffee cup he held out for her.

Taking a seat across from her, he propped his foot over his knee and fiddled with the shoelaces of his government-issued boots. There was a shift in the air around them. *Uh-oh.* By the furtive looks coming her way and the nervous energy whirring off him, he was going to ask her out again. She'd only recently ended things with Puck, and they were nowhere resolved to her satisfaction. Despite her best attempts, her entire soul was focused on the son of a bitch. Even if they weren't in this stalemate, she would've prudently taken time to get over Puck before agreeing to a date. And at this point, with Puck at her door every evening, she couldn't imagine another man touching her.

"So...I was wondering if you wanna go out tonight? It's TGIF and all that." He trailed off as his gaze shot to hers and then scattered nervously.

"Oh, Derick, that's so sweet of you to ask me," she

exclaimed, "but, I'm kind of in the middle of ending a relationship. I'm totally flattered, but it's not the right time for me. Can I get a rain check?" she asked cheerfully. The chances of Puck letting her go, with the way he was coming around, were slim to none, but her head was spinning. She had no idea what she was doing.

Derick's gaze drilled into her. "You're still with that ex-con?"

His tone was cold, edged with disgust.

Ava's eyebrows shot up. "Ahh...yeah. You know about that?" *Crap, crap, crap. My job...* He'd never hinted at anything before.

"Yes, I know," he seethed, his lips twisting in revulsion. "A fucking ex-inmate. Christ, Ava, you could do better than that."

"H-his case was dropped," she stammered out. *Oh, God, how much does he know?*

"I saw you around town with him," he said, giving her a tight smile that didn't reach his eyes.

Ava's head snapped back. *What?* That didn't make sense. It was cold and wintery outside, and they rarely ventured out of the house. It was too cold for more than a short ride, and outside of the few times they'd gone out with Kat or to a party at the clubhouse, they'd stayed home. Anxiety slithered up her spine, raising the hairs on her nape. He was lying. She saw it in the way his eyes flitted from side to side.

"Really? Where?" she asked casually.

He rubbed his mouth. "Where what?" *Hmm, he's deflecting.* Pretending he didn't understand.

"Where did you see us?" she said in a firmer tone.

His nostrils flared. "Around," he mumbled. "I don't remember exactly where."

Ava froze. Not only was he lying, but there was an inexplicable edginess to his body language. His movements were jerky as he flicked at his shoelaces and repositioned his foot over his knee. Questions raced around her head, but one in particular circled back repeatedly. He'd been watching her. Stalking her. It explained the odd feeling she'd had at times that she was being watched. She thought Puck put a prospect on her because he was a biker and bikers sometimes had to protect their women. Instead, it was Derick. The instant the thought pierced her consciousness, she shivered in revulsion. *I'm right.*

Carefully, as if in the presence of a wild predator, Ava pronounced, "Well, it's over between us."

His eyes flew to hers. "It is?"

"Yes, we're in the final throes of a bad breakup, but I need time. It's been a hard few weeks, and after I cut it off with him, I'll need time to recuperate and heal. You do understand that, don't you, Derick?" she asked in a cajoling, sugary tone.

"I guess..." he replied. "I can help you get over him." He looked at her hopefully.

Good God, this man's delusional.

"I wouldn't want to use you as a rebound. You know how that is," she said with a flick of her fingers.

"Not really," he groused.

"As a social worker, I'm going to get through this the right way. There are stages of grief one normally goes through with the end of any relationship. Why don't you give me a few weeks? Then we'll go on a nice date together?" she suggested, holding her breath. Her skin crawled because if he'd been sneaking around and stalking her, then, he could be dangerous. He might be struggling with mental illness. Her heart stuttered. Derick could be the culprit of the destruction at the bar.

Everything fell into place in her mind. It was never the Renegades. It made more sense that this unhinged CO, who was essentially a trained law enforcement officer, had perpetuated the destruction, not a group of middle-aged dads who rode expensive bikes.

Holding her breath, she reiterated, "What do you think, Derick? Can you do that for me?"

"I guess," he muttered, like a petulant child who'd been refused a treat.

A breath of relief whooshed out of her. "Wow, thanks for your understanding and patience, Derick," she lied, holding back the sarcasm that was eager to escape.

"I've waited this long, I guess it don't hurt to wait a little longer," he grumbled.

Her eyebrows shot up again, but she quickly hid her expression and pasted on a fake smile. Through it, she fibbed, "Great, it's a date. Well, I better get back to work."

With a grunt, he got up. A slight sheen of sweat dotted her skin as she impatiently waited for him to get out of her office. Grabbing the cup, she gulped down the lukewarm coffee as she watched him leave her.

Tonight, she wasn't leaving Puck out in the cold. They were going to have a talk.

27

PUCK

They'd gone from living together, sleeping together, and fucking through the night to sharing a single meal in silence or with him rambling on like an idiot.

Puck didn't have any reason to complain after his massive fuckup, but that knowledge didn't make things any easier. The first time they'd gotten together, it had happened organically. Then he'd fucked it up. The second time, he'd pushed, got what he wanted, and fucked it up again. Third time around, they were doing it her way.

Of course, her way sucked ass 'cause there was no sex involved. No touching. No kissing or licking or... *Christ.* There was nothing. Regardless, he powered through it and made sure his ass was parked outside her house by the time she drove up.

Tonight was different, though. Instead of strolling past him and slamming the door closed, she paused in front of him and said in a serious tone, "We need to talk." Continuing to her front steps, she unlocked the door and left it open for him. Swinging off his bike, he followed her inside. He shrugged off his jacket and then got comfortable on her comfy sofa. He had no idea what she wanted. No idea whatsoever.

For the first time in a long time, he wrangled to get his nerves under control. Ava could be ready to tell him to go fuck himself for good, so it was a shock when the first thing out of her mouth was about Officer Dipshit.

"You have access to channels I don't have, and I need you to investigate Derick Cotman. I think he's the one who destroyed the Squad Bar. Like I initially told you, it wasn't the Renegades at fault."

He knew that pussy motherfucker wasn't to be trusted. He'd felt it in his gut the instant he laid eyes on that piss-ass fuck. His enmity had only increased when he caught the bastard salivating after Ava.

"Tell me what you know," he demanded gruffly.

"Recently, he started hanging out in my office during his coffee break again. He'd stopped for a while. Come to think of it, it was when we were together."

"We're still together," he drawled.

Ava rolled her eyes and pursed her lips but didn't otherwise contradict him. "Anyway, today he admitted to stalking me. To following me around. He knew we were dating, which was the first big tip-off. But what really disturbed me was how angry he seemed about it. While I was talking to him, it suddenly hit me that he was the one. He did it. I'm certain of it, Puck," she finished resolutely. "Have you found out who trashed the bar?"

"Nope. It definitely wasn't the Renegades. They've gone out of their way to stay on our good side and help us. They also had a party the night of the attack, with dozens of people in their clubhouse. Not that it's a solid alibi, but Kingdom had a meeting with the president of the mother chapter, the president of the Poughkeepsie chapter, and your father. He walked out of there convinced they had no intention of stirring up trouble. We haven't had any leads up till now. That fucker rubbed me the wrong way from day one. I'm a man who trusts my gut, and my gut told me he was bad news."

"I thought it was because he flirted with me," she sassed.

"That sure as hell didn't help," he retorted. "It was more, though. Something's off about him." He rose to his feet and walked to the exposed window. Staring into the night, he mused, "The bastard's been following you around, huh?" He slowly unhooked the cord from the little hook against the casing of the window and lowered the blinds.

"Yes, at times I sensed someone was watching me. You know that prickly sensation you get on the back of your neck? I assumed it was you, that you'd posted a prospect to watch over me. It never occurred to me it could be a stranger."

Puck dropped the cord and turned to her. "You didn't have a problem with the idea of me having someone watch you?"

Ava gave a small one-shouldered shrug. "Clubs have enemies. Abby told me about the man who attacked her to take revenge on Loki." Her gaze dropped to her lap. Plucking at her slacks, she finished in a soft tone, "I don't doubt you'd do anything to protect my physical person from harm. I doubt you in other ways."

"But it proves you trust me to safeguard you," he contended.

"In some ways. Not in other ways."

He came to her and dropped to his knees. "What do I have to do to prove how much I love you? I'm here every fucking night, enduring your silent treatment so I can be close to you. Angel, you've got to know I've learned my lesson."

She kept her eyes cast down. Bringing a finger under her chin, he slowly raised it until her eyes were level with his. "What do I have to do to prove you're my priority? No matter what. I swear to you, I'll never hold out on you again, never avoid talking to you about something, or put you second."

Finally, her eyes locked in on his. *Thank fuck.* He fell into her wide yellow-and-green splintered eyes. They roved over his face, dipped down to the V where the top buttons of his Henley were undone. Her gaze skated from one shoulder to the other, and then cascaded down his entire chest. On his end, he stared at the silky waves of her burnished hair, her pert nose, and plush lips. He planted his hands on either side of her hips.

"Please," he begged softly. He'd never pleaded in his life, but here he was, down on his fucking knees, begging this woman to give him one last chance. He was ready to do it every damn night if it'd break through her resistance.

"How can I trust it won't happen again?"

Good question. Lucky for him, he had the answer. "We'll do it your way this time."

"My way?" Her lips twisted sardonically. "And what is my way?"

"See a therapist. Stop hiding and avoiding stuff that comes up. Talking. Communicating. See? I listen. I may not have followed, but I know what makes you tick, angel. What makes you feel safe. I should've given it to you from the beginning, but I'm a muleheaded bastard, and I don't like to be vulnerable or admit weakness. You're not just anyone; you're the woman I fucking love, and I'm on my knees, willing to do whatever it takes for you to give me another chance."

She tipped her head down, and her lips gently grazed his. Like gates of a dam swinging open, his hands were all over her. Her hips, her waist, her tits. He opened his mouth, and by the grace of everything that was holy in this twisted, fucked world, she returned the gesture.

Moaning, he deepened the kiss, and her hands tugged at his shoulders and upper arms to pull him closer.

"What is it you need, Ava?" he coaxed. He heard the hunger, the desperation in his tone, and he didn't give a fuck; he was dying to hear her admit to wanting him. For fuck's sake, he *needed* to be needed by her.

"I want you. Now. I need you, Puck."

Pulling deep from a hidden reserve of self-restraint, he paused his caresses to confirm, "You sure?"

"Yes," she breathed against his lips. "But this time around, I'm not going to be meek and quiet anymore."

"Angel, you're a badass when you need to be, and you're meek when you need to be."

"No," she said firmly. "My error was that I didn't vocalize my needs, but I won't make the same mistake twice. You must be taught to pay attention to me, and that lesson starts now," she warned as she pulled him to sit beside her.

A rumble rose from his throat. Ava attempting to take over was sexy as all hell.

Standing, she raised her cable-knit sweater off and quickly divested herself of the rest of her clothing. Watching her strip, he palmed his hardening cock. She gestured for him to stand up, and once he was naked, she planted her palm on his chest and shoved him backward. Stumbling back a step, he landed on the couch, and she immediately straddled him with her firm, slim legs. They both moaned as her wet pussy settled on the underside of his shaft. Moving back and forth, she slathered his steel-hard cock with her juices. Her intoxicating vanilla scent filled his nostrils, leaving him dazed.

Taking his cock in hand, she slowly impaled herself. He let out a guttural sound at the tautness of her wet, hot sex, but she didn't stop or give herself a moment to adjust to his size. It'd been more than two weeks, and her sheath felt so damn good wrapped around him. Breathing through his open mouth, his head dropped back.

A bite on his lower lip snapped his attention to her.

"Eyes on me," she ordered. Drops of blood dotted his bottom lip, and his vision blurred with lust.

Grinning through the pain and oozing blood, he said, "You gonna hurt me, little girl?"

"Punishment for what you put me through," she justified smugly.

"Do your worst," he growled as she slammed down hard on him. Fuck! The pain of his lip mingled with the buzz swarming his body. She'd barely begun, but his body was primed for her after so many days apart. His balls already drawn up in anticipation of spilling. "Ride me," he commanded hoarsely.

She didn't need to be told twice. Holding on to the back of the couch, she took him inside her tight clutch again and again. Breathing harshly, she rode him for gold. This other side of Ava was a shocker. She was by no means a slouch in bed, but he usually took the initiative and dominated her. To witness her taking her fill, *taking him*, greedy and demanding, was like a hit of cocaine. He was so damn controlling that it'd never occurred to him to give her the reins, but holy fuck, he'd been the fool. She had a wicked fire burning in her. It'd been muzzled by the self-restraint she'd imposed on herself over the years. Watching as she slammed down on his wet cock, he'd found himself a wild thing. She bit and nipped wherever her teeth landed. Her nails raking down his chest, leaving a trail of angry red marks. As if in a delirium, she took and took, lifting and dropping on his cock relentlessly.

Yanking his hair, she dragged his head back. Pausing halfway down his shaft, she panted against his lips. Her open mouth slid down his throat and latched on. His hips punched up to get back into her tight heat, but she shook her head. "Nuh-uh. This is my rodeo, bronco."

To show off her control, she moved down with excruciating slowness, a pace meant only to torture him. He bared his teeth and clenched his fists at his sides to keep from taking her by the nape and going dominant on her. She was right. This was her ride, and he was going to honor it if it killed him.

"Babe, I'll be your bronco any fucking day."

She shuddered above him and then dropped the rest of the way until he was buried to the hilt. Breathless, she dropped her forehead on his shoulder. Moving her hair aside, he licked up the side of her throat and murmured in her ear, "When we fuck like this, it's like a sacred space where our souls join."

Her eyes fluttered shut, flickered open, and then she popped back up. His words lit a fire; she quickened her pace, fucking him raw. Angling his hips, he thrust up to meet her, hitting her in her most vulnerable spot. A gasp slipped past her lips, immediately followed by a moan. Aww, hell, her walls clenched down on his shaft like a vise. Writhing her hips, she screamed out his name. Clutching her waist, he lifted her and rammed her down on his cock. "Mother*f*—"

His brain short-circuited.

Ripping her off him, he placed her on her knees. Her hands seized the back of the couch, and he mounted her from behind. His hand slid around to her front, clasped her throat, and squeezed. She was so wet that the sloppy, smacking sounds of their flesh and of his balls slapping against her pussy resonated throughout the room. His fingers on her throat triggered a second orgasm and this time, her cunt milking him was too much.

Releasing his grip, his palms smacked down beside her own, and he emptied himself. Swear to Christ, he had so much come built up from the weeks of deprivation, that he would've given her a baby if she wasn't on contraception. Hell, with the furious intensity of their fucking, he wouldn't be surprised if she got pregnant anyway.

Bowed over her, his chest fell against her slick back. Ava went limp and slumped forward. It took some time before he had enough control over his muscles to move. She let out a small whine when he withdrew. Wrapping his arms around her, he dragged her into his arms and carried her into the bedroom.

Gazing down at her, he promised, "You won't regret giving me another chance."

"Make sure I don't," she mumbled into his chest.

"Never again," he vowed. Laying on the bed beside her, he dragged her until she was lying on top of him. Throwing the covers over her, he settled in and let out his first content sigh in weeks. One hand behind his head, the other cupping her ass, he let Ava pepper his chest with light kisses.

"You know I'm gonna have to hurt him, right?"

She settled her chin on top of her folded hands. Expression calm, she conceded, "Yes, I know."

"You're not gonna give me grief like Abby gave Loki, are you? Letting your social worker side kick in like it did for her?"

Her gaze wandered away from his as she considered his question. He was so damn greedy for her that he shifted uneasily under the absence of her gaze. Thankfully, it returned to him.

"We're both social workers, but we work with different populations. Abby's focused on helping survivors of violence, mostly domestic violence, which is the worst kind. It's so intimate that the betrayal goes much deeper. Some of the people I work with are perpetrators. Violence is in the air you breathe in jail; it's a part of life. I also grew up around bikers. They may not be like the Squad, but they share the same values, so, no, I won't give you any grief. I got chills when he admitted to following me."

His lips twitched. "So you think violence is the answer?"

"Certainly not," she huffed. "He needs to see a psychiatrist or therapist, not get beaten up, but the reality is that he went after the Squad. He took the law into his own hands. I definitely think you should catch him and turn him over to the police."

Puck grunted. "Assuming we can connect him to the crime, a CO's gonna have to do worse than bust up a bar to get real time. If we went the legal route, it would close the window of opportunity we have to make him pay."

"Do you think he's connected to Kingpin somehow?"

"Good question," he replied with a frown. The thought had definitely crossed his mind. They'd find out for sure when they caught Dipshit and questioned him. "He could be out there now, for all we know. He needs to be neutralized. Come to think of it," he said and gently moved Ava off him. He returned to the living room, shoved his legs into his jeans and tugged his boots on. Throwing on his jacket, he scanned the area through the blinds for a few minutes. He didn't see any suspicious activity. Dipshit could be out there, but Puck would take the risk of going to his bike to retrieve his gun. Coming back unharmed, he shucked off his clothes and went back to the bedroom. Placing the firearm carefully on the nightstand, he came back to her side.

"You're cold," she protested as he returned her to her spot on his chest.

"You don't want to warm up your man?" he teased. She grimaced at the last word he uttered. "What?" he demanded, caressing down her spine, ending at her ass. Grabbing one buttock in his hand, he gave it a little swat and tried again. "Talk to me, Ava. We said, 'no more holding back.'"

"I worry." The two words slipped out of her mouth. "You've worn me down yet again, although this time you managed to leave out the blackmail," she ended drily. "But...it could happen again."

"It won't," he replied fiercely. Never had anyone doubted him, and to get that from Ava, of all people, felt wrong. "We grow. We learn. I've learned, and I'm telling you, I'm not going back to a cold bed instead of lying in here with you every night. It chipped away at my fucking soul. After breaking up with you the first time, I was a mess over my mother, and I didn't experience the soul-crushing pain of not having you. Man, did I feel it this time around. I get that you have doubts, but I'll do everything in my power to prove myself. Matter of fact, it's better if you don't trust me. Makes me more determined to prove you wrong."

"Prove it to me now," she prompted, with a gleam of mischief in her eyes.

"Yeah? I'll prove it by thrusting my tongue in your pussy until you scream," he said, turning her onto her back and shimmying down between her splayed legs.

"Humph, now you're talking," she quipped.

And he did just that. If all it took was for him to tongue-fuck her every day, then he'd gotten the break of his life.

28

PUCK

Puck hadn't been in this neighborhood since the last time he bought a baggie from a corner dealer.

Eight years had passed, but some things never changed. He poked his head around the corner of the building he was hiding behind and watched a disheveled man stumble toward the dealer, handing him cash with his shaking hand. To think there was a time he thought that shit was cool. The door of the decrepit bar across the street swung open, and Jiggins sauntered out. Didn't even look up from his cell phone to check his surroundings. Dumb fuck.

Puck tucked his freezing hands into his pocket and followed Jiggins a few blocks, stopping and hiding each time Jiggins paused to chat with the various dealers and runners. He was obviously doing his rounds. So damn confident he was in his 'hood that he hadn't brought a bodyguard with him.

There were a few abandoned, burnt-out shells of buildings ahead. Perfect. Jiggins kicked off the wall of the building he was leaning up against and strolled down the street, whistling a little tune. Puck quickened his pace and, as Jiggins passed one of the empty buildings, took out his switchblade, clicked it open, and ran up to the kid from behind.

Arm around his chest and sharp metal at the base of his throat, Puck growled, "Don't say a fuckin' word, or I will gut you like a hog."

Jiggins gurgled against his knife, pressing his Adam's apple against the gleaming blade. Puck dragged him over the toppled walls of the half-standing building, across debris and rubble, to the back of the burnt-out building. Throwing him down on the littered ground, he straddled Jiggins, knife back on his throat.

"What the—" Jiggins's eyes bulged out. "Puck? The fuck you doin', man?"

"Don't fuckin' act like we're friends when you trashed my place."

"What? I didn't do shit!" he yelled.

But Puck had caught the flicker of his eyelids and the tell-tale twitch below his left eye. Liar. He didn't have time for this shit.

"Motherfucker, don't waste my time. Tell me who else besides you trashed my bar. Tell me that CO Cotman was in on it. Fuckin' dare lie to me, and I'll slit your throat and leave you to bleed to death."

"Relax, relax, Puck," Jiggins cooed. "I'll tell you whatever you want."

Puck's gaze flittered around the building, but there was no one around. Pressing the blade closer until his skin was seconds from getting cut, he snapped, "I fuckin' know you will. Spill already. Figured Kingpin blames me for the bust-up in jail, but what the fuck does Cotman have to do with anything?"

"Cotman works for us, yo. He's got a hard-on for that little social-worker chick you're bangin'. Got his panties in a twist about her."

"This has nothing to do with her."

"It does for him. He's transferring to Green Haven to prep for Kingpin's move once he's convicted. Gonna test the waters. See what other COs might be into makin' some side cash." Jiggins swallowed around the blade glinting in the beams of light pouring down on them from the gaps in the crumbling roof. His eyes glided to the side and then snapped back to Puck. The fucker was holding out on him.

"What does he want with her?" Puck couldn't say Ava's name out loud to this dirty asshole.

"The fuck do I know."

"What else is there? You're holding out on me, Jiggins. I worked side by side with you for weeks. Lived, ate, and slept by you. Tell me fuckin' everything."

Jiggins started to struggle. Fuckin' idiot. Puck pressed his knife until the skin was sliced, blood dripping down the sides of his throat.

"Fuck, man!" he shouted.

"Tell me!" Puck hissed.

"You've got the Romanians on your back."

"The Ro—*what*?"

"The *Romanians*. The Lupu Clan make the Russian Bratva look like Mary Poppins, yo. They supply us from the City, and they sent one of their men up here to seek out any intel on the Squad."

"The one who showed up at my bar. Nikki?"

"Yeah, that's him. He's a crazy fuck. Looks clean-cut in his suit, but he's a nasty, cold-blooded killer."

Scuffing against the rubble on the ground echoed in the vault of the four standing walls of the building. Puck glanced over his shoulder, not surprised to see Whistle working his way toward them. He'd instructed Whistle to cover him but hang back.

"Took you long enough," he muttered.

"You good?"

"You might wanna hear this," Puck suggested. Pulling his knife off Jiggins's throat, he wiped the blood off on his jeans, closed the blade against his thigh, and pocketed it. Beads of sweat rolled down Jiggins's temple, but Puck wasn't worried. Jiggins was more than happy to spill every secret. That was the way of cowards.

Lowering his gun, he said, "Go on. Finish up."

"I don't know why the Romanian mafia is all up your asses. Kingpin doesn't tell me everything, but the mafioso bastard visited Kingpin in jail." Whistle's eyes gleamed a brighter blue, and his jaw tightened. "He hasn't been back. Either he was satisfied with what our men and Cotman did to your bar, or he'll be back."

"Cotman was involved in wrecking the bar? You sure?"

"Sure, I'm sure," he muttered as he pulled himself to a sitting position and used the end of his shirt to clean up his throat.

Puck came to his feet. He gave Whistle a nod. "Guess it's time to pay Cotman a little visit."

※※※

CUTTER, Kingdom, Whistle, and Puck had waited a long-ass time in the dark shadows in Dipshit's house by the time they heard the lock on his front door disengage. The instant Dipshit turned on the light switch, his eyes flashed in shock. Dumbass that he was, he tried to escape, but Whistle, who was by the door, pounced on him. They dragged him down the stairs into his soundproof basement, which they'd already prepped for his arrival. Who the fuck had a soundproof basement anyway? God knows what the son of a bitch had done down there already. He was a sick fuck. It was time he was put down like the rabid dog he was.

"Ow!" shouted Whistle and backhanded Dipshit across the face, causing him to tumble down the last few steps. Sprawled on his back, Dipshit howled when Whistle straddled his chest. "You fuckin' bite me, motherfucker? You wanna see how I bite back? I'll fuckin' tear your asshole to shreds."

"Get off him," muttered Cutter with a swat to Whistle's head as he came down the stairs and passed by.

With a grunt, Whistle swung off Dipshit and hauled him to his feet. Towing him to a chair, Whistle shoved him down and secured his hands with rope.

Puck sauntered up to him and crouched until he was eye level with the prick. "Your life as you know it is over, motherfucker. We know you hooked up with Kingpin in Duchess County Jail, and now you have a transfer coming to Green Haven, don't ya? To supply Kingpin, yeah?"

After his friendly little chat with Jiggins, he had done reconnaissance and caught Dipshit on video with more than one narco in the area.

Dipshit's face contorted from denial to incredulity to anger.

"You can kiss those future plans goodbye, Dipshit," drawled Puck.

"You don't know nothin'," the man spat out.

Puck rose to his feet and towered over him. "You gonna question what I do or don't know? There's one thing I know for sure. You've been following my woman around. The fuck is wrong with you? I ain't gonna let that stand."

Griping him by the throat, right beneath his chin, he pressed his thumb and forefinger inward. "I should end you for that sin alone." His fingers cinched tighter. "You don't follow her." Tighter. "You don't look at her." Tighter still. "You don't fucking *think* about her."

Dipshit was struggling, writhing in his seat, choking for breath as Puck asphyxiated him. Another beat passed before Puck released his hold and stepped back, watching Dipshit gasp for air. Thrusting his head between his thighs, the man hacked and coughed and sucked in oxygen all at the same time.

Puck took a seat opposite him. Examining his nails, he said in a soothing voice, "I want you to know that Ava's under my protection. Squad protection. This is as personal as it fuckin' gets. You want to continue breathing, you're gonna get your sorry ass out of this town." His eyes flicked up and locked in on Dipshit's. "Feel me?"

Dipshit's eyes were bloodshot and bleeding fear. Nodding forcefully, he said, "Yeah, yeah, okay."

"I mean now, asshole. Today. You pack your shit, and you drive away in that car. Tomorrow you call out sick, quit, do whatever you gotta do. We rule this town. Kingpin's not gonna back you on this. He's a bit player compared to us."

"Okay, sure, whatever you want," he stammered.

"Good," said Puck, standing up. "Now. To make sure you don't go back on your word, we're gonna do a bit of work on you."

"No, no, that's not necessary. I hear you loud and clear."

Staring him down, Puck nodded his head. Then he shook it. "Nah, I think it is. I think you've got to feel the pain of having put my woman in an uncomfortable situation." Pulling out a pair of steel knuckles from his jacket, he fitted them over his fingers and flexed them. "Let's get started."

29

PUCK

Puck came out of the shower of his house, wrapped a towel around his waist, and grabbed another one to rub his hair dry.

He'd stopped by his old place to clean up and destroy the clothes he wore when he beat up Dipshit. There was satisfaction in hurting that bastar. Gratification and redress for the times he'd shoved Puck in the back when he transported him to and from the housing unit and Ava's office, but especially for the crime of stalking her.

Looking around his simple bathroom devoid of the beauty products, soaps, and candles that dotted Ava's bathroom, he found it empty. There came a time in a man's life when he had to come to terms with certain things. Moving in with Ava was one of them. Learning about Dipshit had only added to his natural tendencies, and protectiveness surged in him afresh. It was time to put the place up for sale.

Sammi was installed in the loft of her billionaire prosecutor boyfriend. He'd converted half the place to store clothing and whatnot for her business. A light shudder coursed through Puck, thinking about Stanton. Wasn't sure he'd ever like the guy. A little rough around the edges for a rich guy, but he was still the guy fucking his kid sister.

Funny, this place used to be a haven for him. He recalled the pride he felt the day he'd scraped together enough money for the down payment. Now he couldn't stand being in the house alone for more than an hour. Done drying himself, Puck hung up the wet towels, padded into the bedroom, and threw on a pair of jeans. Anticipation of getting to Ava was riding him hard. It had gotten to the point that by the time the sun started to set, he got antsy to be at her side.

The roads were dry, the air crisp. It was still cold as fuck, but he could take her out for a short ride. After shooting her a text to be ready for him, Puck locked up the house and got on his bike.

He pulled up to the curb of her house and waited. Ava came out dressed in layers and a thick jacket. Hooking his arm around her waist, he pulled her in for a deep kiss.

"You okay?" she asked, searching his eyes.

"Now I am," he replied, giving her a cocky smirk. Her gaze followed the upward movement of his lips, glancing over his nose and the crinkles at the corners of his eyes. Leaning into him, she sighed against his lips before grazing them lightly.

He handed her a pair of leather gauntlets and a helmet. Slipping in behind him, she latched her hands around his stomach, and he pulled out. They rode outside of the city, over still country roads, the sun warming their backs. Crossing a bridge over the Hudson river, he drove onto a rocky crag overlooking a large span of water.

They walked to the outcrop, and Ava leaned over the rail. The sun was spread out over the horizon, leaving the sky layered with filaments of tangerine orange and gold. The wind whipped around them, flinging Ava's hair across her cheeks. Puck leaned in, caught a few strands, and lifted them away from her stunning face. Pops of green slivers in her eyes stood out, her skin flushed pink, and her lips were a juicy cherry-red color.

"It's done," Puck said. "If he knows what's good for him—and after today, I'm sure he does—you'll never see his face again. Found out he was supplying Kingpin in jail and requested a transfer to follow him to Green Haven."

"Damn," she murmured.

"Dipshit's absence will slow Kingpin down for a while. We'll have to stay vigilant to keep him in check for as long as he's behind bars."

Ava's hand drifted over Puck's and squeezed. "Thank you. You didn't have to help me, but you did it anyway."

"'Course I did."

"It relieves my guilt over Sasha," she confessed.

"I see you, angel, and I'd do anything for you. Even without the sex, I would've done anything to get closer to you when I was in jail." He leaned close to her. "Wanna know why?" he teased.

She batted her lashes at him coyly and purred, "Why?"

"'Cause I'm in love with you, Ava. You're my old lady, and I want it all. I want my jacket on your back with big ole letters branding you as "Property of Puck," I want the ring on your finger, and my baby in your belly."

She threw her head back, and her laugh rang out across the expanse of space. "Okay, okay. It's yours. You know I love you to death. I never got over you the first time around. And then, to top it off, I can't seem to have an orgasm with anyone else, so..." she paused with a dramatic sigh, "I guess I'm stuck with you."

"Oh, it's my *skills* in bed that did it, huh?"

"Not *only* that," she quipped, "but it definitely tips the scale when you get on my last nerve."

Tangling their fingers together, his eyes turned serious. "I made an appointment with a therapist. Robert something or other."

"I know Robert. He's a good guy. You'll get along with him."

Puck slipped his hand away from hers and sauntered over to his bike. Opening the hard-shell pannier on the side, he pulled out a jacket. He heard her gasp behind him.

Good.

Twisting around, he shot a look over his shoulder and found her covering her gaping mouth.

Walking toward her at a languid pace, he held it up. "What do you think?"

"It's beautiful," she exclaimed.

She was right. It was. He'd had Hoodie, a brother with wicked design skills, make graphics for the back. It had the Demon Squad logo flanked by angel wings, and a bottom rocker etched with the words, "Property of Puck."

Her hand slipped away. Tears glistened in her eyes, the orange sky backlighting her mahogany hair. Yanking it from his hand, she stripped off her coat and slipped the black leather biker jacket on. Stuffing her hands in the front pockets, she gently dragged one of her hands out and opened it. A little black velvet box was nestled in the palm of her hand.

"You didn't," she murmured, her head sweeping from side to side, tears rolling down her cheeks.

"I did," he confirmed with a grin. "Whatcha gonna do about it?"

Taking the box from her trembling hands, he flipped it open and turned it toward her. It was a solitaire, clear and brilliant, just like her. Glints of coral orange reflected off the diamond from the setting sun.

"Whatever you decide, you'll have me forever. I'm not

going anywhere. You make me a better man. Not perfect, never that," he said, one corner of his lips tipping up sardonically. "You've always been in my corner, and if I can be a better man, I'll try. For you."

Tears dropping faster, she silently held out her hand. He grabbed her fingers, feeling the tremor in them, and slid the ring on. He lifted her hand to his lips and gently brushed her knuckles. Releasing her, he opened his arms, and she flew into them. He grasped her tightly against his chest, as tightly as he could, because he was never letting this woman go.

"It was worth it, you know?" she said, her tears wetting the side of his throat. "To be here with you makes the times apart almost worth it."

"I'm a lucky bastard to have gotten a second and third chance," he murmured. Gripping the back of her neck, he pulled her head back and dropped kisses along her cheek down to her chin. "There's no getting away from me now. You know that, right?"

"Yeah, babe, and I love you, too," she murmured against his lips.

His mouth slanted over hers in a bruising kiss.

A kiss expressing everything he felt for her.

A kiss that claimed her for what she was.

His property.

Would you like to read a BONUS EPILOGUE????
Subscribe to my newsletter and get it for FREE: https://
BookHip.com/QNMVHL

THANK you for reading Puck's Property! I hope you loved meeting Puck and Ava. The next book in the series is about Whistle, who meets his match with Tasa in Whistle's War.

A Mafia princess on the run.

A Bratva prince turned biker.

Will their love start a war?

ON THE RUN **from an arranged marriage, Tasa thought she'd found the perfect hide-out. After all, her eldest brother and head of her mafia family would never think to search for her in a club full of rough bikers. With her newfound freedom, the first thing on Tasa's bucket list is to lose her virginity. The perfect specimen comes in the shape of a sexy biker with coal black hair and stunning turquoise eyes.**

It was just her rotten luck to have chosen a man with a possessive streak a mile wide.

WANT A TASTE NOW?

AS THE EMPLOYEES shuffled in for the evening shift, Whistle called them into the office, one by one, for a "conversation."

Tasa threw Jazz a worried look. "Are you sure everything's alright?"

"You've got nothing to worry about. There's a problem, but it began before you started, so he doesn't suspect you. What would be suspicious is if Whistle didn't bring everyone in for a little one-to-one chat," she murmured discreetly near her ear.

Tasa stilled.

"What is it?" she hissed.

If there was a problem, she needed to know ASAP. No way

did she want attention thrown on the bar, especially not by the police.

"Can't tell you the details, but someone's not playing nice."

Fidgeting with the strings of her apron, Tasa gulped. "Will the police get involved?"

"Nah-uh. That's not how it works inside a club. Traitors are dealt with internally," Jazz assured her.

"Okay," she breathed out with relief. That was the way things worked in her family, and she was far more at ease with the idea of an internal form of justice.

"Tasa," came her name in a familiar, low bass tone that sent a delicious shiver up her spine.

Widening her eyes at Jazz, who gave her a reassuring squeeze of the arm, she made her way to Whistle. He studied her carefully as she moved toward him. She noticed his eyes were a few shades darker by the time she reached him. Maybe it was the low lighting in the bar.

He gestured for her to precede him down the dark hallway toward the splash of light spilling out of the open door of his office.

She paused at the entrance for a moment, taking in the small, compact space. The place was surprisingly tidy, with files neatly stacked in a steel-mesh divider and a desktop computer on the desk.

Choosing one of the chairs facing the desk, she perched on the edge of it, waiting for him to close the door and take his seat. Instead, he motioned toward a small couch pushed up against the far wall. Silently following his direction, she skirted around a low table and took a seat right up against the arm of the couch, making sure to put as much space between them as possible.

He grabbed a few files, dropped them on the low table, and slid into the space beside her with the sleek movements of a large feline. Spreading his arm over the back of the couch, his leather cut creaked as he turned to face her.

Despite being winter, but he wore a short-sleeve black T-shirt that showed off an arm of sculpted muscles covered with tats as intricate as lace. Even the knuckles of his fingers, tapping lightly against the top of the couch, were tatted. In her world, a man's tats were his calling card, but even in the civilian world, one could learn a lot from a man's tats. She itched to inspect them closely but didn't dare.

This was the closest she'd ever been to Whistle for more than a passing moment. Close enough for the distinct scent of leather, clean male, and his own cedar-based aftershave to waft up to her.

She shrank back to protect herself from the seductive assault of his fragrance, but despite her best efforts, her nostrils were suffused with that spicy warmth of his. She parted her lips and tried breathing through her mouth, but quickly gave up once she realized she wouldn't be able to go through a whole conversation like that with him. She took a nose full of his delicious scent and promptly realizing her mistake.

His riveting eyes locked on her, and a small notch formed between his black brows. He cocked his head to the side, a small, amused smile lingering on his lips. "You scared of me?"

"What? Of course not," she sputtered, feigning insult.

"Why are you moving away then, baby girl?"

The abraded edge of his voice scraped over her skin like a rough caress. *Baby girl?*

She gave her addled mind a sharp, little shake to slough off the lust weaving itself around her and choking her good sense.

"Um, I'm not. I was just making myself comfortable," she boldly lied, squirming a little in her seat as if trying to find just the right spot.

A cacophony of sensations rioted through her, and she wasn't used to being assaulted by so many feelings around a man. What made her most wary was the inconvenient tug she felt in her heart. Because she could not, under any circumstances, get attached. It would upend her meticulous plan.

"You don't look comfortable," he noted. "Matter of fact is, you look scared."

He moved closer, causing another wave of his decadent scent to assault her senses.

"Is it 'cause I'm a big bad biker?" he taunted in that lilting tone of his.

"No," she scoffed with a hard roll of her eyes. She tossed her head, flicking her hair over her shoulder for good measure.

What kind of prim goody-two-shoes priss did she come off as if he dared ask such an absurd question? By no means was she scared of him, even less so because he was a biker. He was a Boy Scout compared to the cold-blooded monsters she grew up around.

Her gaze scored down his front. Sure, he was *big*, but in no way did that constitute as *bad*.

Angling her head, she spotted the shadows lingering in those vivid eyes of his. Intensity, yes. Maybe a woman who hadn't grown up as she had would've judged him as lethal.

Her?

Meh, not so much.

"I'm not scared of you," she assured him.

He made a disbelieving noise in the back of his throat. A sexy-as-hell, toe-curling kind of noise that had her thighs clenching before she could stop it. She had to consciously relax her muscles, sink deeper into the couch, and fix the mask of disinterest on her face.

His phone vibrated, but he didn't flinch or move an inch to

check it. He simply took it out of his back pocket, silenced the ringer, and laid it face-down on the table, his attention focused on her the entire time. That intensity was like an aphrodisiac.

His gaze roved over her face, questing for what, she had no idea. Then it dipped to the deep cut in the clingy long-sleeved shirt she'd borrowed from Jazz. Jazz had been right that showing a little cleavage, along with show-casing her butt in a tight pair of jeans, did wonders for her tips.

"Hmm, you should be a little scared," he murmured low in that gravel tone of his as he inched closer.

"If you knew what I wanted to do to you ..." He trailed off with a tiny, almost self-conscious shake of his head.

His movements were smooth and relaxed, but she had the distinct sense of being a prey in the crosshairs of a decidedly hungry predator. She may not know him, but she'd be a fool to mistake this guy as a simple biker, and her grandmother had certainly not raised an idiot. He may not be like the *mafie* killers of her world, but that in no way meant she should underestimate him.

Beneath his relaxed posture were ripples of danger, and she'd been around enough savage men to recognize the signs.

He moved nearer still, and her heart tripped over itself as another wave of his leather-clean-male-cedar fragrance hit her again.

She cleared her clogged throat and cheekily asked, "Why's that?"

"I'm the big bad wolf. Could be bad for your health." He'd gotten so close that his lips were but mere inches from hers. "Or I can be good. Very good to you. Depends on how you wanna play this."

"I don't play games," she rasped out through her parched throat.

Damn, the way he pressed close into her personal space was doing something awful to her, ratcheting up a whirlwind of nerves. Suddenly, she worried whether he was on to her. Was he somehow connected to or working with Alex and she'd had the wretched luck of falling in his clutches? Was she about to be expedited back to Sunnyside, all hope of freedom lost?

Licking her dry lips, she inquired, "Why don't you tell me what you're talking about?"

His fingers picked at a lock of her long hair and twirled it around his index finger. Tugging it, he brought her face closer to his and whispered, "We're a family here."

That's not what I expected. "Okaaay, and you're telling me this because?"

"Because I need to know everything about my employees. When Jazz brought you in and vouched for you, you became part of my family. There's a little thief in our family, and it's my job to catch it."

Leaning away until her spine smacked against the arm of the couch, she swore, "I promise you. It wasn't me. I don't have a death wish."

"Didn't say I thought you were the culprit. The stealing started before you showed up on our doorstep like little, lost orphan Annie."

Tasa tried tossing her head back in offense, but his hold on her hair yanked her back in place. She let out a little huff. "I'm hardly lost. I'm most definitely not an orphan, and I'm not a redhead, if you haven't noticed." *Shut up, Tasa.* Maybe if she held her breath and quit scenting him, she'd regain control of her faculties because she was babbling like an idiot.

His beautiful ebony-black brows gathered over his porcelain skin. "In this family, we protect our own. That's what family does." He gave her lock another little tug. "You come to me if you have a problem, if you're in trouble, if you need … anything."

She swallowed hard; the sound audible to her ears. Of course, she couldn't tell him about her situation. He didn't know her, but he'd offered her protection because of her connection to Jazz, and she appreciated the gesture.

He was either unbelievably cocky, or he was *that* confident in his abilities. Tasa had long ago learned to trust her instincts and her gut told her to lean in toward the latter. If she was right, and this was the kind of man with the means to protect her, it would go a long way toward making her feel safe. After independence, safety was her second priority. And if she wagered a guess, she'd say this man didn't speak out of turn, didn't boast, or preen.

Since leaving New York, this was the first moment of feeling completely safe. Her fears melted away like ice cubes on the hood of a car in the blazing summer sun. In that instant, she made the impulsive choice to stay in Poughkeepsie and the Squad Bar. She didn't want to bring her brother to their doorstep, but if she hid out for a few months and moved on in the spring, they'd surely stay under his radar.

"I'm not in any trouble," she replied, the touch of his fingers as they raked her hair, scraping her scalp, and pulling her head back, shot electricity straight to her core.

"Mm-hmm," he replied, clearly not believing her. "Seems like I'll have to earn your trust to get a confession out of you. Don't worry, I'll eventually find out every damn thing I want to know, but I'll give you time."

"How gracious of you," she snapped.

She might trust him to protect her, but he better not hold his breath for her to crack. No way was *that* going to happen. It dawned on her that he'd been watching her, probably more than the few times she'd caught him staring. She suspected that she'd been in his sights since she walked through the Bar doors. He may have kept his distance, but he'd been circling her for a while like any good hunter would.

Having pricked his interest, she could no longer melt back into the woodwork. His curiosity had been ignited. He looked at her as if she was a meal to be devoured, one slow bite at a time. She knew a predator when she saw one, and this one was on the prowl.

There was a game to play here, and while she hadn't picked up on that fact until it was too late, now her best bet was to play it. And she was going to lap up all the sexy male attention that came her way. She'd milk this for all she could, dispose of that pesky hymen, and learn what good sex was really like. There was no doubt Whistle knew his way around the female body. Just their little back-and-forth, testing and teasing, had her thrumming with desire.

"So, how do you expect to *earn* my trust?"

Looping his fist around her hair once, twice, he dragged her close enough for their breaths to intermingle, hot and heavy. His eyes dropped to her lips. Impulsively, she licked them glossy and wet.

His scent hit her bloodstream like she'd gotten drunk on the finest, strongest *țuică*, a plum brandy from the old country. His stare, along with his hold on her hair, made her nerves jangle like a caught gazelle.

She went limp against his hold, as any good prey would, and a rumble of approval reverberated through his chest. His lips moved down the side of her face to the shell of her ear. She felt his warm breath as he praised her, "Good. Good girl."

MORE BY MONIQUE

Steamy Biker Romance Series

Kingdom's Reign (Book 1)
Cutter's Claim (Book 2)
Loki's Luck (Book 3)
Stanton's Sins (Book 4)
Puck's Property (Book 5)
Whistle's War (Book 6)
Her Hidden Valentine, A Squad Novella
(Book 7)

Lupu Family Mafia Romance Series

The lives of these powerful men revolves around three core elements: duty, sacrifice, and family. There's little time for women, and no time for love.
Each one of them will be cut off at the knees, humbled by a woman. Oh, how far these mighty men will fall before they learn the age-old lesson that the only way out is through...

The Chosen Heir (Alex's story)
The Recluse Heir (Luca's story)
The Savage Heir (Nicu's story)
The Perfect Heir (Tatum's story)
The Secret Heir (Prequel to Sebastian's story)
The Bastard Heir (Sebastian's story)
The Princess Heir (Emma's story)

Empire Academy Series
A High School Bully Mafia Romance Series

UNFORGIVABLE (Starlene's story)
UNREGRETTABLE (Crina's story)
UNFORGETTABLE (Gabriela's story)
UNDENIABLE (Zoe's story)